The Cardiff Christmas Club

By Nick Frampton

For my Gran, who made every Christmas magical

Text copyright © 2017 Nick Frampton

All Rights Reserved

This ebook is licensed for your personal enjoyment only. This ebook may not be re-sold or given away to other people.

Also by Nick Frampton:

Fiction:
The River (Book One of The Cities of Life and Death)
Adam 0532

Non-fiction:
Your Big Adventure: An essential guide to travelling, backpacking and gap years

Chapter One

Katy pottered around the echoing flat, adjusting decorations and filling dishes with shiny wrapped sweets. But really she was delaying the inevitable, busying herself with fairy lights and scented candles to distract from the task ahead. When there was nothing else to be done she reluctantly dragged the near empty backpack across the dark stained floorboards and nestled it in to the bottom of the wardrobe. The once blue bag was now bleached grey with the sun and stained brown with mud and the red dust of the Australian outback. Its corners were frayed and two of the toggles were missing, but she loved it and everything it stood for. It had been her constant companion for a year – more than she could say for many of her ex-boyfriends – but now it was time to put it away. It was over. She was home.

She sat on the bed and allowed her mind to wander and a golden haze of sunsets and sandy beaches washed over her. For a moment her senses zinged with the scent of a thousand spices mingling on her tongue. The explosion of flavour drew her back to crowded street markets pulsing with the competing shouts of a hundred traders. But all that was a world away. Outside her window the rain fell in torrents and people hurried from taxi to doorway as quickly as possible, fugitives from the Welsh winter.

Katy never knew how to fill those last few minutes before the start of a party; when the glasses were out, the music was playing and all you wanted was for the guests to arrive. She walked back in to the living room taking a wide angle past the table of crisps and snacks to prevent herself from grabbing a handful en route.

On reflection she conceded that she might have overdone the decorations a little for November. Two strings of fairy lights had been wrapped around the curtain poles; one white and one multicolour; their tiny bulbs flickering in time with one another. Chains of ceramic gingerbread men hung from the picture rail and shiny paper chains – her mother's favourite – were draped over every light fitting, shelf and window frame. On the table sat a miniature Christmas tree from her childhood. It was a little tired, the tinsel had grown thin with age and the coin-sized baubles had tarnished with the years, but there was no way she would part with it.

In a week or two she would buy a spruce to sit in the window and then she would dig out the rest of the decorations. When she had left a year ago and packed her life in to boxes it was the Christmas decorations she found hardest to downsize. In the end she had thrown away only what she had bought herself as an adult. Everything else, from the Murano glass baubles purchased on a family holiday when she was fifteen, to the faded cardboard angels she and her brother had made in primary school remained. The childhood magic of Christmas had never really left her and she wasn't ready to turn her back on it either.

Just as her resolve was wavering and she found herself edging towards a bowl of cinnamon popcorn, the doorbell rang. To her surprise she felt a flutter of anxiety woven in to her excitement as she hurried down the stairs to greet her first guests.

She wondered how much would have changed in the year she'd been away. If nothing else she looked very different than when she had last seen them all. Twelve months of instant noodles and daylong hikes had returned her figure to the slender proportions of her student days. Her once pale skin still had a healthy glow from the heat of the Australian summer. And a smattering of freckles had surfaced on her cheeks, echoing the soft hazel of her eyes. Her hair had also grown out and she'd taken to bunching it in to a ponytail, which simultaneously lifted her brown hair from her shoulders and cleared the straying fringe from her eyes. Even the colour seemed to have changed; the sun drawing out subtle red highlights that she had never noticed before. She wondered if the transformation would seem even starker to the others after a year's absence, compared to her seeing the changes slowly unfolding over time.

In university, where they had all met thirteen years previously, they had been known as the *fabulous five*. At least that was how Tom referred to them – and still did – even if the name registered with no one else. His dogged persistence to unite them even as the years went by and boyfriends flitted in and out of their lives was one of the things she loved about Tom. He grounded her, something she found incredibly ironic, given he was probably the flightiest person she knew.

Tom, Katy, Anne, Siân and Simon: over the last ten years they had been through their fair share of heartache and boyfriends, and at a conservative estimate probably a small swimming pool worth of rosé wine. But all that was changing now; Simon had Adam, Siân was married and even Anne – who had once declared herself undateable – was happily coupled up.

And then there was Tom. Tom: who had been there for every birthday and every Christmas, every hangover and heartbreak; from the first week of university to the day she got on the plane. He had schlepped alongside her to speed-dates and blind dates, equally optimistic but equally hopeless at breaking their run of singledom. Not being in love didn't seem to matter so much when you went through it with someone by your side. But she had changed all that, she had left him behind and in her absence she had been replaced. Tom had found someone, someone who could be to him something she never could. His name was Owen.

She opened the door quickly, casting a warm glow on to the four huddled figures on her doorstep. They were so bundled up against the wind and rain it took Katy a moment to register which of her guests had arrived. But as soggy hats and coats were hurriedly peeled off and hugs were exchanged to a chorus of excited *hellos* she identified her dripping house callers as Siân, Dai, Simon and Adam. She was a little disappointed that Tom and Owen were not the first to arrive, but she hoped she hid it well. The second disappointment came when they all dashed up the stairs towards her top floor apartment without anyone commenting on the Victorian tiling in the porchway, or the marble black and white checkerboard floors. They were commonplace in Cardiff – many of the older houses that had been converted to flats shared a grand Victorian era entrance – but Katy had never lived in a property with one before. She had expected at least one of her friends to comment on the unusual ceramics, with their green floral spray exploding in to a sea of dark purple. It was one of the factors that had finally decided her on the apartment, when in truth there were many larger flats available in her price range.

'The weather's awful outside,' Simon said as they stepped in to the apartment.

'Yes, not exactly Thailand out there is it Katy?' Adam added.

Adam was the longest serving and most established of "the boyfriends." And by Katy's reckoning by far the most handsome. At

23, when Simon had introduced him to the rest of the group he had been good-looking; flawless skin – the type normally reserved for actors in American high-school movies, a dark mop of slightly curled hair and emerald green eyes that seemed to follow you around the room. But at 31 he somehow looked even more remarkable. His hair was still brown without a fleck of grey and his strong jaw (which was clean shaven the first time they met) was peppered with short coarse stubble. His lean torso was muscular and athletic and tapered in to smooth long legs that begged to be put in to shorts and paraded around for the world to see.

Adam dressed only in the finest labels, wearing clothes that looked as if they had been shipped over that morning from Milan or Rome, or somewhere equally fabulous, only to be unveiled on that very occasion and never to be seen again. Simon in contrast would often turn up in a rugged pullover that he had bought from a charity shop years previously. And yet he still looked good in them. Away from his boyfriend Simon would turn many heads himself – both male and female. He had a quiet confidence about him; an effortlessness that people found endearing. They looked happier than ever and Katy was glad. In their early 20s people had said it would never last, but eight years on they were still proving everyone wrong.

Without fail all of her friends had met their partners through some form of organised event or activity. Simon and Adam had blazed the trail, having met at a Welsh language club. They had both moved to Cardiff from the Home Counties and so neither of them knew any Welsh other than the occasional phrase or road sign. They started the same week and though they failed to master the complicated ll-sounds of the class they soon found a more enjoyable outlet for their tongues in each other. They had been together ever since and were both of them still utterly incapable of speaking more than a sentence or two in Welsh.

Anne and Matt were next. They met at a book group, Anne having convinced herself that she needed to find someone cultured and with a passion for art and creativity. By the time they were married the closest either of them came to literature was watching a movie adaption at the multiplex cinema whilst they fed each other popcorn and wrestled over the armrest.

Siân and Dai had met at cookery classes at the local college. Dai doggedly pursued Siân throughout the eight-week course, trying to impress her each week with his knowledge of pastry and bread making. Yet in the fourteen or so months they had been together since, Katy was pretty sure they had lived off a steady diet of takeaways, meals out and oven-bake lasagne and chips.

When Dai became the latest addition to the boyfriend collective, Katy's friends' lectures about the virtues of joining clubs and societies to find a man seemed to increase tenfold. Just as Anne and Simon had done before her, Siân seemed to take every opportunity to present Katy with some pamphlet or flyer for hot yoga, ice yoga, mountain climbing, bell ringing... even Nordic yodelling. The club juggernaut became an unbearable agenda, resisted only by Katy and Tom who staunchly refused to give in.

The problem for Katy was that people joined these clubs under the pretence of being cultured or sporty or deeply troubled by the state of peace in the Middle East. But really they wanted someone to watch TV with on a Thursday night and to cuddle up in bed to on a Sunday morning. There was nothing wrong with that, but "the clubbers" (as Tom and Katy called them), were insufferably proud of their achievement at finding someone against all the odds. But they missed the point – they failed to understand that if Katy was going to make time in her busy life around work, the gym and the seemingly endless list of other priorities (including finding a man), then it had to be something she was passionate about. It would need to be something exciting, a hobby or a pastime that she cared about, and not something that she'd drop as soon as there was a crumpled pair of boxer shorts lying on her bathroom floor.

So she had resisted, turning down offers of painting classes, poetry marathons, yoga sessions, cake-bakes and even litter picking. If she was going to meet a man...no *when* she met a man, any shared interests would be just that. Something they could enjoy together always, and not just a brief stop on the highway to marriage and kids.

By the time the doorbell rang to announce the arrival of the final guests they had already got through two bottles of wine and Katy was beginning to feel the slightest bit tipsy. She had already sidestepped a thinly-veiled discussion about the new wave of spin classes being run in community centres across the city and managed to quash a suggestion that she accompany a work colleague of Siân's to a pottery course starting in the Bay.

Perhaps it was for this reason that she practically pounced on Tom when he arrived, grateful that at last she would have an ally in proceedings. But then she remembered Owen: the boyfriend. But more than that, the boyfriend that Tom had met at some arty film club that Simon had told him about. Tom was one of them now – a clubber.

'So how many were there Katy?' asked Adam cheekily, as he opened a fifth bottle of wine.

'How many what?'

'You know,' Simon chimed in. 'Holiday romances. How many dashing young men threatened to steal you off us and keep you loved up on some beach?'

'Yes, how many? We're all boring and coupled up now, we want to know about all the men!' Adam chuckled.

'Oh you know, a few.'

'How many is a few?' Matt asked, sounding genuinely curious.

'More than three, less than a football team.' Tom said, a little louder than Katy was expecting.

'Tom! Just you know…a few. Talking of footballers though, you should see the Aussie Rules football players, they literally wear the shortest shorts you've ever seen and every one of them looks like a model.'

'Oh so three *and* a football team then!' Tom squealed.

Katy picked up a breadstick and threw it playfully in his direction. 'You can't judge everyone by your standards Tom!'

'Hey, he's a good boy now, aren't you?' Owen grinned and hugged Tom close to his chest.

Katy felt a sudden pang of jealously, she was happy that Tom was happy, of course she was. It was just that suddenly she was the only one – the only one of the fabulous five who hadn't found a partner. And suddenly she felt a lot more alone that she had ever felt before.

'I'll make a start on dinner; you must all be starving the way we've torn through this wine. I know I am.'

'I'll help,' Owen offered.

'It's no bother really,' Katy replied. 'Stay and enjoy.'

'I need an excuse to put down this glass of red wine and anyway…' he smiled, 'it gives everyone else a chance to tell Tom what they *really* think of me.'

In her tiny kitchen Owen looked like a giant, towering over the worktops and unable to move around freely without nearly knocking something or other over.

'I'm sorry,' he kept saying, 'it must be the wine.'

But it wasn't; it was what happened when you put a 6ft 2 man with broad shoulders and the solid build of a rugby player in a room that had been built for a 5ft something city executive who would only use a kitchen for storing takeaway menus and heating up pizzas.

Katy could certainly understand Owen's appeal – he looked like a man who could take care of you. He had broad arms, which strained at the fabric of his sweater around each bicep, and the outline of a torso that bore witness to countless hours at the gym. His face was strong and masculine. A thick-cropped beard sat beneath bright blue eyes and warm slightly freckled cheeks that hinted at summers spent outdoors. Then of course there was the real clincher, the thing guaranteed to make any woman (or in this case any man) go weak at the knees. Beneath the finely sculpted and chiselled exterior Owen was a teacher – a man who willingly devoted his life to teaching children to read and tie their shoelaces. No wonder she had an involuntarily flutter of excitement when he eased by her to reach the fridge and his tightly knotted thighs brushed against her hips.

'Will I do then?'

'I'm sorry?' Katy garbled, as a bright red flush of embarrassment rushed to her cheeks. It was ridiculous but for a moment she almost felt as if he had read her mind.

'For Tom…'

'Oh, of course,' Katy replied a little too eagerly.

'You're not mad with him then?'

'Mad, why would I be mad?'

'He was worried you might be…well that you might be disappointed that things changed while you were away. And what you'd say – you know, he's told me all about the curse of the clubbers – he didn't want you to think he'd abandoned you for them.'

Suddenly Katy was hit by an enormous wave of sadness. It might have been the wine, or perhaps she was getting a second wave of jetlag, but whatever the reason she felt her eyes pricking with tears and heard a tremble in her voice.

'Of course not. I don't think I could ever be mad at Tom, not really. I'm just glad he's found someone.'

She realised that the wobble in her voice probably made her words seem unconvincing, but she was speaking the truth. She was happy for Tom, and for Owen and for all her friends. But for the first time in her life she realised she was properly alone. She was 31 and single in a city where everyone around her was blissfully coupled up.

For the last twelve months Katy had been surrounded by people. Every waking moment, and every sleeping moment too for that matter, had been spent in the company of others. In the daytime she had gone on group hikes and busy tours and at night she had slept in crowded dorm rooms echoing with the coughs, splutters and snores of her fellow travellers.

Out there travelling the world, backpacking in unfamiliar countries, where she often couldn't even speak the language, she had felt a strange confidence – a surety that she could do anything she set her mind to. And though they had been modest achievements; they meant something – ordering a meal in Japanese, navigating the bus network in Thailand, surviving spiders in the outback and hiking trails in the rainforest.

Now she was back in a city that she knew, surrounded by people she loved, but somehow she felt more of an outsider than ever. Things had changed while she was away, the world had moved on and though she and Tom would always be there for each other he had Owen to think of now. She needed her own life, and she needed something to focus on over the coming months. But as the evening begun to draw to a close she became increasingly certain it wasn't a man she wanted. Not yet anyway. Tom and Owen, Siân and Dai – they had all been ready to meet someone – it was why they had joined every club they could think of in the first place.

A year ago she had considered it, she'd be on the verge of cracking and had steadily leafed her way though a series of ads, listings and prospectuses trying to figure out what interested her. But then she had made the biggest decision of her life, to leave it all behind and explore the world. And because of that things were different now; she wasn't the same woman who had got on the plane at Heathrow twelve months earlier. For the moment love could wait; she needed friends like her, and to be around single people who weren't constantly obsessing about meeting *the one*. She wanted to meet people just like the friends she had made travelling; people who were more interested in seeing the world than finding someone to hide away from it with. The only thing was *could she?* It was easy enough to bond with someone when you were sat on a hostel decking overlooking a beach, with tropical waters lapping at the shore, and all the time in the world to enjoy it. Easier still when you could stay up to four o'clock in the morning drinking beer and playing cards with people you had only met hours earlier. You could share things with them, because you might never see them again, or you might just keep bumping in to them at every hostel for the following two months. But either way people were rarely looking for love, some fun maybe – and she had had one or two travelling flings herself. But they were just that, there had been no expectations and she had enjoyed not having the pressure to try and turn it into something more. But could that work in Cardiff, where the backdrop to her daily life would be a nine-to-five office job and the closest she got to a palm tree was the coconut shampoo she bought at the corner shop?

As her guests slowly filed in to taxis and disappeared in to the night Katy became more and more convinced that that was where the challenge lay – in bringing her experiences travelling in to everyday life. Katy dismissed her earlier sadness as nothing more than a passing wobble and retrieved a half finished bottle of wine from the kitchen. She poured herself a large glass of red and then a half bottle of white swiftly followed. By the time she crawled in to bed it was nearly three in the morning and already her head was beginning to pound and a hazy fog of alcohol was settling on her brain.

The pillow felt hot against her head and she adjusted it, turning it over and smoothing over the stuffing. Just as she felt herself drifting off she had a flash of inspiration that she wanted to remember. She groped in the darkness for her battered laptop, which had survived a year of bumpy bus journeys and an assortment of spills and knocks. A glass of water tumbled from the bedside table and crashed onto the floor below. Katy swore loudly and patted the carpet around her bed until she located the glass and hurriedly returned it to its previous resting place. She then turned her attention to the laptop and a bright white screen burst into life in front of her. She thumbed away at the keys for what seemed like an age before something appeared that made sense. It took another two attempts to turn what she had in to something intelligible and readable. When Katy was finally satisfied with what she'd written she pushed the laptop to one side, hearing it clatter to the floor. She winced at the noise it made as it clanged against the bed frame and threatened to split her spinning head in two. She closed her eyes and tried to breathe evenly, ignoring the waves of nausea and within minutes she was asleep.

Chapter Two

Katy arrived at the bus stop with just enough time to see a departing flash of green before the bus disappeared in to a side street. For the briefest of moments she considered chasing after it and then the smell of a passing bin lorry triggered a fresh wave of nausea in her stomach. Her head, not wishing to be out done, suddenly started to pound again and she instantly dismissed all thoughts of heavy physical exertion for at least a week. Travelling may have increased her alcohol tolerance, but last night she had launched a one-woman assault on her body and the end result was undeniably: wine 1, Katy 0.

The walk in to town took less time than she imagined. Headache aside she was probably the physically fittest she had been since university and the paving stones disappeared beneath her feet with ease. It was incredible how much had changed in a year; shops had closed and reopened, butchers had become bakers and florists had become newsagents. One or two pubs had disappeared and four or five new ones had sprung up to fill the void. Had she been there for the past year these changes would barely have registered, but taken all at once it was a little disconcerting. As she reached the city centre she tried not to look too hard at the shops and focused on the landmarks she could rely upon; the bridge topped with its row of stone animals, the castle – stalwart sentry of the high street, and her personal favourite the arcades.

Cardiff had what seemed like innumerable arcades; small covered shopping streets squeezed improbably between buildings. Some of them linked with one another, while others ran in parallel, but each had their own distinct character. After ten years in the city she still couldn't name all of them, but she could describe every one of them in detail. Whenever anyone had asked her about home it was one of the things she mentioned. They were the backbone of her surrogate city and she spoke of their Victorian grandeur with pride.

Waiting just outside one such arcade was Tom, framed perfectly by an archway of high-glassed ceilings and wooden frame shops. He was wearing a short maroon scarf, a blue sweater and a black jacket that she suspected belonged to Owen, given it was at least two sizes too big on him. She smiled, not just because it was good to see him, but also because it was good to see him so contented.

'I'm so sorry I'm late, I missed the bus and…anyway it's so good to see you. Properly I mean.'

'I know - I've missed you Katy. A year's a long time!'

They hugged and Katy felt herself relax in to his arms. She could have happily remained cocooned in the comfortable familiarity of his touch for hours, despite being stood in the middle of a busy street.

'Let's get coffee,' he said eventually. 'My head's killing me.'

Katy laughed and followed Tom in to the coffee shop where he bought them both extra large lattes and the biggest chocolate muffin imaginable.

'So, how was it really – being back last night?'

'It was lovely, I missed you all terribly. It's been amazing this last year, I loved every minute of it – but – well it's just so good to see you all.'

'And Owen?'

'He's lovely.'

'He is! And have you seen his arms?'

Katy laughed: 'Yes, impressive!'

'And he plays rugby Katy, as in actually gets all muddy and sweaty with a bunch of lads for fun. It's literally the hottest thing I've ever seen.'

'Well it's good to know he's ticking all your boxes,' Katy said with a smile.

'He is really. I mean putting aside how good he looks in shorts for a moment; he's an amazing guy. He's sweet and clever and I've been wanting you to meet him forever.'

'How long have you been together now? Five months?'

'Nearly six. It's wonderful Katy, I can't believe I waited this long.'

'It's serious then?'

Tom's response was stifled by a huge chunk of muffin and he quickly cupped his hand to his face to stop a shower of crumbs covering the table. But the grin when he removed his hand said everything. It was serious.

There had always been boyfriends with Tom. Some he had fallen for and some had fallen for him, but the two had never married up before. It was the one area of Tom's life that remained completely unfathomable to Katy. He would introduce her to someone and she would find him charming, attractive, funny – everything she wanted in a man herself – only to have Tom dismiss him a few days later. Then he would turn up at her flat giddy with excitement over someone else and when she eventually met him he would turn out to be aloof, or rude, or wholly unsuitable in some other way. What all the men had in common however was that visually they were carbon copies of Tom – slim, clean shaven, well-dressed and young-looking, or just plain young in some cases. Owen however didn't fit that mould at all; he was five years older than Tom and looked as if he could have come out of the womb with a full beard. His hair was unstyled and cropped short and shock horror he actually had to buy his t-shirts from a section other than the XS rail.

'You never said last night – if there was anyone special while you were away? You mentioned a few guys in emails, but by the time I next heard from you they always seemed to have moved on.'

Katy felt a pang of guilt at his question. There had been times when there had been a few weeks between her replies, when the internet had been too difficult to access, or too expensive, or she had simply been too busy having fun.

'No, no one really. There were some lovely guys of course, but they were all too young to take seriously.'

He seemed to pause and she was surprised. She couldn't imagine any question that he could be apprehensive about asking. Over the years they had talked about everything, and nothing was off limits, especially after a few drinks.

'I saw David the other day.' Tom said, tentatively.

'Oh,' was all the response she could manage.

David. Shit.

'He's moved back. He's got a job at the Heath.'

'You spoke to him?'

'Of course Katy, you were together four years. I could hardly ignore him.'

'No – sorry, I just – I just wasn't expecting him to be *here*.'

'He looked good.'

'Tom!'

'Well I knew you were thinking it. I could practically hear the question turning over in your head.'

'Good? Not heartbroken, or fat, or I don't know – sad?' she asked, hearing the slight desperation in her own voice.

'It's been a year, what do you expect?'

'I know, I mean I want him to move on. That's why I ended things; I wanted us *both* to move on. I just wanted him to do it far away from here.'

'London didn't work out. Apparently.'

'What do you mean *apparently.*'

'Oh come on Katy. Are you that naïve? You go travelling for a year and it just so happens he moves back a few weeks before you're due back. He still loves you.'

'He said that?'

'No. But why else would he be back?'

Katy didn't give an answer. She couldn't think of anything at all to say. She had thought that morning that the hangover was as bad as it could get. She'd been wrong.

'Is there anything still there? For you…?' Tom asked quietly.

'Oh God. Did he ask you to ask me?'

'No, of course not. We both know I'd never take his side over yours…I just wondered.'

Katy sighed. The silly thing was she had gone travelling to forget David. But she had found that being away reminded her of him more than anything. Whenever there was a beautiful sunset, or a dish she had never tried before, or when things on the road got just a little too much it was always him she thought of. Always David.

They had lived together, holidayed together, loved and fought under the same roof for years – it was only natural that he was in her thoughts. But as time had gone on she had made peace with her decision. She loved David, but they weren't right for one another. It had been a relief when she returned home knowing that he was in London. Finding out that he was actually in Cardiff was the last thing she had expected.

'So what next?'

'Next we shop. I have no winter clothes, I had to borrow plates and glasses for last night and there's only so long a girl can live without a hairdryer.'

'Wow, you really went all out on the downsizing,' said Tom, a genuine note of surprise in his voice.

As they left the coffee shop and stepped out in to the bracing air Tom squeezed her arm. 'I wasn't asking about shopping…'

'I know. But it's all I feel capable of right now.'

Chapter Three

Shop windows the length of Queen Street were filled with golden stars, glittery presents and sweater-clad mannequins surrounded by cotton snow. Already there was a sense of panic in the air, even though there were still four more weekends before Christmas. The streets were crowded and as Tom and Katy weaved through their fellow shoppers they were blasted with alternate volleys of warm air and Christmas tunes as shops fought for their custom. Katy was handed one leaflet and then another advertising sales and it didn't take long for the two of them to tire.

'Let's go down here,' Tom said as he turned a corner, leaving the chaos of the high street behind. All around St John's church there were small pine huts bursting with holly wreaths, cards and gifts. Katy stopped to look at a stall selling garlands of dried fruit. There were rows of them, all hanging from the arches of the hut. Each one was a feast of citrus interspersed with pinecones and cinnamon sticks, and held together with brown twine. They were finished off with long trails of berry red ribbons. She breathed in deeply, savouring the earthy smell of spice overlain by the sweet citrus hum of oranges and clementines. It reminded her of her childhood, when the school bus drove them round the nearby villages to sing carols.

At every village the bus would stop and empty it's cargo of children onto the pavements and they would take garlands just like the ones from the stall as gifts for elderly villagers. Her mum would remain in the back of the bus, surrounded by the richly scented orange strings and with an old guitar on her lap. And while all the other children sang along to *We Three Kings* or *O Come All Ye Faithful*, Katy would stand silently and watch her mother singing in perfect harmony, eyes closed in bliss and strumming at the weathered six strings of her beloved guitar. Then when they were home and Katy and her brother no longer had to share their mum with the rest of the school she would jump in to her mum's lap and bury her head in the orange scented wool of her mum's jumper. In those moments Katy was entirely in awe of her mother, who literally sang her accomplishments to the world, whilst Katy's own voice trembled and shook at the slightest bit of public attention. In the years since, Katy's confidence had grown and she had become an adult in her own right; accomplished and competent, yet she still felt dwarfed by her mother – a glittering goliath of womanhood she felt she could never live up to.

It was some moments before Katy realised that she had lost Tom. She had been so engrossed in the stall she hadn't noticed that he had wandered on ahead. By the time she caught up with him he had already ordered two Glühweins. Beaming at her he thrust a large ceramic mug of the steaming wine in to her hand and took a large sip of his own.

'Just what you need – hair of the dog!'

The wine went down much better than she expected. A few hours earlier the very thought of alcohol would have turned her stomach. But after wandering around in the cold, the hot spiced drink was surprisingly welcome. The first mugful quickly disappeared and a second swiftly followed.

By the time Tom went to fetch a third the stall had become much busier as shop and office workers finished for the week and gathered to meet one another over drinks. Whilst she waited, Katy absently flicked through her phone checking for messages and deleting junk emails. The last email she came to looked like spam at first but there was something about the title that sparked a vague memory in her. She opened it up and felt a hot pulse rush to her temples as she read.

RE: Christmas Club

Dear Katy,

What an excellent idea. I shall see you on Saturday.

From Cerys

P.s. I hope you don't mind me emailing, you didn't say in your message whether we should just turn up or let you know in advance, so I thought best to email.

Katy felt her face erupt in a flush of heat, but it wasn't caused by the Glühwein. A wave of panic swiftly followed and she pushed her way through the crowd towards the bar, leaving a trail of angry people in her wake. Accusations of pushing in sparked up all around her and she felt the embarrassment growing in her cheeks. She ducked her head down and focused only on the back of Tom's head. When she was close enough to reach she tapped him on the shoulder and pulled him gently away from the bar.

'What's going on?' he asked, stepping aside from the crowd. He looked like a dejected puppy, his cheerful demeanour disappearing as he watched his spot at the bar being filled by two men in suits.

'I was just about to be served,' he added, a little sulkily.

His objections fell on deaf ears. Katy's mind was already racing through all the mortifying permutations – all of them far worse than missing out on a mulled wine.

'God Tom, I think I may have done something really stupid.'

They caught a taxi from the end of the street. The whole journey Katy anxiously watched the meter as it ticked upwards – painfully reminding her not only of how slowly they were progressing, but also how much it was going to cost her. When they finally reached the flat she thrust £20 in to the cabbie's hand through the divider and hurried to the front door, not waiting for the change.

The keys were like butter in her hands, slipping uselessly through her fingers. There were only three keys on her chain but it took her four attempts before she found the right one. Once in the flat she ran straight to the bedroom and reappeared a moment later, laptop in hand. She flipped the lid and stared impatiently at the screen. It responded painfully slowly, gradually fading from black to colour and opening up on the last page she had visited the night before. It was a local online message board that allowed people to post ads. Katy had used it lots just before she went travelling, selling off furniture and boxes of unwanted household items. But the page in front of her wasn't for selling goods, it was a socials page and there right at the top of the page was her name and the same words she recognised from the email: Christmas Club.

Katy clicked on the advert title and a new page opened up. She raced through the whole message without breathing, desperate to see how bad it was.

Christmas Club

Everybody is welcome to the first meeting of the Cardiff Christmas Club – this Saturday!

There are only two rules.

1. *This club is all about Christmas, and only Christmas. Nothing else. You have to like Christmas. Humbuggers, spoilsports and miseries are not welcome here.*

2. *Under no circumstance at all must anyone at Christmas Club be looking to find a boyfriend, girlfriend, husband, wife or significant other. This is not that kind of a club – this is about Christmas (see point one for more details).*

I'm Katy, 31 and I'm not looking for a boyfriend (or a husband)…or a girlfriend either. Not that it would matter if I was. But I'm not. Anyway – this Saturday Christmas Club – 5pm at The Flying Duck pub. See you there. I shall be wearing a Santa hat.

By the time she had read the message through a second time tears were rolling down Tom's cheek. He had balled his hand in to a fist and was biting so hard on his fingers that Katy could see the skin around his teeth was pinched white. The stifled guffaws rocked through his body and he was almost bent over double with the effort at trying to contain his laughter. In a moment she could tell he would lose all self-control and explode in a shrieking mess of hilarity.

'It's not funny Tom. Somebody has emailed me. They're coming to this. They're going to turn up *tomorrow* at the pub expecting some crazed Christmas lunatic who hates men.'

Katy heard a loud thump behind her and turned round to see Tom sitting on the floor rocking backwards and forwards practically screaming with laughter. She picked a cushion from a chair and threw it at him.

'It's *not* funny Tom.' But even as she spoke she realised it was and felt a smile creeping across her face.

'Oh God,' she said again as she sat down beside him. 'Of course I can't go.'

Suddenly there was a lull in the wheezing, spluttering cacophony of Tom's mocking and he looked at her in deadly seriousness.

'Katy Winters, you are absolutely 100% going to go to that pub tomorrow. Even if it means I have to drag you there in your little Santa hat myself.'

Chapter Four

Tom gave Katy a wave while he waited to be served. He hadn't been in *The Flying Duck* pub for years and to his knowledge neither had Katy. He wondered what had dredged it up in her thoughts to pick it as a venue. When they were students they had drunk there regularly and the place hadn't changed much since. The wine was still cheap and so was the décor. Peeling white and fuchsia walls framed a dark carpet, heavily patterned with Fleur De Lys and beer. It was a place they had outgrown as their salaries grew and their nights out became fewer and more treasured. That they were suddenly back there years later spoke volumes to Tom.

He was worried about Katy. On the outside she looked better than ever; she had never needed to lose weight, but the 10lb she had dropped travelling made all her features sing a little more. Her skin was a delicate sun-kissed shade of bronze from a year in warmer climes. The smile that he loved to see had returned, and her hair, which had grown out to shoulder length while she was away, looked incredible tied up in a loose ponytail. She was single-handedly discrediting all he had ever heard about the damaging effects of sun and salt water.

But there was a change on the inside that worried him, she was different than the Katy he had tearfully hugged goodbye at the airport. Most of the changes were positive; she had clearly had an incredible time and seen and experienced things he could scarcely imagine. She was more confident too, of that he was sure. And he wouldn't have said she was unhappy – but there was something not quite right. Maybe she was just disappointed to be back, after all he had heard about people having "travel blues" when they returned. But the very fact that she had started her own club, albeit in a drunken haze, worried him. Katy had always been staunchly resistant to the "club delusion" as she called it. In truth it had never really bothered him, but she had been insistent and as ever he had stuck by her. That she had now done a complete U-turn worried him.

It was his concern for Katy that caused Tom to make her to go to *The Flying Duck*. At first he had laughed, of course he had. The idea of her drunkenly ranting in to the internet about the clubbers had seemed so funny at first. But the more he thought about it there was something incredibly sad about it; something that reminded Tom of his younger self.

Before Tom came out his sexuality had been a dark and heavy secret and he carried it with him every day. He hid it from friends and family and felt the weight of it gradually dragging him down. Sometimes the burden got too much and he had cried for help, but nobody had noticed. At least nobody until Katy.

They had met in fresher's week and had instantly hit it off. They were in the same halls and quickly identified that they had one or two of the same lectures, crossing over in their year one choices of art and photography. At the end of the first week, they were in a grubby basement bar in town and everyone around them was dancing. The place was full of students, most of them first years and there right in the middle of it all was Katy and she was dancing arm in arm with the most carefree man Tom had ever seen. Free – that was how Simon appeared: free.

Simon was good looking, but he wasn't *the most* attractive man there. Yet in the dismal light of the basement bar Simon shone and Tom was utterly captivated. Simon was gay and it wasn't something he was hiding, or apologising for, it was just another part of him, just as his eyes were green and his hair hazel brown. When Tom realised he was staring he quickly looked away as a sad lump of envy formed in his throat. He wanted to be like the boy on the dance floor, he just didn't know how.

As soon as the song ended Katy was by his side, playfully asking who had caught his eye. Tom could tell then that she knew, he had been uncovered and he felt sick to the core with worry. Outwardly he laughed it off, feigning ignorance, but for the rest of the night he was aware of it, like a shadow growing across their burgeoning friendship. She knew and he knew that she knew, and that would never go away.

He had only known her a week, it wasn't *so* bad he tried to tell himself. It wasn't like it was one of his friends from home or his family. So maybe she wouldn't speak to him again - a week ago he didn't even know her, was it really something to be so upset over?

For the following two hours Tom put himself through utter torture. All the time his eyes kept drifting to Katy, looking for some sign of the rejection or ridicule that would surely come his way. And then he would steal a glance at Simon and his heart would sink at the knowledge that the life he needed was so close but felt utterly out of reach. He got drunk; ridiculously and utterly drunk and then his paranoia got worse and he knew he had to leave, before he said something; before he slipped up and gave the game away completely. He stumbled towards the stairs, already battling the lurching feeling in his stomach that told him he was going to be sick. To his horror Katy followed him, collecting her coat from the cloakroom and catching up with him before he could slip away.

In the fresh air of the open street his queasiness settled for a moment and he was struck by a moment of what felt like clarity. He kissed her, willing himself to enjoy it and convincing himself that he could make it work. His whole life reeled in front of him, she was fun and kind and his parents would love her – they could have a family and he'd be happy enough. And he'd do right by her; he wouldn't cheat on her or hurt her. It wasn't what he wanted, but perhaps it was enough, and no one, no one but him would *ever* know otherwise.

Katy kissed him back, lightly pressing her lips against his. She didn't return the roving advance of his tongue, but she didn't push him away either. It was…nice. Her lips were soft and sweet with the tang of orange juice. He ran his fingers through her hair. *I can do this*, he said to himself, over and over. *I can do this.*

They caught a taxi back to the halls, sitting in the back with hands outstretched, bridging the gap of the no-man's land of the middle seat. But the closer they got to the hall the more he began to panic. He wasn't sure what to say…what to do.

He fumbled with the front door key and they let themselves in as quietly as possible, aware of the dorm rooms around them and the slumbering people inside. He led her towards his room and just as he went to unlock it he felt a hand on his. Katy smiled at him and kissed him gently on the cheek before whispering 'goodnight' and heading to her room across the hall.

On the one hand he was relieved, grateful that he had been spared the embarrassment of finding out he was unable to perform, but on the other he felt his torture grow. He could feel the lie spiralling out of control; he could see it growing the next morning and the one after that until there was no telling what it would become.

But nothing Tom feared came to light. The next morning he woke up to find a note from Katy pushed under his door, inviting him to come to her room when he was up. She greeted him with a huge steaming mug of coffee and a plate piled high with buttery toast, a little cold but delicious all the same.

Somehow she knew exactly what he needed. She spoke when the lump in his throat became too big to squeeze out the words and was quiet when he found his strength. Katy led the way, so that all he had to do was follow. But when it came to the final leap it was his to make alone. At last he said the words that had haunted him his whole life out loud. He was gay; and the world was still turning.

From that day their friendship was cemented. Katy introduced Tom to Simon and he helped Tom continue the journey that Katy had begun. In the months that followed Anne and Siân joined their ranks and the five of them became a unit. They were like a family, with Katy and Tom as the dysfunctional couple at its heart. For ten years they had been there for one another unfalteringly, right until the day Katy stepped on to a plane. Tom had worried that the time apart would cause them to drift, and that was even before Owen had arrived. But when Tom woke the morning after reading Katy's message with a knot of anxiety in his stomach the size of a football, he knew two things. The first was that they would always be in each other's lives and neither boyfriends nor continents could separate them. The second was that something was very wrong, Katy's message had been a cry for help and this time it was his turn to answer.

Chapter Five

Tom set the cups of coffee down and squeezed onto the bench beside Katy. She refused to wear the Santa hat, but as a compromise it sat on the table in front of them so that people would see it as they came in.

'I still can't believe you made me come,' she moaned to Tom.

'You had to come, you couldn't just have stood that woman up.'

'I could have emailed her and told her it was cancelled.'

'And then you would have spent all evening worried that she hadn't got your email, or that someone else would have turned up without getting in touch first. We'll stay for an hour, see who comes and then I'll buy you a glass of wine and you can forget all about it.'

'No, wine is what got me in to this mess in the first place. We'll stay for *half* an hour and then you can take me for the biggest, chocolatiest, most expensive cake that you can find in Cardiff on a Saturday night.'

'Deal,' he grinned. 'I can't stand that you're thinner than me now anyway – it'll be good to fatten you up.'

They sat and talked, both of them glancing at the door every few minutes waiting to see if anyone arrived. When it was 5 o'clock Katy started to hope that no one was coming and decided that if nobody had arrived by quarter past they would leave. She started to imagine the cake she would order, it would have to be one of those triple layer ones; sponge then chocolate filling, more sponge and chocolate filling on top. And she'd have it with cream and ice cream and chocolate sauce too if that was an option.

'You must be Katy.'

'Sorry?' Katy said, a little flustered.

'The hat dear. You are Katy yes? From the Christmas Club?'

'Oh, yes.' Katy replied, trying not to sound too disappointed. 'And you're...Cerys?' she asked hopefully, thinking that at least if only one person turned up they could call the whole thing off without too much fuss.

'Yes, and this must be your lovely husband all cwtched up beside you.'

Cerys struck out a hand, which Tom shook in muted bewilderment.

'You know, I did think your ad a little odd – all that talk about not looking for boyfriends and everything. But of course it makes sense now. You've already got yourself a man – and you don't need another one do you. One's more than enough to take care of! Right, I'll just get myself a whisky and I'll be right back.'

'My God,' whispered Tom, sounding more than a little shocked.

'I know – she actually thought you were straight.'

Cerys had delivered her opening address without pause or hesitation and only stopped to take breath when she left them for the bar. She spoke with a strong Welsh lilt that reminded Katy of her aunt. But there the resemblance ended, where Katy's aunt had been a mild and meek woman, Cerys seemed anything but. She was like a whirlwind in a wax jacket, elbowing her way up to the bar and ordering a drink with near military efficiency.

The door of the bar opened again and a young woman stepped in, shaking the rain from her umbrella as she nervously ran her eyes over the room. Her eyes seemed to settle on Katy and Tom and she walked over to them quickly, not making eye contact with anyone en-route.

'Are you Katy – about the Christmas Club?'

'Yes, nice to meet you.'

'Sophia.'

'And I'm Tom.'

Sophia sat down opposite Katy and put her bag on the table. Katy didn't know a lot about fashion; she knew the shops she liked and rarely deviated from them. But she could tell the bag was expensive, and it wasn't just her bag either. Sophia's coat was thick and luxurious and around her neck hung a small string of pearls.

After a minute of rummaging in her bag she pulled out a small black leather bound notepad and a silver pen in a felt sleeve and placed them on the table in front of her. Sophia opened the notebook, flicking to an empty page and then wrote in big letters at the top: *Christmas Club (first meeting).*

Katy felt a flutter of panic – she wasn't sure what exactly the woman was expecting that she thought she would need to take notes.

'I really hadn't planned anything, um…formally,' Katy offered apologetically, wondering if the woman was expecting some sort of agenda or schedule.

'Oh, well that's OK – I guess we can make it up as we go along. Are you expecting many more people?'

At that moment Cerys returned from the bar, hesitating for a moment before taking a seat next to Sophia. Cerys eyed up the new arrival the way Katy imagined a vet would look at a newborn calf.

'Are we expecting any more?' Cerys asked, ignoring Sophia.

'Well Sophia has just joined us,' said Tom, 'And it's only just gone five so we'll wait a few minutes more.'

Cerys boomed her name at Sophia by way of introduction and then thrust out a palm, extending it so far that the younger woman was forced to scrunch her own arm against her chest to give them the room to shake hands.

'Sophia,' and then she added, 'I'm Swiss. But I'm studying in Cardiff now.'

'Tom and I both went to university in Cardiff too,' Katy jumped in, grateful for the conversational lifeline.

'Ah is that how you met then? Lovely!' exclaimed Cerys.

'Well we're not actually a couple. We're just friends.'

The reaction from the two women couldn't have been more different. Cerys looked genuinely surprised and even a little disappointed maybe. Whereas Sophia took one glance at Tom and then proceeded to tap her pen impatiently on the pad, unsure why they were wasting time stating the obvious.

'More candidates I think,' Tom whispered. He gently nudged Katy and gestured subtly to a couple that had been stood at the bar previously but were now starting to drift over towards the table.

When they realised they had been seen the woman from the couple stepped forward a little tentatively and waved a hand in their general direction.

'I'm Jenny and this is my husband Chris. We weren't sure if we could join or not.'

'I'm sorry?' Katy asked, becoming increasingly flustered.

'Well we're married you see. So we're not looking for anyone because well we've already found them,' she added with a giggle as she beckoned her husband to step forward. 'So I said that was OK – but if you're only looking for single people, well then obviously we can't join.'

'That's a good point,' Cerys chipped in. 'I'm single, well divorced which I guess isn't the same thing. Oh don't worry yourself dear – it's a long time ago now,' she added, looking at Katy.

'I'm single too,' Sophia added thoughtfully – 'and the two of you?'

The whole evening was becoming increasingly surreal and Katy wondered how she had found herself discussing relationship statuses with complete strangers. Suddenly she realised that everyone was staring expectantly at her; waiting for an official judgement on whether married couples were eligible.

'Of course you can join – take a seat,' Tom said. And he shuffled up so that Jenny could sit beside him on the bench.

Chris followed, grabbing a chair from a nearby empty table and positioning himself between Jenny and Cerys. Chris seemed reluctant to put down his beer and clung on to it firmly. He gave a brief nod to the assembled party and then tilted his head towards the small TV in the top right of the bar, which was playing football. Katy was left with the distinct impression that coming along was definitely Jenny's idea, and she looked like the kind of woman that you didn't generally say no to.

'Super,' Jenny added. 'What have we missed?'

'Nothing really,' Sophia replied.

Katy felt the blow of the young woman's verdict on the evening so far keenly and her heart sank a little deeper, knowing she had nothing planned.

'Well perhaps we should all introduce ourselves – I'm Jenny, and this is Chris and we've just moved to the area. We thought it would be a lovely way to meet people in time for Christmas.'

There was an awkward pause for a moment as people waited for Chris to continue the introductions. When he stayed silent, Jenny cleared her throat a little and Katy thought she saw the table wobble a little as if a firm nudge had just taken place underneath it.

Chris gave the group a small wave in response and then seeing his wife's disappointment raised his glass to the rest of them. When it was clear that no further greetings were coming Cerys stepped in, amply filling the void and causing the tables around them to glance in their direction.

'Cerys, and I'm from Cowbridge. Oh and what brilliant timing – here's Rhodri. He must have found a parking spot after all.'

Katy looked up to see a tall man with chestnut brown eyes and a wave of dark black hair. He pulled up a chair and sat on the edge of the table to the right of Katy. As he moved Katy caught the slightest draft of cologne, it was rich and spicy like burnt orange and ginger. She smiled, but like Chris opposite him, Rhodri's eyes had already drifted towards the flickering screen and the two-dozen men chasing a ball around a green field.

'I'm Sophia, from Bern in Switzerland. All my family are away over Christmas and it didn't seem worth going home. So I'll be in Cardiff for Christmas.'

'Rhodri, I run the farm next door to Cerys.'

'And I'm Katy and this is Tom.'

'Perhaps you could tell us a bit about the club? Why you set it up?' Sophia asked.

Katy started to speak before she had fully decided what she was going to say. She couldn't tell if Sophia was goading her on, or simply eager for something more to happen. Either way she could feel the pressure piling up. For twelve months she had been her own person, experiencing freedom in a way she never had before. There had been no deadlines, no client meetings, Council Tax bills or spam insurance calls. She had been answerable to no one and the closest she had come to a routine was following her stomach's demands for regular meals.

But suddenly people wanted something from her, they wanted answers and ideas and plans. And she had none. There was never meant to be a Christmas Club, people were never meant to turn up.

'I hadn't really thought that far if I'm honest. I wasn't sure anyone would show up. I'm sorry; it's all been a bit of a mistake. I've been away for a year and I guess it's just been a bit hard adjusting to being back and for a moment I thought it would be a good idea to have something to focus on, something positive and I really do love Christmas – but, but it was a stupid idea and I'm sorry but I think I've wasted all your time. I'll buy you all a drink.'

She felt tears pricking at her eyes and a lump forming in her throat. Her head felt hot and clammy and she could feel the thorny blush of her skin turning rose red above her chest. Tom placed a supportive hand on her left leg and cleared his throat nervously.

'It's not worth getting upset over.'

To her surprise the words of comfort actually came from her right, from Rhodri. Somehow she hadn't expected it – the gentle, soothing voice didn't seem to match the strong, almost gruff exterior. But then he leant back in his chair and returned his gaze to the screen and she wondered if she had mistaken dismissiveness for kindness. Perhaps he was as disinterested in the whole evening as Chris clearly was, but if so why had he come?

'So you don't have a plan at all?' Sophia asked. As she did so her pen wavered across her notebook as if readying herself to strike out the words she had only just written, before returning home frustrated at having her evening wasted.

'Well, perhaps someone else would like to suggest something,' Tom said. 'You all came; at least one of you must have had some thoughts?'

Katy wondered why Tom was trying to pursue this so doggedly. Surely that had been their escape? Embarrassing and mortifying yes – but they had nearly been free and now he was trying to drag it out further. He had wandered right past the elephant in the room and proceeded straight to the dead horse – and he was well and truly flogging it.

But it turned out Tom wasn't the only one intent on dragging things out and Cerys quickly took up the reins: 'Well, actually there was something I was hoping for some help on – and it certainly fits the bill. Every year I make holly wreaths for the village. They're quite popular and all the money goes to the village hall and the Christmas fayre. Normally I'd have made a start by now, but this year – well – I'm rather behind…'

For the first time since she had arrived at the bar Cerys' voice dropped below booming. Come the end she even sounded a little subdued. Her head dropped from its proud, horizontal position and her eyes drifted down to the table.

'I have all the ribbons and the wire,' she added 'and they're really quite fun to make.'

'How many do you need?' Sophia asked, her interest picking up for the first time.

'Two hundred.'

A muted wave of gasps swept the table and even Chris tore himself away from the TV long enough to register his surprise. Whatever people had imagined coming out of Christmas Club, it was clear that they weren't expecting it to sound so much like hard work.

'Two hundred?' Jenny repeated questioningly.

'Yes, well give or take, sometimes we need a little more. Or a few less.' Cerys added hastily.

Across the table the number 200 and the words *holly* and *wreaths* had appeared in Sophia's book, each evenly spaced and written in large sloping script. Beneath this she started to scribble what looked like a series of numbers.

'There's seven of us, 200 holly wreaths. That's only 30 each, well it's 28 and a half – but obviously we'd each want one ourselves so that makes it 29 and a half so 30 just makes sense really – that way if the first one is rubbish it doesn't matter.'

Sophia seemed to have worked it all out, and to her thirty holly wreaths probably didn't sound a lot. But Katy knew it wouldn't be so easy for the others who had jobs and families making demands on their time that a 20-year-old student couldn't imagine.

'Six,' Chris interjected. 'There's six of *you*. I just came along tonight – in case, well you know – the advert did sound a bit crazy. No offence.'

The funny thing was Katy wasn't offended at all, the advert had sounded crazy. If one day she was married and she announced she was coming along to something like this then she would hope her husband would check it out with her.

'That's a lot of work,' Jenny added. 'I've just started a new job. I wasn't expecting such a big time commitment.'

'November and December are my busiest times,' said Tom. And they were, Katy knew that – it was the time of the year when he had to finish lots of portraits and commissions ready for people to give as Christmas presents.

'I understand. I knew it was a big ask. And anyway there wouldn't even have been six of us I suppose – and split five ways its just too much.'

Katy didn't understand what Cerys meant; why there would only be five of them? But before she was able to ask her Rhodri was speaking, his voice solid and sure like granite.

'We could do it. It'd be hard work. But it's doable. I could probably take on a few more than my share, and if anyone else could do the same we could probably make it easier for Tom and Jenny and anyone else with lots on.'

Cerys gave Rhodri a look that Katy couldn't quite figure out. The older woman was surprised definitely, but there was something more. Katy wondered how they knew each other and whether it went beyond being neighbours. There was no obvious romantic link; Rhodri was a good 30-40 years younger than Cerys and there had been no mention of Cerys having a daughter.

'Katy?' Sophia prompted.

'I'm sorry?' she replied, having completely lost track of the conversation.

'I was just saying I could probably take on a few more too. And I wondered if you could also – just until you start work?'

What happened next Katy would never have predicted. A few hours earlier she had wanted nothing more than for the whole thing to go away. Then in the previous half hour somehow things had changed. As soon as the pressure of directing the group had been lifted and someone else had put forward an idea she had started to relax. To her even greater surprise she even found herself wanting to take part. Although she knew almost nothing about Cerys, she got the impression that she wasn't a woman who asked for help easily. For her to have come along and met a group of strangers and bring up the holly wreaths it was clearly something that she was struggling with. If that wasn't a good enough cause for Christmas Club then what was?

'Yes, actually I think I could. Tom, Jenny, if the rest of us could make 40 each, do you think you'd both have time to make 20?'

They both seemed to hesitate a little. Katy figured that neither of them had any idea how long it would take to make a holly wreath. Not that she did herself. But after a moment Tom agreed and Jenny followed suit.

'Excellent,' Katy said, feeling suddenly optimistic about the whole thing. 'Then it's settled – the Cardiff Christmas Club has a plan. Let me get everyone a drink and then Cerys – you can talk us through what we need to do.'

Katy stood up to go to the bar but straight away found she was hemmed in. To go to her left would mean asking Tom, Jenny and probably Chris to move. But somehow that was more appealing than trying to squeeze herself past Rhodri.

The decision was made for her when Rhodri scraped his chair forwards, pinning himself against the table and clearing a small space behind. She stepped in to the gap, grateful at least that she didn't have to walk in front of him, but even so she was aware of how close they were. Although he was sat down the back of his head was near hers and as she brushed by she could see the dark 'v' of his hairline cutting in to the nape of his neck and leading her eyes down his broad muscular back. Suddenly aware she was staring she lifted her head to find Tom watching her, his blue eyes twinkling and a small smile on his face. He stood up as well and followed her to the bar, leaving Jenny talking to her husband, who at the mention of a drink seemed to have perked up a little.

'So – Christmas Club then?' Tom said, by way of a greeting.

'Yes, not exactly what I had planned for this evening. But you know actually I'm really pleased. It's going to be a few weeks before I get a job, maybe it won't be until the new year even. It'll do me good to have something to focus on. And it will help Cerys, and it's for charity.'

'Right, so it's nothing to do with the six-foot tall dark-haired, stunningly attractive man you've been sat next to all night?'

Katy instinctively shushed him, painfully aware from past experience that Tom was rarely as quiet and discreet as he imagined himself to be.

'No! Anyway it wouldn't matter if it were, would it? You remember the message – no one looking for a boyfriend, girlfriend, husband or wife need apply. He's probably already got some perfect blonde wife waiting for him at home baking mince pies and stirring pans of homemade mulled wine. And even if he were single then that means he's not looking, which is perfect because I'm not either.'

'That's good.'

'Really, why?'

'Definitely one of us, you can tell. He's as gay as Christmas.'

It wasn't unusual for Tom to claim the attractive men they saw in bars as playing for his team. In fact if Tom's assessment of the male population of Cardiff was correct then the chances of future generations ever being born was pretty slim. But Rhodri? She couldn't see it.

'He can't be gay. Surely. You don't really think he is do you?'

Tom paused before replying, dragging out his answer like he was a presenter on a TV talent show.

'No, of course not. But if you're not interested why does it matter?'

She couldn't believe she had fallen for it. To make things worse before she even had the chance to argue with him about it, he was gone, drifting back to the table with the first of the drinks, an infuriatingly smug look on his face.

The rest of the evening seemed to disappear in a blur. In many ways it reminded her of travelling, just with an average age about a decade and a half higher. But the feeling it gave her; of meeting new people, sharing stories with strangers and making plans to see and do things you hadn't expected – that was exactly like travelling. It was what she missed the most. So when the time came to finally say goodnight and bring the meeting to a close Katy was actually a little disappointed that it was over.

Jenny and Chris left first, followed by Sophia. Then when only the four of them remained Rhodri excused himself and headed to the bathroom. After he had left the table Cerys turned to look behind to see he was gone and then leant in taking hold of Katy's hands in her own.

'Thank you,' Cerys said sincerely. The words caught in her throat as a bubble of emotion raced to get out in to the open, manifesting itself in a suppressed gulp of air.

Katy didn't know what to say, Cerys was a proud woman and she didn't want to embarrass her by making a fuss. Instead she just smiled and when she felt the tremble ripple through Cerys' hands and shudder against her own she pretended she hadn't noticed it and gave her the space to regain her composure in her own time.

The door to the gents toilets opened and Rhodri re-entered the bar, stooping to avoid the low doorframe as he did so. Immediately Cerys withdrew her hands and got to her feet. She gave Rhodri a quick wave and then suddenly seemed in a hurry to leave. She stopped just long enough to give Katy a quick kiss on the cheek, leaving behind the heady waft of her well-waxed jacket.

'That'll be me off too then.' Rhodri added, more formally than Katy expected. She leant in to give him a goodbye hug and then decided better of it, sticking a hand out in front of her. He shook it slowly and she couldn't tell if he was relieved at her last minute withdrawal or disappointed. Or perhaps she was overanalysing as per usual and he hadn't even noticed.

Katy suddenly regretted wearing flat shoes, she felt dwarfed standing in front of him. Her eyes were at the level of his jaw and she found herself staring at the thick carpet of dark bristle on his chin admiringly. As soon as she realised she was doing so her eyes fluttered upwards and fell on his; two dark chestnut discs gazed back at her. She smiled and looked away, embarrassed by their proximity, but not before she stole a quick look at him.

There was something incredibly refreshing about Rhodri. She had spent the last year surrounded by permanently tanned and toned 20-somethings; their muscles artificially shaped by hours of repetitive curls, squats and weight lifts. Compared to Rhodri they looked ridiculous and frivolous; strange creatures that probably spent more time fussing their hair in one day than he probably had in his whole life. Not that she hadn't enjoyed the view when they had strolled in front of her on the beach, impossibly short shorts riding up their near flawless legs. But there was a whole different appeal to Rhodri, something raw and irresistible. He was rugged and almost wild; from the stray chest hairs that curled unchecked over the top button of his shirt, right through to his wayward hair, which he had unsuccessfully tried to squash in to a cap. It was almost as if was fighting a losing battle to rein himself in.

Rhodri leaned in towards her a second time and for a moment she thought he was going to hug her after all. But then he stuck out a hand and shook Tom's vigorously before turning round and heading for the door. The two of them watched him leave. Despite the time of year he had no coat and only a thin checked shirt to stave off the cold. His unbranded jeans clung tightly to him, picking out the defined shape of his bum before tapering in to solid legs that would put the average rugby player to shame.

'Wow,' said Tom, craning his neck to watch Rhodri's behind disappear in to the dark November night. 'It's a good job I'm spoken for and you're not interested, else we'd really be in trouble.'

Katy managed a half-hearted murmur of agreement, but she wasn't sure it was good enough to convince even her.

Chapter Six

Katy's alarm clock went off at 7:00am. The shrill chirp disturbed her from her dream and she felt a moment of disorientation. It was the earliest she had been awake in quite some time and it was very tempting to turn off the alarm and stay bundled up in the duvet for another few hours until she woke naturally. Instead she wearily swivelled to sit on the edge of the bed, fumbled in the dark for the handle of her bedside table and opened the drawer. Her new running kit was at the top with all the tags still on. She pulled each one off, snapping the thin plastic wires that attached the cards and dressed quickly before the chill could set in and she changed her mind altogether.

By 7:15am she was running along the pavement, dodging rubbish bags and leaf piles. It was cold and dark, with the only light coming from the soft glow of streetlights and the passing headlights of cars. Katy loved this time of the morning, when the city was just waking up and the streets were quiet. She crossed the road and ran over the small bridge into Bute Park. She weaved her way through the trees taking the narrower paths north through the park until she came to the weir. The river was running high, sending clouds of spray in to the air as the water turned over on itself. She ran over the suspension bridge, smiling involuntarily as it bounced beneath her feet and even if only for a moment she felt like she was seven years old and care free again.

At the other end were the playing fields; a huge open expanse of green that seemed to last forever. In the distance she could see the castle towers reaching skywards and the creeping spider legs of the Millennium Stadium. It was a view she had seen countless times, but one that never failed to fill her with joy. She had been all around the world in the previous year, but Cardiff still held a special place in her heart.

She ran in to the open field, abandoning the paths for the bounce of springy grass beneath her feet. Away from the river it was much quieter and the majority of people in the fields weren't moving around much. Instead they allowed their dogs to do the running for them as they chased after tennis balls and sticks. There was only one other runner, a man in a black t-shirt and shorts with a beanie hat pulled low over his head.

Katy's step faltered a little as she tried to work out whether she should move to her left or her right to avoid him. It seemed silly that she should have to adjust her path at all really, given how massive the park was, but they were definitely on a collision course. She swerved right just as he went left, so even though they had both moved they were no better off. Katy smiled and gave a flick of her wrist to indicate she was going right and he responded; not with a thumbs-up or a sign he would go left, but a wave.

Katy looked again at the running figure that was growing closer with every step and her stomach flipped. He looked so different: his distinctive sweep of chestnut hair was hidden by the beanie and the clean-shaven look was gone. A designer shadow of stubble framed his upper lip and then arced along his jawline, masking the dimple in his chin.

'David,' she managed, as much in confirmation to herself as a greeting to him.

He stopped a few feet from her and smiled, revealing a perfect line of piano-key white teeth behind a mist of ice-cold breath. He pulled off the beanie and a coiled wave of hair bounced jack-in-the-box like from his head.

'Katy – it's good to see you.'

Tom was being gracious when he had said David looked good – he looked incredible. He had never been out of shape, but in the time they were together he found it harder to fit exercise in to his routine. He worked long hours at the GPs, often making house calls on evenings and weekends. Then there were the added commitments that came from merging two lives in to one; nights out with different friendship groups, family visits, weddings, trips to see two sets of parents and two sets of university and school friends. When life squeezed you in every direction somehow going to the gym didn't seem as high a priority. And when they did have a free evening they chose to spend it with a takeaway and a bottle of wine. It wasn't necessarily the lifestyle either of them would have chosen, but it was the one their lives allowed them at the time.

But a year on Katy couldn't help wonder if she had been the problem. David looked fitter (in every way) and there was a sparkle in his sky blue eyes and a cheeky playfulness to his grin that she hadn't seen in years. She dreaded to think what she looked like to him. It was so unfair – men exercised and the glisten of sweat accentuated their masculinity. It made them seem physical, strong, athletic…Hell; he looked sexier than she could ever remember. In contrast she imagined herself red-faced and breathless with her hair clinging damply to her forehead and her eyes puffy and plain without make-up.

'I heard you were back,' he said, his breath a little laboured but his voice even and strong. 'How was it?'

She didn't know how to answer; it was a difficult enough question at the best of times. After all how could you sum up a year of incredible experiences in to a neat sentence or two? But it was impossible to imagine the right thing to say to the man you left behind.

'It was good, really good. I thought you were in London?'

Katy balked at her own directness and the almost accusatory tone in her voice. She didn't own Cardiff; he had as much right to be here as she did. She just wished he wasn't.

'It didn't work out. I missed Cardiff. I –'

He tailed off and she was left wondering how else the sentence might have ended. *Did he miss her? Did she want him to?*

'I guess it just wasn't right for me; too many people, no hills…no rugby,' David continued. As soon as he had spoken he laughed nervously at his own joke. David hated rugby; it was the one part of living in Cardiff that was completely alien to him.

'How long have you been back?' Katy asked

'Just over a month now. You?'

'A week. I was at mum and dad's for a bit first.'

'How are they?'

'Good. They asked after you. I told them you were in London.'

She had done it again, making it sound as if he shouldn't be there.

'I saw Tom, he must be excited to have you back – I'm amazed he lasted the year to be honest.'

Was there a dig there? David had been jealous of Tom at times, he didn't always appreciate their closeness – was he referencing that, or was he hinting at the trail of abandonment she had left behind?

'He has a boyfriend now, I'm not sure he's had time to miss me lately.'

An awkward silence settled between them and she wished she could think of an excuse to end the conversation before there were any casualties. But she had nothing – she had nowhere to be and not a single plausible reason entered her head.

'I have practice in an hour,' he said, and her heart flooded with relief at the get-out, 'but we should meet up properly.'

'Yes – of course. You still have my email.'

He laughed softly; 'Yes Katy, I still have it.'

Of course he did. She winced at the awkwardness of it; they had spent four years entwining their lives and then had only two months to pull them apart. He didn't just have her email address, he had DVDs they had bought together, CDs, ticket stubs from theatre trips. There was probably even some clothing of hers still mixed in with his; t-shirts that they had worn around the house interchangeably. And she was no different. When she returned from travelling she had four boxes to her name; and one of them was his – a cardboard coffin filled with a jumble of photographs and boxer shorts, souvenirs and sunglasses – none of which she could bring herself to throw away. You didn't walk away from four years of living with someone without some baggage. You could travel round the world but the heartache only followed you; a trail of disappointments and regrets that never quite left your side.

'I'll email you then,' he said.

For a moment it looked as if he planned to hug her goodbye, but he stopped and started to jog awkwardly on the spot, not quite leaving but not committing to staying either.

She smiled and brushed her hand against his arm. Instantly she regretted it as she felt the sloping rise of his bicep flexed warm beneath his t-shirt. She had meant it as goodbye, a familiar note of finality to their conversation, but instead she worried she was starting something else entirely.

'Goodbye David.'

Katy started to run, only turning to look behind her once she had covered a good part of the field. He was still standing where she had left him, no longer running on the spot but legs planted firmly on the ground. She wondered what he was thinking and felt a familiar wave of guilt wash over her. It was a pain that she knew well, a nagging hurt that countless beautiful sunsets and miles of sandy beaches had failed to lessen.

Chapter Seven

The apartment felt cold and empty when she returned. The run home had been a struggle and by the time she stepped through the front door all she could manage was to flop on to the bed and pull the duvet over her aching legs. Once she was bundled in she reached out a single hand and pulled a cardboard sheet the size of a clipboard towards her. It was the first day of advent and she opened the window on the brightly coloured calendar to reveal a chocolate reindeer hidden behind a layer of silver foil. On the inside of the cardboard was a picture of a family carol singing; mum, dad and two beaming children. If only life were that simple; everything packaged away in neat little compartments as perfect and wonderful as an advent calendar.

She ate the milky chocolate, which coated her tongue in a layer of sweet fuzz and pulled the duvet around her shoulders. It was after lunchtime when Katy made her second attempt at the day. She felt groggy and even a hot bath hadn't eased the weariness that had come over her since her run. As she passed through the living room she spied the pile of CV's that Simon had printed for her at work and dropped round the day before. She had planned to spend the day trawling the many employment agencies and recruitment specialists in the city, but it would have to wait. Instead she raided her freshly stocked kitchen; pulling out butter, flour, sugar, nuts and a large tray of eggs.

She poured the ingredients in to a large china bowl, measuring them by sight rather than in ounces. She rubbed the flour, sugar, butter and ground almonds together in her hand and let the mixture slowly ball to a crumb. With greasy fingers she then broke an egg in to another bowl and beat it with a fork before adding it to the rest of the mixture and placing the whole thing in the fridge.

Whilst the pastry chilled she poured a can of soup in to a pan and gently heated it on the hob, stirring in a gentle figure of eight. The liquid was thick and a vibrant red; the rich tomato musk filling the kitchen and causing her stomach to rumble. She tore a chunk of bread from a loaf and dipped it in while the soup was still on the heat, testing to see if it was ready. It tasted delicious and reminded her of her student days when she would eat soup every day, sometimes twice a day and never tire of it – which was lucky given it was all she could afford back then.

Even when she and David had been earning good money she had always bought canned soup. As soon as winter came round every year she would stock the cupboard with rows of tins, preferring their simple pleasures to the more fanciful carton alternatives found in the chilled cabinets.

After she had eaten and washed up she removed the doughy mixture from the fridge and rolled it directly on to the worktop. She cut out thin discs using the rim of a wine glass and then pressed them into a muffin tray. Katy then spooned heaped measures of mincemeat from a jar into each pie base before topping with a pastry star. It covered most of the mix but left small triangles of mincemeat that would bubble up over the top when they went in to the oven. She brushed them with a little milk, and then seeing as it was out poured herself a large glass, which she carried through to the lounge as she placed the finished tray in to the fridge.

Katy flicked through a binder of DVDs to the backdrop of her gently humming oven as it warmed. They were arranged by theme; a large romantic comedy section shifting in to comedy and then drama, then a small number of science-fiction and fantasy titles (most of which were David's), before she arrived at the back of the binder where there was a double sleeve of Christmas films. She ran her fingers over the smooth plastic pockets as she decided which film to watch before arriving at a decision.

Katy put the disc in to her new DVD player, which chugged noisily in to life – causing her to instantly regret choosing the cheapest model available. Instead of flicking through the trailers she watched them all, smiling at the idea that every year she watched the same clips of the same films so that she knew them by heart, even if she hadn't seen the movies themselves.

Ten minutes in to the film she put the mince pies in to the oven and swapped her glass of milk for a hot chocolate. Twenty minutes later and the apartment filled with the rich waft of spices and warm citrus peel.

Baking was in Katy's opinion, the closest thing to alchemy, transforming humble materials into golden treasures. And it transformed her too; she took great pleasure in the knowledge that she had created something from nothing.

    She emptied most of the tray on to the rack to cool but carried two mince pies back to the sofa to eat while they were hot. They were delicious, the pastry crumbly and short and the filling hot and rich. They were sweet but not so much as to be sickly and when she had finished the first two she guiltily went back to the rack for a third. She told herself that they were best straight from the oven and so it wasn't quite so bad to eat three. And she could always run an extra mile or two the next day to make up for it. But when she thought about the chance of bumping in to David again she changed her mind. She returned the pie to the rack and picked up a clementine from the bright red bowl at the end of the worktop instead. Perhaps she would take a day or two off from running.

Chapter Eight

Katy couldn't decide what to wear. It was very unlikely that any of the agencies she called in to would want to interview her on the spot. And even if they did, that wasn't the same as an employer interviewing her, but she still wanted to make a good first impression. Her options for doing so however were limited by two major factors. The first was the weather, which was blowing a gale, with rain crashing against her window with a worrying force. The second was the sorry state of her wardrobe. Suddenly getting rid of all her clothes before travelling seemed like a mistake and she wished she had kept a few more choices.

In the end she settled on a purple blouse with a dark grey jacket and dark denim jeans. The jeans weren't ideal but they would be warm and offer some protection from the downpour. Over all of this she put on a long black raincoat, tied with a fabric belt at the waist.

Knowing that an umbrella wouldn't last more than a few minutes, Katy called for a taxi so that she could at least get in to town without getting too wet. Once there she would have to hope for the best and dash from office to office using as many covered walkways and indoor shopping centres as she could. She had no set appointments so she planned to start at the furthest end of town and work her way back to the centre.

The taxi took nearly half an hour to arrive and within a minute of being in his company Katy could tell the driver was in a mood as foul as the weather. The windscreen was steamed up and the cabin was stuffy from the streams of hot air blasting from the vents. The noisy racing of the windscreen wipers formed a frantic backbeat to the chorus of exasperated gasps and sighs coming from the driver. The closer they got to the city centre the more agitated he became and Katy started to wish she had caught the bus instead, even if it had meant getting a little wet.

Given how miserable the journey turned out to be Katy changed her mind and decided to start in the city centre. She jumped out of the taxi near the castle and proceeded to work her way through her list in reverse order.

Each of the agencies greeted her politely and made positive murmurings when she talked about her experience and previous employers. A few arranged to carry out a more detailed interview at a later date and two even printed out details of potential positions for her to read over at home. All in all it was a successful morning and by midday she was done. It was still raining heavily and so she pottered around the shops for half an hour killing time until Simon was free.

Katy arrived at the coffee shop with ten minutes to spare and took the opportunity to peruse the wide selection of cakes. The café was known for its generous portions and she hungrily eyed an enormous wedge of carrot cake with creamy white frosting and a fondant icing carrot on top. There was a growing queue and so she decided to take a seat to keep out of everyone's way. She chose a spot by the window and before long she recognised Simon running across the road towards her. He was dressed in a silvery blue pastel suit and a pink tie. It always amazed her how different he looked at work – so much more grown up than the Simon she was used to.

'I'm sorry I'm late,' he said, reaching in to kiss her and showering her with rainwater in the process.

'It's OK; I think I'm early actually. Would you like a coffee?'

'I'll get these. Latte?'

Simon joined the queue and she felt a mini jolt of disappointment as the prospect of a slice of the carrot cake plummeted. Buying a slice yourself and passing it off as an impulse was one thing – ordering it whilst someone else queued for five minutes was quite another. There was a downside to having body conscious gay men for best friends – they were much less forgiving when it came to food.

Simon eventually returned with a coffee in each hand and a small square of granola in a bag. He pulled it out and broke it in half giving her a conspiratorial wink.

'Don't tell Ads, he's got me on a diet.'

Katy looked incredulously at Simon's tiny waist and wondered how long her own slimmer figure would last if she indulged in cake at every opportunity.

'How's work?'

'Oh you know, busy, stressful, poorly paid – the usual. It's nice to have you back actually. We were always the ones with proper jobs. I've missed not having you around to keep me company amongst all the artistes.'

Katy laughed – whilst technically Tom was the only 'artist' the rest of their friends worked in creative jobs in theatres and museums and schools. It was only Simon and Katy who sat behind a desk all day chained to a computer.

'Well I'll be re-joining the ranks again very soon hopefully.'

'It went well today then?'

'Yeh, I think so – a few potential leads at least.'

'Great, fingers crossed.'

'I saw David yesterday.'

Katy hadn't planned on saying anything, not yet at least. But the moment there was a slight pause in the conversation she had blurted it out. It was as if the words couldn't leave her mouth quick enough. Simon didn't respond straight away, instead he let out a big exhale of breath somewhere between a sigh and the noise people made when they got really bad news from a doctor.

'Tom said he got hot.'

Katy smiled; she should have known that would be the detail Simon would focus on.

'Yeah, he did.'

'I heard majorly hot - as in slam me up against the kitchen wall, don't wait for the bedroom, take me now hot.'

'Tom's words or yours?'

'Well Tom painted the picture, I added the details.'

Katy couldn't help laughing. Her friends were no help at all, but it was funny hearing them talk about David that way. For years he was just, well, David – all of a sudden he was David new stud about town, as if he was a completely different person.

'He looked good.'

'Oh come on Katy, don't give me that – are we talking cute guy in a bar hot, movie star hot or all out shag me now sports magazine hot?'

'Simon! It's just David ok. David after some, well ok a lot, of gym time.

'But it's not though is it – this is hot new David. This is post-London David. This is *left his job and moved back to Cardiff for you*

David. Who knows what this David is capable of, or what he looks like naked?'

Katy laughed again: 'I imagine much the same as old David, just maybe with a slightly less wobbly tummy.'

'Wobbly tummy?! From what Tom said we're talking proper six-pack, rippling abs, v-line crotch.'

'How did Tom get that from bumping in to David in the supermarket? I can't imagine he whipped his top off in the frozen foods section so Tom could have a look.'

'Oh you know – you can tell when a guy's ripped and then you just imagine the rest yourself.'

'Just how much time have you boys spent lusting over my ex-boyfriend?'

'Honestly? Hours – this is big news. I mean we had Owen to get excited over for a while, but he's kind of boring now. David – this David, is a whole new exciting topic of conversation.'

'He's still just David. Still working too much I expect, still incapable of emptying the washing machine when it's finished, or picking up his socks from the bedroom floor.'

Simon didn't say anything but something about his mood changed. His smile hardened and his brow furrowed. The good-natured humour of the past five minutes disappeared and something more serious filled the void. Suddenly Katy felt like she was going to get the kind of lecture she hadn't had since she was 17 and her dad told her she wasn't allowed to get on a motorbike with Tommy Jackson ever again.

'So what was it like? Forget what he looked like for a moment. How did you feel?'

His tone was softer than she was expecting and she wondered if she had misjudged the situation.

'It was strange, really strange. Like déjà vu – it was new but also really familiar.'

Katy wanted to tell Simon everything, including heading back to bed the moment she got home and then trying to bake away the awkwardness. But she was worried she might sound crazy, hell – she was worried she was crazy the way she had crumbled after seeing David.

'But it was good to see him?'

'Yes – and no. It was scary how easy it would be just to go back and act as if the last year had never happened. As if I might lose myself all over again.'

'But it did happen, you've changed and so has he from the sounds of it.'

'I'm not sure a six-pack counts as personal growth. We split up for a reason and I'm not sure I want to go back. I'm not sure he would either.'

'He came back for you Katy, I'm pretty sure he's already made that decision.'

'Yes – he probably has.'

'And that's a bad thing?'

'Yes, because that's what he always did – made the decisions for us. He had everything mapped out; how many kids we were going to have, where we were going to buy our first house, when we were going to get married. Neither of us ever stopped to think if we wanted those things.'

'You don't want kids?'

'No – I do. But not like that, not as part of some masterplan sandwiched right between buying a sensible car and picking out his and hers matching wardrobes.'

'Ok and you should tell him that. But don't you think the guy deserves a second chance?'

'What if we've already had our second chance? What if this is it – a chance to start over with someone new. He didn't exactly look like being single was doing him any harm.'

'So you're not going to see him again?'

'I told him to email me.'

'An email? Jesus Katy. You practically married the guy, doesn't he at least get your phone number?'

Their lunch date wasn't exactly turning out the way Katy had planned. She had been right to think a sermon was coming her way; Simon had just lulled her in to a false sense of security by starting softly on her. She wondered when all her friends had suddenly become members of the David Barratt fan club, because it certainly hadn't felt like that when they'd been together.

'Maybe I don't want to call him OK. Or see him, or deal with him. Perhaps you should all think about that before deciding what's best for me like some big boys club I'm not a part of.'

She could feel her eyes pricking with tears for the second time in 24 hours. But this time she was angry, she was pissed with Tom for stirring things up, with Simon for pushing her, but most of all she was furious at David for coming back and not leaving things alone. She must have had a face like thunder because when Simon spoke again his voice was softer and he reached out across the table to hold her hands as he spoke.

'I'm sorry. I just don't want you to lose out. Sometimes it's easier to give things up than it is to keep them going – but that doesn't always mean it's the right thing.'

'I didn't give up Simon, it wasn't working. We fell in to a rut that wasn't going to go away.'

'And you did the right thing, I agree. David was a jerk, he didn't put the effort in – I know that. But it sounds as if he is now. C'mon Katy I get it, believe me. I've been with Adam seven years now, seven years! And some days I see a hot guy walk down the street or in a bar, or in a meeting and I think damn I could be with that guy. I fantasise about what my life could be like and we'd be shagging 24/7and going to fancy restaurants and taking expensive holidays. And maybe it would be like that for a few months, but then life would happen and we'd be too tired to go out and we wouldn't stay up till four in the morning shagging or dancing because there'd be deadlines and reports and early meetings. So we'd end up sat on the sofa and as I'd be looking at this 6ft 2 blonde-haired, blue eyed, Scandinavian supermodel; with his amazing six-pack and perfectly round ass I'd be thinking about Adam, my Adam – little man-belly and all.'

'Adam doesn't have a man-belly!'

'A little one, well it's certainly not a six-pack. But that's not really the point. A new car is always going to look more exciting than one you've driven round in a bit.'

'But it's different for you. I've seen what you two are like, how he looks at you; like he could practically devour you on the spot. And you adore him!'

'I do. But that doesn't mean he doesn't drive me crazy. On the outside you only get to see the good stuff. Of course he seems perfect to you; you don't have to wash his pants, or tidy up after him. Real life – it's just not that sexy day to day, but it's real and I'd choose Adam over a fantasy guy every time.'

'Is that what this is about: the other night with Rhodri?'

'I just think it would be the easiest thing in the world to walk away from David, especially when there's someone shiny and new dangled under your nose. But it doesn't mean you should.'

'Look, can we just forget all this? I'm not interested in Rhodri, or David. Actually the only person I'm really interested in right now is me. And I wish you'd all just accept that and leave me alone. I clearly have enough men interfering in my life already without adding any more to the mix.'

'I'm sorry Katy, shit, I'm going to have to go soon – I have a meeting at two o'clock. Look I just think give the guy a break. If Ads and I ever split up and we had a second chance I'd like to think his friends would give me the benefit of the doubt. But I promise I won't bring it up again and I hate that we're going to have to leave it like this. I'm sorry – really.'

'I know you're just trying to help. I just wasn't expecting it all. I thought that door was closed, now not only do I find it's open but it feels like you're all queuing up to push me through it and I'm not ready.'

Simon genuinely looked sorry and Katy could tell he felt awful about leaving when there was still some tension between them. They hugged and when he kissed her on the cheek goodbye she tried to return his warmth, but she was angry and she had never been good at hiding that.

As he crossed the road he turned and waved to her. Katy waved back and watched him jog away in the direction of his office. She waited a minute or two and then set off in the opposite direction, but not before she had ordered herself a slice of the carrot cake to go.

By the time Katy arrived home and removed her phone from her bag she had received five texts. The first three were from Simon – all variations on an apology. The fourth was from Adam:

Simon's an idiot. A well-intentioned loveable idiot. But an idiot all the same. Just don't be too hard on him – he means well. A xx

Any residual annoyance she felt fell away and she instantly replied to them both to set Simon's mind at rest. She had never doubted that Simon had meant well, but he had gone about it entirely the wrong way. And the text she had received from Adam only served to prove the point she had been making. If she had got in to a fight with Simon when she and David were together, then David would have shrugged it off with disinterest. If he were to comment he'd probably just say her friends were always attracting drama. And although there would be an element of truth in that, it wasn't what she wanted to hear. Adam got that, he knew Simon was upset and that was enough for him to want to sort it out. Her and David had never had a relationship like that.

When she had smoothed over the situation with Simon she reread the fifth message and was surprised at the smile it brought to her face.

Hi Katy, it's Rhodri. Hope ur still on for holly wreathing tomorrow. The farm's a little hard to find + I remember you don't have a car. Shall I pick you up? How about outside The Flying Duck at 9? See you tomorrow.

Chapter Nine

Katy heard the 4x4 approaching long before she saw it. The car was a rumbling giant of a vehicle that slowly spluttered its way towards her. It was a dark crimson red but splashed liberally with mud. Behind a dirty windscreen she could just about make out the figure of Rhodri towering over the steering wheel. He waved and slowed down to a stop just outside the pub. Katy quickly dashed round to the passenger side and opened the door. The cabin was much higher than she expected and she had to stretch to reach the door handle. When he saw she was struggling Rhodri leant over and gave her a hand, pulling her a little more firmly than she would have liked on to the seat. She landed with a small bump, overshooting the seat and careering in to Rhodri's muscular body, her face slamming embarrassingly against his chest.

The car exploded in a fluster of apologies and then slumped in to an awkward silence that Katy feared would last all the way out of the city. When it became clear that Rhodri would not be the one to break it she started to rack her brain for a point of conversation, *anything* to advance them past the memory of the face dive.

'I've never made a holly wreath before,' she managed eventually.

A huge look of relief came over Rhodri's face and he set upon the new conversation in frenzied enthusiasm.

'Well we won't be making them today. Just collecting the materials really. We'll need holly obviously – a good mix of leaves and berries and stalks. Then there's the moss, which is harder to find and even more of a bugger to harvest. So today we'll be doing that – then there'll be a good day or two of the actual making to come later.'

'Oh,' Katy said, suddenly looking down at her clothes and wishing she had known they were going to be wandering around hedgerows and fields, rather than sitting in a warm, dry kitchen.

'Don't worry it's not as bad as it sounds.'

'No – I just didn't realise what was involved I guess.'

It was too late to ask Rhodri to turn around and anyway she didn't want to admit her mistake any further, but the jeans were brand new and her top was about as windproof as a feather.

'Do you think I might be able to borrow a jacket from Cerys?'

She felt Rhodri's gaze run over her, his investigation seeming a little more thorough than necessary to assess her lack of coat before he returned his eyes to the road.

'I'm sure I can find you something. You'll need some wellies too. I'm not sure I've ever seen less practical shoes.'

Katy blushed, they had been the second pair she had tried on – he should have seen the first.

It was strange but in the ten years she had lived in Cardiff, Katy had rarely ventured out to the immediate countryside. They had driven up to the Brecon Beacons of course, and she had been to Swansea and Newport and to Penarth. But as they left the city Katy was amazed how quickly the houses fell away and the land stretched in to sweeping green fields. It was cold out but the sky was a cloudless blue and in the winter sunshine Katy almost felt as if they were driving through the Swiss countryside.

As the roads began to narrow and the hedgerows closed in on them Rhodri's choice of vehicle began to make a lot more sense. After a while Katy barely noticed the spluttering engine or the jolting of the seat. There was something about Rhodri that held her attention, something more than his obvious good looks and impressive body. After a while she realised it was the way he spoke; he was careful with his words, efficient almost. He didn't ramble on the way she did when she was nervous. Instead everything seemed very deliberate and considered. As a result when he did speak she found she really listened, eager to catch every word he said. Normally when she first met people, especially men, she was incredibly conscious of the silences and would say almost anything to fill them. With Rhodri it was different she was content just to be in his company and allow conversation to come to them naturally.

'We're nearly here,' he said after a little while. 'Just over this ridge.'

Sure enough a few minutes later they crested a small hill with a little lane leading off to the left that ended at the door of a beautiful white stonewash cottage. The gravel driveway crunched under the wheels and the noise sparked a chorus of dog barks. A moment later and two chocolate Labradors were racing excitedly towards them. Rhodri slowed down and yelled for them to be quiet. Katy couldn't help but laugh, as the dogs seemed to pay him no attention whatsoever.

The front door opened and out came Cerys in the same wax jacket as she had worn to the pub, but this time paired with a flat cap and grey gardening gloves. She waved warmly, flashing a pair of secateurs at them in the process. Behind Cerys stood Jenny and Sophia – both seemingly better dressed for the activity than she was. Sophia was wearing combats and a large grey hoody spotted in paint. It looked as if it had probably once belonged to a boyfriend given how much it swamped her. Jenny was wearing jeans and a large red sweater with an equally bright raincoat over the top of it.

'And here's our leader!' Cerys boomed as Katy got out of the car.

'Oh, no – its everyone's club, and it's your idea.'

Katy half expected Sophia to produce a notebook from under her hoody and make a note of the suggested transfer of ownership. However no one seemed to seize on the idea and so Katy supposed that for now she would have to act as reluctant figurehead.

'So where do we start?' Katy asked.

'What are you wearing dear?' Cerys asked, even more bluntly than Rhodri.

'Well I hadn't quite realised what was involved.'

'I said I'd find Katy something to wear at mine,' Rhodri added, stepping in valiantly on Katy's behalf.

For a moment it looked as if Cerys was going to say something else but then she changed her mind and turned to close the door on the cottage, before striding off down the lane away from them.

'Cerys!' Katy called after her. 'You forgot to lock the door.'

Rhodri smiled and Katy couldn't understand what the joke was, but instead of chasing after Cerys he shooed the rest of them down the lane in pursuit.

'I think we'll risk it,' Cerys shouted a few minutes later, clearly stifling a laugh.

'So, where are we going?' Jenny asked.

'Oh it's not far dear – just to the farm across the way. Here we go.'

To Katy's amazement Cerys scaled the five-bar wooden gate and started walking in to the adjacent field. Not only was she surprised at the sprightliness of the woman, but also her brashness. Katy was quite sure that you couldn't just wander on to someone else's land, even in the country.

'Um won't the farmer mind?' Katy asked, loudly enough so that Cerys could hear.

'I don't know dear, why don't we ask him…Rhodri?'

Cerys practically bellowed Rhodri's name, even though he was only a few feet behind her.

'This is all yours?' Sophia asked in wonder.

The farm seemed to stretch out in every direction, with row upon row of ploughed soil laid out in ridges in front of them.'

'Welcome to Windmill Farm,' Rhodri answered a little bashfully.

The rest of them climbed over the gate, both Jenny and Katy managing it with far less grace than Cerys had displayed a minute earlier. As Katy straddled the top bar she had horrible visions of getting stuck or losing her nerve about jumping down to the other side and having to ask for help. In the end what spurred her on was the sudden realisation of what she must look like, sat atop the fence with one leg either side whilst she contemplated the drop.

She landed a little clumsily and with a noisier squelch than she would have liked, but safely and relatively mud-free. Last to come over was Rhodri. He put one foot on the lowest rung and then with a spring, vaulted the rest of the gate in a single move, hurtling his muscular body over as easily as if he were a man half his size.

Katy stole a glance at his bum as he walked away and marvelled again at how tightly his trousers seemed to cling to his defined shape, leaving little to the imagination. She looked away worried she was being obvious, but to her left she could see Jenny and Sophia rapt in equal appreciation. In fact Jenny looked practically ravenous. Katy smiled, Sophia she could understand: to a 20-something-year-old student Rhodri was about as perfect a specimen of the rugged older man as you could get. It was Jenny and Katy that should know better; Jenny was married and as for herself Katy was barely a year or two younger than Rhodri.

'Come on ladies,' Rhodri suddenly called, turning round and briefly flashing them his broad chest and incredible smile.

'Coming,' they replied in unison, happily following him across the field.

Chapter Ten

The field sloped down in to a small wooded gully that was overgrown with cowslips and bindweed. Katy could hear the sound of a small stream and a chorus of birds singing overhead. Cerys led them along the line of bushes until they came to an opening where the low-lying shrubs had been cleared. The ground underneath them was springy and damp, with roots running across the surface like thick veins. It was a cool damp spot, sheltered from the winter sun by a thick canopy of gnarled trees.

'This is the best spot for the moss. Katy – why don't you and Sophia stay here with me whilst Rhodri and Jenny go and start on the holly clippings?'

Sophia's face was etched in disappointment and Katy wondered what she was more upset about: was it spending the day in the shady cold of the gully, or was it spending it with Cerys and Katy whilst Jenny had Rhodri all to herself?

But then Rhodri chipped in: 'I was going to take Katy up to the house for a change of clothes. There's no way she can be picking moss like that. I'm surprised she's made it this far to be honest. How about you ladies handle the moss and Katy and I can do the holly. It's best up by the house anyway.'

Katy was only mildly put out by the third commentary of the day on her poor wardrobe choices. And anyway, it had been worth the clothing cock-up for the look on Jenny's face – she was practically seething at the last minute substitution. In fact none of the women looked too happy – Cerys included.

Katy wondered if Rhodri had picked up on it too, because before there was any opportunity for discussion he was striding up the field and Katy had to half run after him to catch up. She picked up her pace, conscious that she couldn't spend all her time chasing after Rhodri like a teenager enjoying the rear view a little too much. What she hadn't accounted for was the difference in the length of their strides. Rhodri's long legs easily powered him back up the hill and with each step he seemed to get further away from her.

It had been a wet, mild winter, with few frosts and the soil beneath her feet was still soft. Katy found herself sinking, the wedge of her heel digging in and dragging her back. Within a few more metres she would lose Rhodri over the crest of the hill.

'Oh, bollocks to this!' Katy stopped suddenly and then leaned over and pulled off her right shoe and sock, balancing precariously on the other foot as she did so. When the shoe was in her hand she stamped her right foot firmly in to the soil whilst she removed her left shoe. She hadn't spent the last year hiking mountains and walking through creepy-crawly filled rainforests to be defeated by a bit of Welsh mud and a few worms. Within a few minutes she had caught Rhodri up, her sudden appearance at his side causing him to stop, his eyes instantly falling on her muddy feet and growing wide in disbelief.

He started to speak but only managed some indistinguishable splutters, none of which really passed as words. She imagined she looked completely bonkers covered in soil, but she didn't care – there was something incredibly liberating about the feel of the earth between her toes and she wasn't done having her fun yet.

'Why have we stopped? Come on, I thought we were heading to the house?' she said, stifling a laugh as she marched off in front of Rhodri.

The house looked like it should be on the front of a Christmas card and Katy could only imagine how perfect it would look dusted in snow. The walls were a rich sandy red stone intermingled with grey and covered over with a red tiled roof. There was a small garden marked out in hedgerows and the house itself was decorated with thick strands of ivy.

'It's beautiful!' Katy exclaimed out loud as she stopped to drink it all in.

'Yes, my grandparents built it. They came to Wales from the Netherlands when my mum was just three years old. Apparently my grandmother fell in love with the place and insisted they move. They lived here for forty years before moving back to Holland to retire. And now my parents have done the same.'

'They live in the Netherlands?'

'Yes, it's just me at Windmill Farm now. But I have a couple of farmhands to work on the land with me and they stay here sometimes so it's never too quiet.'

It was lovely, there was no denying it, but Katy couldn't imagine living so remotely on her own. Other than Cerys' place they hadn't seen another house for quite some time before they arrived at the farm.

It was also the first time that Rhodri had given a clear signal that he was single. There had been no mention of a wife or family sharing the house. Perhaps he preferred it that way. It was strange but whenever she heard the phrase 'married to the job' she always had visions of city boys hunched over computers until 2am. But being out in the open surrounded by fields and fresh air, there were worse occupations to devote your self to.

Rhodri let them in to the house through the kitchen and as he removed his muddy boots she suddenly looked down sheepishly at her own feet and wondered what she should do. As if reading her thoughts Rhodri appeared with a huge pile of towels.

'Normally its only the dogs I have to worry about traipsing mud all through the place. But it seems I'm going to have to be just as careful with you!'

'Yes, sorry, I suppose it was a little silly,' said Katy as she struggled to remove the soil from her toes.

'Actually, I was quite impressed. I can't imagine the other two being so happy to get their hands…or feet dirty.'

Rhodri disappeared in to the heart of the house, leaving her alone in the large country kitchen. In the centre of the room was an enormous oak table with generations' worth of scores and scratches etched across the top. It was a table decorated with the battle scars of countless Sunday roasts, Christmas dinners and family parties. Katy could imagine Rhodri seated at the table as an infant, surrounded by his parents and grandparents, all excitedly watching him; from his first mouthfuls to his first day at school, right through to the day he took over the farm.

Her own parents had a modern table that they had bought after she left home for university and they were constantly replacing and upgrading their furniture so that Katy barely recognised the place from one visit to the next. In contrast Rhodri's kitchen felt lived in and every item looked loved and cherished, nursed from one owner to the next. A soot-bottomed kettle hung over the sink, its copper sides tarnished and dented. In the corner of the room there was a tatty old dog bed, faded and well worn, and the wooden worktops bore the same weathered look as the dining table.

Overhead she heard Rhodri plotting his path for her in a series of footsteps and clunks, as drawers and cupboards were opened and closed. She wondered what exactly he would bring down – anything that belonged to Rhodri would completely swamp her and anyway she wasn't sure she would feel comfortable wearing his clothes.

When he did finally reappear he handed her a wrinkled carrier bag. She was surprised to find if full of women's clothes and in a similar size to hers.

'Oh,' she said, a little louder than expected.

'Everything OK?'

'Yes I just wasn't – yes, of course everything's OK – thank you. Is there somewhere I can change?'

'Bathroom's just through there,' he said, pointing to a door to the right of the range cooker.

Inside the bag was a faded concert t-shirt from a group that Katy had never heard of. The picture on the front was of an exploding drum with cymbals flying out like shrapnel in every direction and the year 2003 in bold purple print. Katy put it on and then pulled out the next item; a chunky blue wool knit sweater that looked as if it had only been worn a handful of times. It was incredibly soft and as snug as a favourite blanket. Katy wondered who the clothes belonged to – the t-shirt was way too small for Rhodri, and she couldn't imagine that his retired mother was that in to The Caerdydd Cymbal Slayers. The jumper could have belonged to her, but it was a fitted style and though it was a few seasons old was still quite modern.

Katy returned to the kitchen in her new outfit, still perplexed as to where it might have come from. Rhodri had mentioned some farmhands but surely he wouldn't lend out their clothes without permission.

'The jumper's lovely,' Katy said, fishing for detail without appearing rude.

'You should keep it, I've been meaning to take it to the charity shop forever, I just haven't got round to it.'

'Oh, I didn't mean…well if you're sure?'

'Of course, it looks good on you.'

Perhaps she should have considered a career in espionage Katy mused. She might be rubbish at finding out information but at least she would be well dressed as a result. The truth was she just couldn't figure Rhodri out and the owner of the clothes was yet another mystery she couldn't fathom. She knew it shouldn't bother her, but it did and she found herself wanting to know more about him. But most of all she wanted to know if he was single…and if so why?

'Right, Cerys will be wondering where we've got to soon – get these boots on and we'll make a start.'

As soon as he had finished speaking he was out of the door, leaving her to pull on the thick boot socks he had left by the front door. She then turned her attention to the wellies, which looked like two miniature submarines that had somehow become beached on Rhodri's doormat. They were colossal and swallowed her feet and most of her lower leg with ease. For the first time she was sure she was wearing something of Rhodri's. The man didn't have big feet – he was walking around on tree trunks!

Katy eventually waddled out in to the garden, her feet slipping and flopping around in the boots as if she were walking on ice. She must have looked ridiculous and although he tried to hide it there was an unmistakeable smirk on Rhodri's face when he saw her. He was waiting for her with two large wooden trugs and a handful of empty rubble sacks. In one of the trugs there were two pairs of secateurs and some gloves.

Despite there being ample holly bushes in the garden, they walked along the hedgerow a short distance in to the field before Rhodri stopped and laid everything down on the ground. He patiently showed her where on the holly to make the cut and how to hold the bush without getting pricked by the pointy leaves.

Having spent her whole life living in apartments it was probably the closest Katy had ever come to gardening and she was surprised how enjoyable it was. They each took a trug, placing the woven basket to their right and filling it with clippings. It was the perfect container for the task and made for a large target – so even Katy's most wayward of throws found its way home. When the trugs were full they then transferred the contents into the rubble sacks, which were much harder to hold and keep upright.

'So do you do this every year then?' Katy asked.

'I try to help Cerys out where I can but I don't often have the time. It's the first year I've ever known her properly ask for help though.'

Katy thought back to the pub and the tremor she had felt in Cerys' hand. They had barely begun with the task of holly wreathing and already it seemed impossible to think that Cerys normally took it all on herself. If nothing else came of Christmas Club it had been worth it just to lighten that load.

As they worked Katy couldn't help but keep stealing glances at Rhodri. Where her own cuts were deliberate and carefully considered he attacked the holly with a barber's speed, wielding the secateurs like they were an extension of his hand.

'So how come a Christmas Club anyway?' Rhodri asked.

'I don't know really. It wasn't exactly planned. I guess I've always loved Christmas, it feels like that one time of year when anything is possible and it brings out the best in people. I suppose I wanted a little bit of that – something to get involved in, something positive.'

'Well you've certainly found something to get stuck in to – Cerys will have you threading holly through wire in your sleep by the time she's done.'

Katy laughed, in part because she could see it happening already.

'But why now?' Rhodri continued.

'What do you mean?'

'Well you've just got back from travelling; you must have lots of people wanting to catch up with you – friends and family. Then from what you said the other night you've a job to look for and work you'd like to do on the flat. It sounds like you have plenty to do.'

Katy stopped what she was doing for a moment while she thought about what Rhodri had said.

'I'm not sure I'm ready for any of that. Of course I'm happy to see people. But this past year for me has been about new experiences and pushing myself to do things I didn't think I could. I'm not sure I'm ready to give all that up. I think everyone just expects me to pick up exactly where I left off with friends, work...dating, everything. And I'm not sure I can. I'm not sure I want to.'

It wasn't until she said it out loud that Katy was fully able to make sense of how she had been feeling since she got back. Somehow she had been able to say to Rhodri what she had failed to explain to her parents, her brother, Tom, Simon – or any of her old friends. Perhaps because he didn't know her it was easier, because she wasn't trying to fit any expectation or idea of who she was with him.

'That probably sounds crazy,' proffered Katy. She was uncomfortably aware that pretty much everything Rhodri had seen of her, from the drunken meandering post that started it all, right through to running barefoot across his field was a little out there and completely out of character. Or at least it would have been a year ago, but maybe Katy needed as much re-education as everyone else on who she was and what passed for her usual behaviour now.

'Actually it makes a lot of sense. A few years ago my-'

Before Rhodri could finish his sentence he was interrupted by a loud shout from behind. Katy looked up to see Cerys, Sophia and Jenny walking around the edge of the garden. Katy couldn't see any moss, but she did spy a huge flask and a stack of food containers and decided that was far more enticing.

Five minutes later they were all sat in a circle on some fallen logs, sharing steaming mugs of mulled wine and rounds of delicious sandwiches. The first were crammed with thick slices of ham carved from the bone and generous chunks of richly tangy cheese. Next Cerys produced some salmon and cream cheese sandwiches, lightly peppered with watercress. To finish they had shortcrust mince pies served in little red napkins – two in each bundle.

'How are you getting on?' Rhodri asked between mouthfuls.

'Another hour should do it,' Cerys replied. 'The girls have been marvellous.'

Jenny practically beamed at Cerys' assessment and Katy suspected it was as much the joy at being thrown in with the younger Sophia as 'one of the girls', as pride in her moss-collecting prowess.

'I can't believe how much we've collected,' added Sophia. 'It's hard work – but it's actually quite fun. And Cerys has been telling us *all* about you Rhodri!'

Katy felt an unexpected pang of jealously, she had spent all morning with Rhodri and he had given away very little. Suddenly it turned out the others were being let in on all his secrets.

'Hardly,' Cerys said, a little sternly.

'Well we've been having plenty of fun of our own – Katy's even been running around in the mud barefoot.'

Sophia gave Katy a look of absolute horror. Collecting moss was one thing, but getting muddy feet was clearly quite another. It was only when Katy looked past Sophia that she caught a glimpse of Cerys out of the corner of her eye. She was frowning and looked more than a little displeased. Katy was beginning to worry that the older woman had taken a dislike to her for some reason.

'It was only on the way up to the house – my shoes were slowing us down. But we've been hard at work ever since. Look.'

Katy gestured towards the bulging sacks of holly in a bid to try and win Cerys over. But as soon as she had done so she felt incredibly needy, just like the kind of child she had hated when she was in school, the type who never did anything without bringing it to the attention of the teacher.

'That does look like a lot. I can't say how grateful I am to you all. Thank you.'

If there was any iciness towards her it had disappeared and a second round of the mulled wine left Katy feeling a lot warmer and fuzzier. The five of them chatted easily and Katy could have happily spent the rest of the afternoon grazing on mince pies and getting to know the others. But after half an hour of pleasant conversation, Cerys announced it was time to return to their respective hedgerows and mossy banks to fill the last few sacks.

All of them except Sophia rose with a chorus of groans and gasps that was followed by much arm stretching and leg shaking to limber up after being sat on the logs in the cold for so long. Sophia gave them a funny look and started to walk down the hill.

'Oh to be young again.' Cerys said wistfully.

'You're not doing so bad.' Rhodri said, helping her to her feet.

'No, I can't complain. Right – see you soon.'

After the warmth of a hot mug in her hands the secateurs didn't seem quite so appealing and it took a while for Katy's fingers to work properly. She took her gloves off and rubbed her hands together for a moment, trying to coax them in to life.

'Here, let me.' Rhodri said, striding towards her.

He stood facing her, taking off his own gloves and then he cupped his hands around hers, encasing her in the warmth of his body. He then lifted their sandwiched hands towards his face and blew gently on to the sides where her little fingers were exposed to the cold air.

'Better?' he asked.

The touch of his skin against hers was like the embrace of a warm bath at the end of a long day, wrapping her in soothing pleasure.

'Much better. Thank you.'

Standing so close, their hands touching in unexpected intimacy, Katy felt the heat creep from her hands in to her cheeks. Her mind started to race and she wondered what it would be like to kiss him, his strong arms wrapping around her, his stubbly chin sparking against her neck and his hot lips upon hers.

A loud chirp from her phone ruined the moment, disrupting her thoughts and sounding completely out of place in the stillness of the farm. Katy tried to ignore it and hoped Rhodri would to do the same. But then it pinged a second time, seemingly even louder than the first and the spell was broken. Rhodri released his grip on her hands and took a step back.

'Sounds like someone's keen to get hold of you.'

Katy removed the phone from her pocket; she had two new emails – both from David. The subject line of both emails was the same and appeared in massive writing at the top of the screen: *Date night.*

It was a term they had used often in their time together. They had both committed to a day a week when they carved out time for one another in their busy lives to do something a little different. At first they had been quite adventurous, driving up to the Beacons to watch the sunset, or trying a new restaurant that David had read about in the Sunday papers. Then as time went on their dates became less imaginative. Cinema trips became DVD nights at home and before long it was clear date night had died a death. Occasionally one of them would try and resurrect it, normally around an anniversary or birthday, but any revival was short-lived. Like a lot of their relationship, eventually they both just stopped trying altogether.

It could just have been harmless nostalgia, but Katy didn't think so. David was setting out his stall and making his intentions pretty clear and Rhodri had doubtless seen enough to reach the same conclusion.

'It's nothing, I'll read it later.'

There was no reply except the frantic swoosh of the secateurs hacking a swathe through the holly bush. *Men.* Katy thought with some exasperation, they never said anything when you wanted them to. Then when you finally got them out of your head that was when they decided it was time to start talking. She picked up the secateurs and let rip, taking out her own frustrations on the innocent holly bush.

-

It was three-thirty when they finally finished and the last sack had been filled. Since email-gate Rhodri and Katy had barely said more than a few words to one another and she feared that the lovely day was going to end on a low note. They packed up and were about to set off down the hill when Rhodri steered them down a different path than the one they had taken before. They followed the hedgerow round to the left and as they dipped back down towards a river they came across a small copse of trees.

'Are they Christmas trees?' Katy asked excitedly, forgetting for a moment the frostiness that had settled between them during the last couple of hours.

Rhodri laughed before correcting her: 'Well technically they're Nordmann Firs, but I guess Christmas tree will do. My mum planted them years ago. I wondered if you wanted one for your flat?'

'Oh I couldn't.'

'Of course you can. Every year I say I'll cut one down and put it up in the farmhouse, but I never do. Mum will be delighted to hear that someone's actually enjoying one for once. Measure up when you get home and then we'll pick one out and cut it down tomorrow.'

'Thank you!' Katy beamed, and instinctively gave him an enormous hug. It was only when it was too late and her arms were outstretched around his giant shoulders that she began to think that maybe it wasn't such a good idea. She pulled away before she got too comfortable and the two of them parted awkwardly, limbs bumping and tangling with one another in a clumsy dance.

Katy heard the rumble of a throat being cleared loudly and looked up to see Cerys standing over them. It was almost like the woman had a knack for appearing just at the worst moment.

'I came to see how you were getting on. Sophia and Jenny are just getting ready to leave. I said I'd check to see if you wanted a lift home Katy?'

'That would be great actually, if it's no bother for Jenny.'

'I'm sure it will be fine. I'll let them know you'll be down in a minute.'

Rhodri walked her back to Cerys' house and they set their sacks of holly down by the front door where Cerys was waiting. Katy said goodbye, giving Cerys a small kiss on the cheek and then she waved to Rhodri on her way to the car. It felt odd not to give him a parting hug, but she was acutely aware of Cerys' eyes burrowing in to her and watching every move.

Sophia was already asleep in the back by the time Katy reached the car, so she got in the front alongside Jenny.

'What a day!' Katy exclaimed, nodding towards the softly snoring figure of Sophia.

'I know, I'll have to let Chris know he's out of luck – I don't have the energy for anything more than a hot bath and some cocoa.'

Katy giggled a little; surprised they were at that level of sharing already. But feeling emboldened she asked the question that had been bugging her at lunch.

'So what did Cerys say about Rhodri then? Sophia said she'd told you everything.'

'Oh, just that she was relieved that you weren't interested in finding a boyfriend. Turns out Rhodri's well and truly off the market – he's married.'

Chapter Eleven

Katy woke to a beautifully warm and blissfully quiet apartment. After a year of sleeping in bunk beds and dorm rooms, being in her own room in a normal bed was a novelty. She still half expected someone to crash in from a bar in the middle of the night, or to have her sleep punctuated by the competitive snoring of other travellers. Small as her apartment was, it was a hell of a lot more private and spacious than she had grown used to. She was so comfortable lying under the thick duvet that it took a while for the memory of the day before to seep in and dampen her spirits.

The emails from David had taken her by surprise; they were funny and sweet all at once, and his idea for a date was perfect – a sunset walk along the barrage followed by dinner and drinks in the bay. The restaurant he had suggested was one she had always wanted to go to, but one they had never been able to justify the prices for when they had been together. Back then it was exactly the kind of evening she would have loved. But that was different; they were in a relationship then.

She had hoped he would suggest something simple and low key: go to a pub, have a few drinks and a chat. But sunset walks and gourmet restaurants were definitely not part of her plan. They were the kind of things that got you in to trouble. David had arranged the sort of night capable of making her forget all her good intentions and all her resolve to leave things in the past exactly where they belonged. He was bringing out the big guns and she wasn't sure she was ready for the assault.

The other man that had managed to get well and truly under her skin was Rhodri. As much as she told herself it didn't matter and that she wasn't interested, it was obvious that she was lying to herself. Everything about the man fascinated her and she couldn't help but stare at him whenever she was in his company. There was something beautifully rugged about him; from his un-fussed hair to his brawny arms. It was like someone had sculpted him from clay or hewn him from granite; carving a man out from the earth and releasing him unchanged in to the world. He was exactly the kind of man she was hard-wired to find attractive – if sabretooth tigers started roaming Cardiff she didn't fancy their chances against Rhodri. But his physical prowess wasn't the problem. What bothered her was that he had lied, or at the very least he hadn't told her the truth. Katy had replayed the events of the previous day over and over in her head after she went to bed. Every way she looked at it, he had had chances to tell her he was married and it certainly hadn't come up when he was holding her hands in his and looking in to her eyes like he could devour her on the spot. He had flirted with her and he was married and that was about as sure-fire a way to piss her off as she could imagine.

Between her frustration with Rhodri and her anxiety over her date with David, Katy would have happily skipped the return trip to the farm. But it wouldn't have been fair on any of the others to duck out over something so trivial. She wished Tom was going to join them, but he was too busy with work and Jenny wasn't able to make it either. Katy resolved to pay as little attention to Rhodri as possible, despite the reduction in their numbers. And the first step to that was independent travel, so she had cancelled their lift arrangements the moment she got home the previous evening.

The result of Katy's stubbornness was three buses and a forty-minute walk to reach the farm and by the time she arrived she felt like a sweaty mess, despite the wintery temperatures. The front door was ajar and the others, including Rhodri, were already in Cerys' kitchen huddled around a tangled mess of moss, holly and chicken-coop wire.

Katy's eyes flitted instantly to Rhodri's left hand, which confirmed what she had already known – there was no ring. He smiled at her and she smiled back as politely and impersonally as she could manage, before turning her attention to Cerys and the mountain of shrubbery on the table.

Although there was a gap right next to Rhodri, Katy sandwiched herself between Cerys and Sophia, nudging the younger woman towards him in the process. After all Katy reasoned to herself; if you wanted to divert a man's attention, putting a 21-year-old with breasts up to her chin between you seemed to be a pretty good shout.

With the woman buffer established, Katy was able to focus on the wreaths, determined to get through her target for the day in plenty of time to get dressed up for her date with David at three o'clock.

The most difficult part of each wreath was bending the wire in to a circular frame and it was also the most important step, as it was the foundation for everything else. The first two she did were decidedly wonky and would have been better suited to making papier-mâché Easter eggs than holly wreaths. The third was on the cusp and just about usable, but the fourth was a near perfect circle and Katy couldn't help but let out a small whoop of satisfaction when she finished it. At her outburst Rhodri appeared by her side, running his hand along her arm to pick up the wire wreath and turn it over in his fingers.

'It's really good,' he said, putting it down on the table and resting his hand on her shoulder.

Katy thanked him and then excused herself to use the bathroom, shrugging his hand away in the process. He wasn't making it easy for her.

'Did I do something wrong?'

'I'm sorry Katy,' said, a little flustered to find Rhodri waiting for her in the corridor.

'You've barely spoken to me today.'

'There's just a lot to do. I have to leave early.'

Katy made to leave but Rhodri didn't budge and there was no way she could get past without squeezing up against him.

'Come on Katy – something's up. You cancelled me picking you up and then you go out of your way to avoid me all morning. What's going on?'

'It's nothing really, it doesn't matter.'

His usually warm brown eyes had darkened to a burnt bronze colour and a temper was visibly brewing on his brow.

'Ok, I was pissed off you didn't say you were married. We spent the whole day together. I'm surprised it didn't come up.'

'Cerys told you?'

'No, she told Jenny and Sophia and they told me in the car on the way home. It doesn't matter who told me. Actually it doesn't matter at all. You're married – great. It's nothing to do with me anyway.'

She made a second attempt at the corridor, coming to a stop right in front of him, her feet almost touching his. But instead of stepping aside he took hold of her arm in his hand. It was frustrating how her body responded to his touch, a ripple of lightning sparking through her. She wasn't scared; his grip was too loose, his touch too gentle to cause any fear. She was excited.

'I'm separated and I didn't tell you because…because it's not something I love to talk about. I had fun yesterday, a lot of fun and I didn't want to ruin the day by bringing it up. I nearly did at one point, just before lunch but we were interrupted before I had a chance.'

'Oh…'

Katy felt instantly ridiculous; she had been punishing him for not telling her something that she had no right to know about – especially when talking about it clearly upset him. And it wasn't as if she had rushed to tell him about her date with her ex-boyfriend.

'I'm sorry. I - I'm not sure what I was thinking to be honest. God you must think I'm absolutely crazy. Can we forget this morning ever happened?'

'Deal,' he said, relaxing his grip and stepping aside so she could walk by. 'Oh and Katy, just so I'm clear do you need a list of everyone I've ever dated? Or just the one's I married?'

'OK, OK – I get your point!'

She playfully shoved him but her hand collided impotently with a wall of muscle and he didn't even flinch.

'Don't start something you can't finish Katy Winters,' he said, flinging his arms out wide and ducking down like a rugby player. But before he could scoop her up in a giant bear hug Katy was gone, speedily walking back to the kitchen her heart pounding in her chest.

She tried to hide her smile as she re-joined the others, but she needn't have worried. Cerys and Sophia were too engrossed in their work to even look up. They had started on the next stage of the process, pushing clumps of moss in to the wire frame and then wrapping a thinner strip of wire round the outside to hold the moss in place. Katy picked up a handful of moss and started to do the same on her own wire frames. The moss was still surprisingly damp and much fluffier than she had expected. It was amazing what a transformation it made too, turning the slightly bleak looking frame in to a lush looking circle of green.

When Rhodri returned he slid himself in next to Katy. Unlike the rest of them he carried on making the wire frames and between them they started a bit of a production line. Rhodri twisted and bent the wire in to shape, Katy and Sophia dressed the frames with moss and then Cerys pushed in sprigs of holly in a tight arrangement. By the time Cerys had finished, only small islands of moss were visible and the whole wreath was ringed in dark green holly and ruby red berries.

'They look beautiful,' Sophia said, admiring one of Cerys' wreaths.

'She's not quite finished with them yet,' Rhodri piped up.

Without saying anything Cerys disappeared in to the next room and came back with a large tatty cardboard box that looked on the verge of collapse. She put it on to the table and opened the flaps to reveal a treasure chest of ribbons, each one a different colour and size. After a brief rummage she pulled out a wide purple ribbon that was tapered at each end. Taking the wreath in one hand and the ribbon in the other, Cerys carefully looped a stretch of the ribbon round the top of the ring to form a hook and then wrapped the ribbon loosely round the sides before finishing in a large bow at the bottom.

It looked wonderful and although she had only played a small part in its making Katy still felt a bubble of pride from seeing the finished wreath. If they all looked as pretty and festive then Cerys would have no problem selling them in the village. There was only the small matter of making the other 199 to worry about.

Katy clearly wasn't the only one buoyed by the completion of the first wreath. A large tartan tin was suddenly produced from one of the kitchen cupboards and Cerys lifted the lid to reveal a mound of golden biscuits the colour of tropical sands. Each one was crammed with citrus peel jewels and rich dark currants. But best of all was the smell; a hit of cinnamon that seemed to fill the room with festive spice.

A second container appeared, this time from the fridge. It was filled to the brim with little pastry vol-au-vents, each one cradling a little parcel of salmon and cream cheese. Finally the last of the mince pies from the previous day were brought out on a large silver plate. Katy eyed the yummy looking offerings hungrily and resigned herself to another hour running in the park the next day to make up for it. Holly wreathing had turned out to be a much more gluttonous activity than she had imagined!

They worked through lunch, although Katy wasn't sure that pushing moss in to wire interspersed with wolfing down pastries and biscuits really counted as work. Not that she was complaining. To add to the festive cheer Cerys had fetched an old stereo from the living room. It was covered in big paint splodges and the sound was decidedly tinny, but there was something charming about listening to old Christmas carols through a crackling speaker. It wasn't the kind of Christmas music Katy normally listened to, which tended to be more poppy and modern, but it had a lovely nostalgic feel. It reminded her of her grandmother and the old radio that sat in the corner of her kitchen and had continued to work right up until the day she died, despite bearing the brunt of countless milk splashes and flour storms.

The pile of completed wreaths started to grow and Katy soon became an expert in layering the holly sprigs and threading the ribbon carefully round the edge. It was nice being able to alternate the tasks whilst getting to know her fellow Christmas Clubbers. The biggest surprise was Sophia. When they had first met Katy had thought her a little rude, but in the relaxed environment of the kitchen she was anything but, and she was actually rather charming.

It was only in the middle of Sophia telling a story about a disastrous first date with a guy from her course that Katy suddenly realised the time. It was 2:15pm and she only had 45 minutes to get to her date with David. She started going in to panic mode and wondering what elements of preparation she could jettison and still make it in time for sunset.

'I have to go, I'm so sorry guys. I had no idea of the time.'

'You're leaving?' Rhodri asked, a note of disappointment in his voice.

'Yes, I'm sorry I'm really late.'

'I'll drop you back; we'll go right away. I'll be back in under an hour if you're OK to carry on for now Sophia?'

To Katy's relief Sophia was happy to stay – she wasn't sure they had time for any delay at all. She said a rushed goodbye to the two women and then dashed to the 4x4 in rapid pursuit of Rhodri, who was already sitting in the front seat starting up the engine. They hurtled down Cerys' lane at breakneck speed, the wheels bumping and jolting over every pothole. Rhodri was certainly making an effort to get her home quickly and she felt a flash of guilt at the knowledge that he was speeding her towards her date.

'I thought it was just an excuse this morning,' he said quietly.

'I'm sorry?'

'When you said you had to leave early, I thought that was just something you'd said because you felt awkward around me. I didn't realise you actually had to go.'

'Oh, I'm sorry,' Katy said, a little surprised by the disappointment in his voice.

There was a brief silence and then Rhodri suddenly started gabbling at an unbelievable speed as if he was unable to get the words out quickly enough.

'I was going to ask you if you wanted to cut down the tree tonight. I thought we could pick one out and then take it back to yours later. But before we did that I was thinking you could have come round for dinner. After we left the others I mean – I was going to take Sophia home and then come back and I was going to cook and well…I didn't think you were really going so early.'

He tailed off and Katy was left trying to process everything he had said in such a short space of time. She had never seen him nervous and although she felt some guilt at the situation it was nice to see that he wasn't entirely superhuman.

'I'm sorry, that sounds lovely, really. It's just I have –'

'A date,' he interjected, sounding thoroughly miserable at the prospect.

Her heart sunk, in all the drama of finding out Rhodri was married and then the discovery he was separated she had forgotten that he had probably seen the email from David the day before. She had given him a hard time and in the end she had been the one keeping secrets.

'Yes, it's a little complicated. It's my ex.'

'I see.'

But he didn't. How could Rhodri be expected to know what the evening meant when she wasn't sure herself? It was confusing enough that David was trying to rekindle their relationship, without Rhodri trying to start something new entirely. She wanted to say something to make him feel better, aware that he was clearly smarting from the rebuttal. But she couldn't think of anything that would help.

They drove the rest of the way in silence and Katy feared that the awkwardness from that particular car journey wouldn't be so easily dismissed. But to her surprise when Rhodri pulled up outside her apartment block he got out of the car and stood beside her on the pavement.

'I had a great day again. It's beginning to become a bit of a habit around you.'

Katy smiled at his kind words and was grateful that he didn't seem to be bearing too much of a grudge. What she hadn't counted on was him acting as if the date conversation hadn't happened at all.

'So about the Christmas tree, when would be a good day for you to come over?'

'Oh, um, well I guess Tuesday would be OK. If you're sure you don't mind?'

Even as she spoke Katy's mind was going in to overdrive wondering if she was pretty much the worst person ever for arranging a date minutes before getting ready to go on another one. Not that either of them she intended as *date* dates.

For a horrible moment she wondered if it counted as two-timing, but then Rhodri already knew about David. All she had to do was tell David later and everything would be out in the open. It wasn't like she was looking for anything more from either of them. It was just two different evenings with two different friends; she just had to make it clear that there was nothing more to it than that.

'Tuesday's great. Do you like lasagne?' he asked.

'Please don't go to any trouble, there's no need to make dinner honestly.'

Katy hoped he wouldn't be offended, but she already had one romantic dinner too many happening that week. She couldn't face a second.

'OK – just the tree it is…I guess I should let you go get ready for your date.'

'I'm sorry.'

'Hey, it's OK. Just try not to have too good a time.'

Katy smiled guiltily. Then, before she could say goodbye, Rhodri lunged at her, kissing her on the cheek and scooping her waist towards him with his arm. He held her close for a moment, his chest thudding in time with hers and his strong legs pressed against her thigh. It seemed to take every bit of his strength to resist going for her lips. She could hear it in the hungry gasp of his breath as it danced on her cheek, hot and moist in the cold winter air. He let her go as suddenly as he had taken hold of her and as he took a step back she could see the fire blazing in his eyes.

'Tuesday then,' he said breathlessly, and with that he got back in to the car and drove away, leaving her stunned and reeling from the electricity of his touch.

Chapter Twelve

Katy was fifteen minutes late by the time she arrived in Cardiff Bay. It was still light but the day was rapidly fading away and she hoped they would still have time to walk to the barrage before the sun disappeared altogether. She hurried from the taxi in to the wide-open courtyard where they had agreed to meet. To her left was the bronze arc of the Wales Millennium Centre, rising from the ground like a pre-historic creature. Enormous letters had been carved into its armadillo-like shell, the words towering above passers-by like a message left by giants.

Katy looked around but there was no sign of David. She walked towards the giant metallic tower in the centre of the plaza where a number of figures stood sheltering from the icy wind. There was a movement from one of them as a gloved hand emerged from the pocket of a long winter coat and waved in her direction. She looked again and was struck again by the transformation. The smart winter coat hung nicely on David's slimmed down frame; accentuating his athletic body and making him look taller than usual. Around his neck was a bright fuchsia and teal striped scarf that she would never have imagined him wearing. To top it all off his wayward hair had been styled into a fashionable mess; a kind of undulating wave of bedhead-chic that straight away she wanted to run her fingers through.

'I'm so sorry I'm late.'

'It's OK. It's reassuring to know not *everything's* changed,' David said smiling.

Somehow his remark put her at ease, she was glad they were acknowledging the divide of the last year, even if it was jokingly.

'I got you something,' he added, and rummaged in his coat pocket before producing what looked like an enormous keyring. She pulled off her gloves and took it in her hand, beaming with recognition as soon as she turned it over. It was a small green disc with red writing on which read *Nadolig Llawen* – Welsh for *Merry Christmas*. The decoration was strung on a length of thin gold twine knotted at the top so it could be hung on a tree.

'It's lovely – thank you.'

'I thought you must have your tree up by now. So I wanted you to have something Welsh to welcome you home.'

'Thank you, really it's perfect. And actually I don't have a tree yet, I'm getting one this week.'

Katy felt a small knot of guilt as she evaded talking about Rhodri. Already she could tell that she wasn't cut out for mass dating and she wondered how anyone could live a double life when she was struggling to juggle even two dates.

'Well let me know if you need help picking it up.'

She couldn't answer him directly; instead she tried to swallow down the lump in her throat and suggested they started to walk before it got too late.

There were lots of couples in the bay. Some were off for an early dinner, others going for a walk like them and it felt strange to be a part of it. When they were together, Katy almost didn't think of herself and David as a couple. That was the problem of spending every day together she supposed, you ended up taking one another for granted. Suddenly though everything felt different, on the way in to town she had found herself wondering if he would kiss her when they met, if he would hold her hand – all things that she hadn't thought about with David for a very long time. Such things were automatic when you were in a couple, but having that uncertainty back was exciting; it was new, even if they weren't.

They chit-chatted as they walked, mostly about little things; where each of them was living, David's new job, and places Katy had been to travelling. They both skirted around the difficult questions; why she had left and why he had returned and of course the thorny issue of whether there had been anyone else for either of them in between. It was nice being able to talk without recrimination or tension. Between splitting up and Katy leaving they had only met up a few times. At first it was practical things like divvying up possessions and sorting bills, but afterwards they met up to try and be friends. For one reason or another though it never seemed to go too well and they would end up sniping at each other. After a few attempts they both stopped trying, it was just easier that way.

The year apart seemed to have soothed some of those old hurts and allowed some of the things they loved about one another to resurface.

David was funny, incredibly so – often people didn't see it at first. He was intelligent and he worked hard and he was a Doctor. And sometimes people wrote him off as a result, (though she suspected his sessions in the gym meant that happened less and less these days). But when given a chance to let his humorous side show he had the ability to make Katy laugh at almost anything. So they walked round the bay to a soundtrack of David putting on silly voices, poking fun at himself and generally playing a bit of a fool in a way she found utterly adorable.

In turn Katy found herself falling back in to some of her old habits and not in the way she had feared. David was one of only a few people she could really talk to, and probably the only one of them who was both a man and straight. She was able to be herself around him and she had missed that since they split up.

It had been a perfect choice of activity and both of them were enjoying being back in one of their favourite spots in the city. To their right a handful of boats putted around the harbour, each one leaving a trail of white foam in their wake as they headed back towards their mooring for the night. Whilst over the open water to their left they could see the opposing shapes of Flatholm and Steepholm islands silhouetted against the setting sun.

When they reached the barrage – a set of giant metal arms that lifted the road to allow boats to pass in and out of the harbour – they stopped to watch the sun finally dip in to the sea and turn the sky a beautiful purple-pink. Just as the light began to fade away David slipped his hand in to hers and squeezed it gently. It felt good – better than that, it felt like coming home.

Rather than walking back the way they came they caught the waterbus back to Mermaid Quay; where all the bars and restaurants were. It was too early for dinner so they ended up going for cocktails first. David ordered his usual drink of a whisky sour, which Katy could never drink without wrinkling her nose and pulling a silly face in disgust. She in turn ordered something fruity and luminous coloured that when David had a sip of he pursed his lips and complained at its sweetness.

At 6pm they headed to the restaurant and asked if they could take their table early as Katy was already beginning to feel a little light-headed and wanted to get some food before drinking any more. The restaurant was stunning, all decked out in a tasteful silver and blue theme for Christmas, with a candle on every table and gentle piano music coming from the corner. The waiter took their coats and Katy couldn't help but run her eyes over David who was wearing a tailored duck-egg blue shirt with a little 'v' of his chest showing where the top two buttons were undone. As he leaned in to pull out her chair Katy could smell his aftershave, it was earthy and warm and a brand she didn't recognise on him.

All in all she was struggling to remember why she had thought the date was such a bad idea. He was attractive, attentive, funny, sweet and most importantly of all he was David – the man she had loved for four years, even when he wasn't always all those other things all of the time.

Dinner itself was incredible and Katy couldn't remember eating so well or so much for a long time. And at the end of it she even enjoyed the mini struggle over how they would split the bill, again something they hadn't worried about since the early days of dating. Everything about the evening was going perfectly, so much so that she didn't want to ruin it by bringing up Rhodri. It had been a long time since she and David had been able to spend an evening in each other's company without it ending in an argument and she didn't want to jeopardise that.

After the meal they caught a taxi back to Katy's apartment, even though she lived further out than David did. He paid for the taxi and sent it away. As the car disappeared into the night and she was left alone with David on her doorstep the enormity of the moment started to hit home. *Was he expecting to come up and if so what then...* They had had sex countless times, probably in the hundreds – but suddenly the thought seemed overwhelming. She wasn't ready, however much she wanted to. And she did: a big part of her was practically screaming at her to take the second chance, to sink in to his arms – a place she had always felt at home – and never let go. But it was too soon. She knew that, she just wasn't sure if David did too.

'I had a great night,' he said.

For the first time since they had met up hours earlier there was a little awkwardness and nervousness that hadn't been there after the first five minutes. David shuffled his feet a little, rocking his weight from one side of his body to the other with his hands in his pockets.

It was cold outside and Katy gave an involuntary shiver, but she didn't want to be the one to say goodnight. She didn't want to walk away from him again when he had put himself out there; she just wasn't ready to invite him upstairs.

'Oh, you're freezing. Come here,' David said. He opened his long black coat and wrapped it around her, pulling her body close to his. David's arms embraced her, his hands linking in the small of her back. She felt the immediacy of his body, the nearness of his lips to hers and felt the soft exhale of his breath as it clouded the icy air in front of her eyes. He leaned in further, gently parting her lips with his, allowing his tongue to flick delicately against hers. And then they were kissing passionately, in a way they hadn't done for years. She felt the urgency in his touch: the desire, and she realised how much she had missed that. It had been so long since she had felt truly wanted by him in a way that made him lose control.

It was no different for Katy; she wanted him, she wanted to kiss a trail of warmth down his neck and onto his chest. She wanted to unbutton his shirt and let her hands run over his torso. Katy's mind was racing, her pulse quickening and a hunger was building uncontrollably in her heart.

Suddenly something changed, David seemed to hold his breath and she felt his grip on her loosen. She looked in to his eyes and there was a cool sadness there where moments before there had been nothing but fire and heat.

'I should go,' he said, before adding; 'I've had the best night. I've missed you Katy, I've *really* missed you.'

Katy hugged him, but not like they had been moments before when it had been all about desire, feverishly caressing and exploring one another. She hugged him in a way she hoped conveyed all the things she felt but didn't know how to say: that she was sorry, that she had never imagined there would come a time when they would be near strangers to one another and that she had never stopped loving him. It was just that one day she had come to realise that maybe that wasn't enough. But leaving him was the hardest thing she had *ever* done and it was her biggest regret in life that they had failed to make it work. These were all the things she didn't know how else to say to him.

'I missed you too.'

Katy watched David walk away down the street, his black coat blending with the night. The darkness eroded his silhouette, gradually swallowing his body so he grew smaller until she could barely make him out at all. When he had disappeared completely she unlocked the front door and made her way up to her empty flat. She piled her clothes on a chair and then climbed in to bed without even switching the light on. And there she lay alone except for her guilt and the confused knot of unrest in her stomach until sleep finally came for her.

Chapter Thirteen

The next few days Katy tried to keep herself busy. She spent Sunday morning writing Christmas cards and catching up on her emails. After lunch she looked over the details of the jobs from the recruitment agencies. They were all perfectly good options; reasonable pay, central Cardiff location and the work itself she knew she could do. But they didn't excite her and so rather than applying for them she ended up flicking through her travel photos, reliving her time away on her laptop screen.

When she got back to the beginning of the album she carried on, going through older folders from before she went away. There was a strange contrast; her travel photos covered everything in an erratic and seemingly disconnected string of images. The pictures meandered through meals she had eaten, strangers she couldn't even remember the names of, road signs, landmarks, sunsets and hazy blurs of campfire drinking. But the photos from before travelling covered only the major events; birthdays, Christmas parties, the occasional night out and some holiday snaps. There were people she deeply cared about, and saw regularly like Anne and Matt who barely featured. Tom was there a lot and of course David: David and her in Paris, hiking Snowdon, at her work's Christmas do in 2013 and David picking up his community award.

Why was it that she had only documented the major events; the things that happened once or twice a year and ignored the memories that were made every day? And why had it taken her ten plane journeys and a year away to appreciate that there was joy to be found in all those little moments that made up a life? Time she supposed – normal life was too busy and hectic. Work and all the other "necessities" that filled her days got in the way of the things that really mattered; like taking the time to watch the sunrise, or spending a day reading a book without feeling guilty about all the things she hadn't done. But worse than all of that, modern life ground her down. It stripped you of your energy and chewed you up your whole life until it spat you out in your final years, when you were too old and too tired to do the things you wished you'd had the time for when you were younger.

Katy and David hadn't pushed each other away; life had done that. It was the constant chipping away; the splintering demands of late nights and deadlines, admin errors and speeding fines, traffic jams and red-lettered bills, midnight supermarket runs and flat tyres. Each one was so trivial and so small, but they piled up and up and it was hard not to take it out on the person you were closest to.

By the time Katy finally got on the plane she was exhausted; seven years of secondary school had been followed by three years of university and ten years of work. Of course there had been a lot of good times, but she had applied herself to every one of those things and they had taken from her far more than they had given back. She had walked away from David because she didn't know who she was anymore, because she was tired and not the kind of tired that a weekend away or a few days off work would cure. Their relationship had been steadily suffering for six months and there were times when Katy felt they were more like flatmates than boyfriend and girlfriend. They were two people trundling along under the same roof who now and then managed to stay awake long enough for a ten-minute fumble before they fell asleep. Things had drifted and neither of them had had the energy to put it right.

Katy's hand hovered over the keyboard. The tide had turned; what had started as a pleasant diversion had become something maudlin and introspective. She put the laptop away and walked over to the bookshelf. She ran her finger along the spines as if reading them like braille until she stopped at a thin blue book with well-worn lines of silver running down its edge where the print had cracked with use. Katy opened the book at the title page and read the inscription:

Katy,

One year of loving you has made me happier than all of the 27 years without you put together. I know paper is for wedding anniversaries but you can't blame a guy for starting early.

This was my favourite book in school; it's been with me everywhere since I was 15; every dorm room and every house for the past 12 years. This book has been to India and Thailand, America and Swindon(!). I'm giving it to you now, knowing that it'll still be with me always, just like you. And when we're old and grey it'll still be sitting on our shelf, as constant as my love for you.

Love always,

David XXXX

Katy carried the book back to the sofa wishing there was a way she could reach out to the David who had written those words – the 27 year old who was still full of all those hopes and dreams, a man so sure they would be together forever.

   Katy started to read, immersing herself in the story that had captured the imagination of a teenage David – and her heart – when he had given it to her. She didn't stop to eat and when she wanted a drink she made it with the one hand whilst holding the book in the other. She carried on reading when it grew dark and didn't stop when night settled in. It was only when she reached the final page and the story was told from beginning to end that she put it down. She was too weary to go to bed, instead she pulled the blanket that she kept on top of the sofa over her body and instantly fell asleep, still clutching the copy of *On the Road* that David had given her all those years ago.

Chapter Fourteen

Katy woke early on Monday morning, her stomach grumbling loudly. She cooked some bacon and eggs and piled them on to three slices of toast. She was going round to Anne's for lunch later in the day and so it was silly to have such a large breakfast. But having not eaten the previous evening she was ravenous and there was no way she could wait until lunchtime.

After breakfast Katy hunted around for her phone, eventually uncovering it wedged down the side of the sofa. She plugged it in and waited for the thing to chirp in to life. There was a message from David. She toyed with the idea of telling him about her late night Kerouac adventure, but in the end decided against it.

He was going to London for a week later in the month and was keen to see her again before then. She replied positively; there was no point pretending she didn't want to see him. She did, desperately so. Having him back in her life was definitely a good thing. Only time would tell how far they should take it.

Anne had also texted her, suggesting she come over early. Katy had no other plans for the morning so she set off straight after breakfast, taking a leisurely meandering route to the house. It was a crisp winter day and despite most people being in work, the park was surprisingly busy with mum's taking toddlers out and students enjoying the sunshine. In the middle of the park, near the café, a brass band was playing Christmas carols and Katy stopped to listen. There was something magical about the deep, rich rumble of trumpets and horns in the stillness of the park that brought the songs to life in a way that no studio recording could ever hope to match. Katy ended up staying to the end of the set, figuring that she was early anyway. When they finished Katy put a £5 note in to the open music case of one of the trombonists and thanked the group with a wave.

Anne didn't work on Mondays, it was something that Matt and she had put in place for when they had children. Anne was off Mondays and worked from home on a Friday, whilst Matt was home every other Wednesday. The arrangements were in place, but the babies hadn't followed. Katy knew they had been trying even before she left and it was sad coming back and finding out that nothing had changed for them.

When Katy arrived Anne was in the garden, taking advantage of the dry day to tidy up the flowerbeds. They sat on small metal patio chairs and nursed their warm mugs of coffee whilst making a fuss of Anne's ginger cat Eric; who flitted between them chasing attention.

'So,' Anne began. 'I've been getting near daily updates from Tom about your love life. Maybe it's time I heard it from the horse's mouth as it were.'

'Charming,' Katy said.

'Oh, I think we're all just a little jealous of the attention. So come on then, tell me everything.'

'Well David's back and he's basically a walking gym advert now. But he seems different too…more relaxed I suppose.'

'I don't think being charming was ever David's problem.'

'No, I guess not. But I'm impressed with how he's handling it all. I really think this past year's changed him for the better – given him some perspective. We had the most wonderful date the other day. And he's even started phoning me again. I can't remember when we last did that. It's just like it was when we first got together – the other night we talked for hours, about nothing at all really, but it was lovely. And I've missed that; I've missed having him in my life.'

'Have you told him about Rhodri?' Anne asked gently.

'No. I can't. Not yet anyway. I don't want to lose him. When I came home it seemed like the worst thing hearing that he'd moved back. I just wanted us to get over each other. But I'm not sure that's possible, and I'm not sure I want to. I'm not planning on jumping back in to anything; not at all. But I can't bear the thought of losing him again either.'

'And has something happened with Rhodri for him to get upset about?'

Katy thought about the question, but it was impossible to answer. They hadn't slept together which is what people normally meant when they asked that, they hadn't even kissed. And yet Katy couldn't explain the spark she'd felt when his lips brushed her cheek the last time they'd met, or the excitement she'd felt when he'd hugged her, their bodies closely entwined. And there were no words for the way he'd looked at her when he warmed her hands in his in the cold air of the farm – as if there was no one else in the world.

'We've been texting a lot,' Katy said eventually. 'Just silly things and a few flirtations thrown in I suppose. You know how it is when you first meet someone you're attracted to? Sometimes it's hard to stop thinking about them – even if you know it won't lead to anything.'

Anne laughed. 'I remember. So you are attracted to him then?'

'Yes, I mean how could you not be? The man's gorgeous.'

'And David?'

'He's David, I think I'll always love him.'

'Well it sounds like you're screwed then,' said Anne.

Katy laughed and playfully threw a chunk of biscuit in Anne's direction. 'Helpful, thanks!' The moment it landed on the floor Eric was beside it, tentatively sniffing the crumbled oat square.

'Just be careful,' Anne said more seriously as she fussed Eric's neck with her left hand. 'You know David can get a little…intense. He's been through a lot. You both have. Just try not to forget why you left him. If all those things are really gone, then great, but don't be swayed just because you miss having him around. And don't jump in to something too quickly with Rhodri either. They're big boys, make them wait until you're ready.'

It was good to talk about David with someone a little more level-headed, someone who was capable of remembering the good and the bad. Ever since Katy had returned she had felt under pressure to feel a certain way about David. The boys had clearly all lost their heads over the thought of David's buff new exterior and David himself was acting just as crazy. Hearing Anne's perspective on it all made Katy realise that she was being too hard on herself. She hadn't forced David to come back to Cardiff and he couldn't expect her to act as if nothing had happened.

Katy left Anne's house with a stomach full of cake but a decidedly lighter and clearer head than she had had for days. When she got back to the apartment she put away David's book and gave the place a quick tidy. She then filled out applications for three of the jobs she had been given the details for and emailed them off to the recruiters. She wanted to change her life and maybe long term they weren't the right jobs, but she also had a flat to pay for and a fairly regular need for food and electricity that required she earn some money.

Riding the wave of efficiency Katy then phoned round the long list of banks, companies and credit card issuers she had accounts with to update them of her new address. The final phone call she made to her mum, who amongst other things was very pleased to hear they would be receiving less mail for Katy.

By the time her mum had finished telling Katy about the dogs, the cat, her dad's progress on the extension and the ins and outs of the neighbour's relationships, they had been on the phone for an hour and not really talked about anything of importance. Katy had missed that; her phone calls home whilst travelling had been short and almost business-like, both sides checking the other was well, healthy and broadly eating what they should be to stay that way. There was something comforting about her mum's meandering return to form and Katy made no attempt to cut her short, not even when the topics started to repeat.

Katy went to bed in a much better frame of mind. And with neither the guilt she had felt on Saturday or the fervour of the previous night's reading marathon to cloud her thoughts she slept well, surrendering her mind easily and slumbering late in to the following morning.

Chapter Fifteen

The late start to the day meant that Katy was only just putting away her breakfast bowl when she heard the spluttering arrival of the 4x4 outside the apartment. She quickly brushed her teeth and checked her appearance in the mirror before grabbing a coat and dashing down the stairs. Parking in her street was a nightmare and Rhodri was hovering in the road, hemmed against a long line of stationary vehicles.

Katy jumped in to the cabin, a little more gracefully than the first time, and they scooted down to the end of the street before anyone else could beep their horn in annoyance at the minor inconvenience the 4x4 had caused them.

'Friendly bunch,' Rhodri joked.

'I know, last week I accidentally dropped a bin bag in the road and I thought someone was going to lynch me because I had to stop traffic for a minute to pick it up.'

'Can't say I have that problem a lot.'

'No,' Katy mused, 'I guess you don't where you live.'

'Get the odd sheep traffic jam mind, when the Thompson's move their flock.'

'Wow, it's all go in the country.'

'It is, you should try it sometime.'

Katy had expected there to be some flirting, especially after the nearly-kiss at the weekend and the changing tone of their increasingly frequent text messages. But she had at least hoped they would have made it outside of the city boundary before he started.

'Mind you,' he continued, 'this'll be the third time you've been to the farm in a week Winters – I'm starting to think you might be a good country girl after all.'

'I grew up in Norfolk, it was hardly the middle of London!'

'That's English countryside though. Whole different thing entirely.'

'How about you just drive? I think I preferred it when you didn't say as much,' Katy said, hoping he would take the joke in the spirit it was intended.

'Yes m'lady,' he replied haughtily, before descending in to a deep belly laugh.

They pulled up on the driveway outside Windmill Farm and Rhodri disappeared in to the house while she waited on the doorstep. It felt a little odd not going in and she had thought they might have a coffee or something first, but he had promised he would only be a few minutes. Katy wondered if Cerys could see the farmhouse from her cottage. It was strange being so close and not popping in to say hello, almost as if they were sneaking around behind her back.

'Ready,' Rhodri called, appearing by her side with what looked like a picnic hamper.

'What's in there?' she asked.

'Just a few tree cutting essentials, don't worry.'

'OK,' she answered, a little warily.

'So suspicious, now come on – you've got work to do,' Rhodri said, marching off over the field.

There was already an axe waiting for them when they arrived at the copse of trees. On the floor beside it there was a small pile of logs, some thin white netting and a long length of frayed blue rope.

'Wow, you country folk really are relaxed aren't you? I've never once seen you or Cerys lock your doors and now I find you leave axes and rope just lying around. Do you have a death wish or something?'

'It's OK, first sign of trouble and I'd just yell and Cerys' dogs would see them off.'

'Jasper and Henry? Only if your attacker could be killed by vigorous licking!'

'Hmm, I see your point. Well let's just say it's not a big worry out here. Right – pick a tree and get started.'

'Me?' Katy asked as she eyed up the clutch of enormous tree trunks and the equally weighty looking axe.

'Yep, you want a tree, don't you? Don't tell me you expect the man to do all the heavy work while you sit and watch.'

The truth was that was exactly what Katy had expected. Not that she thought it was Rhodri's job or any of that macho bullshit, but the thought of wielding an axe within a mile of anyone else really wasn't a good idea.

'Ok, I'll get you started,' he said, smiling at the stunned look on her face. He was enjoying himself way too much for Katy's liking.

Rhodri told her to stand with her legs slightly apart facing the tree. He then picked up the axe and stood behind her in a similar position. She could feel his warm breath fluttering on her neck and the press of his waist against her hips. He brought her left arm across her body and twisted her hand round so that the palm was facing upwards. He then stretched out her right arm in the same way. When he rested the axe in her hands she was worried it would be too heavy to lift, but he held on to it, taking all the weight. Rhodri counted them in to a swing and then they moved their arms in unison. The blade bit heavily into the tree with a satisfying thud. They pulled the blade back out and there was a small 'v' shaped cut in the side where the axe had found its mark. Rhodri led them in to a second swing, and then a third, all the time guiding the blade and bearing its weight.

The groove in the tree started to grow, getting deeper and wider as the axe bit further and further in to the trunk. Even though Rhodri was doing all the real work, Katy could feel the ache settling in to her limbs with every blow. It wasn't just the swinging motion that was taking its toll, but the recoil when the axe hit the tree. The force of the blow echoed up the handle and in to her arms. So when Rhodri suggested she finished on her own she looked at him as if he had lost his mind.

'Trust me, I know you can do it,' he said.

He let the full weight of the axe rest in her hands and then gently backed away. Katy looked round anxiously, worried that he might be in the way if she swung too wildly or dropped the axe, but he smiled encouragingly and gestured for her to carry on. Nervously she pulled the axe behind her and then swung it forward with all her might. It hit the tree but a little north of its mark and so she tried again. The second time she connected in just the right spot and was rewarded with an impressive shower of splinters.

'Perfect! That should just about do it I think,' said Rhodri, as he stepped forward to take the axe from her weary hands.

'Really?'

'Yep, now help me give it a push.'

The two of them found a grip on the tree, weaving their hands between branches until they were both touching part of the main trunk. The tree resisted at first, reluctant to be severed from its roots. But as they continued to shove at it Katy heard the final sliver of wood begin to splinter and crack as the tree slowly fell towards the floor.

Rhodri levelled off the base with the axe and then picked the tree up by its trunk and held it out towards Katy.

'There you are, your very own Christmas tree. Cut by your own fair hands.'

Katy gave a clap of excitement – it was the best Christmas tree she had ever had, not just because of it's nice symmetrical shape and vibrant green needles, but because she had picked it and cut it down herself, even if she had had some help along the way.

'It's perfect, thank you so much – I love it!'

'I'm glad. It's not like we can put it back and get another one!'

Between the two of them they managed to manoeuvre the tree into the netting and then Rhodri tied the rope around it to keep the branches contained. When the tree was completely wrapped up and ready to transport Rhodri laid it on the ground and turned his attention to the woodpile.

'What are the logs for?' Katy asked.

'I thought we'd have a fire to warm up.'

Katy was already fairly warm after all the chopping and then trying to force the tree into the net, both of which were very physical tasks to be doing in a thick winter coat. All the same a fire would be nice she thought and so she mucked in, fetching small twigs and kindling that would help the logs catch.

'You've done this before,' Rhodri said, sounding impressed.

'A fair bit – I've had more campfires in this last year than most boy-scouts I'd imagine.'

'I'll leave you to it then.'

Rhodri handed Katy a lighter and then proceeded to unpack the hamper. Inside were a frying pan, a small milk pan, a flask of water, a pint of milk, a small loaf of bread and a large sandwich bag filled with sausages.

'You said no dinner!' Katy protested.

'I'd hardly call a cup of tea and a hot-dog dinner! I promised I wouldn't go to any effort and cook a big lasagne. This is *completely* different.'

Katy made a show of reluctantly agreeing to him cooking the sausages, but inwardly she was delighted. She only hoped that her rumbling stomach would keep quiet long enough that it didn't show her up as a fraud.

Before long the fire was crackling away and a thin wisp of woody smoke was snaking in to the air. There were few things as rewarding for the senses as an open wood fire, and Katy could only imagine how good it was going to smell once the sausages were cooking.

'Milk and sugar?' Rhodri asked, holding a mug of tea out towards her.

'Just milk thanks. You're very well prepared!'

'Well it's not often I get to have tea with a beautiful woman in the woods.'

Suddenly it was there again; the admission that he liked her, the comment that took them beyond the realm of friends and into something more.

'Rhodri, about the date I went on the other night. It's – well it's complicated. He's my ex. We were together for four years and then we split up shortly before I went travelling. He moved away but he's just come back to Cardiff and I think, well I'm fairly sure he wants to start things up again.'

'And what do you want?'

'I don't know. But I won't hurt him again. Until I know what's happening – well I'm guessing I'm saying that I can't get into anything else right now.'

Rhodri put his mug down on the ground and stared into the fire. Katy couldn't judge his mood, she wasn't sure whether he was sad, or frustrated, or angry.

'It's OK,' he said eventually, 'I guess I kind of knew that something was going on. It's not exactly a surprise that someone was waiting for you when you got back.'

'Really?'

Rhodri laughed quietly and then said: 'I imagine you're a pretty hard girl to get over Katy Winters. He was stupid enough to let you go, I bet he's not going to let the chance to get you back slip away as easily.'

'Well he didn't let me go exactly. I finished it with him and then it was another four months before I left.'

'But he could have gone with you, or at least tried to.'

'I'd never thought of that. I guess they've always seemed like two different things; we broke up and then I went travelling – I think the time for second chances had already passed by then.'

'You're telling me if he'd asked to come with you, you'd have said no?'

Katy thought about his question for a moment before replying.

'No, I guess not. Actually I think it would probably have saved us.'

'And now?'

'I don't know. I'm sorry. I don't want to lead you on, or mess him about. I don't want to be unfair to either of you. I kissed him the other night. Well he kissed me I suppose. But I didn't exactly stop him.'

'You're feeling pretty bad about this aren't you?'

'Yes. I really am sorry,' Katy replied.

'Don't be. I'm not sure I've ever met anyone so honest. I wish everyone was more like you. The world would be a much happier place. You've done nothing wrong, not to him and certainly not to me. So stop giving yourself a hard time.'

'Thank you,' she said, relieved at his reaction.

'I'm not giving up mind.'

'I'm sorry?'

'Hey, don't get me wrong – I'm not going to make things awkward for you, or try anything on. You've got stuff you need to work through and I won't get in the way of that. But I like you Katy and if he's stupid enough to stuff things up a second time I'll be here waiting. So you better get used to having me around for now. All's fair in love and war after all.'

Katy was a little taken aback at his frankness, but there was also something incredibly sweet about it. He knew there was a chance that she was going to get back together with David and he wasn't going to stop that happening. But he also liked her enough not to give up, and it was hard not to be flattered by his attention.

'Ok, well I think I can live with that.'

'Good.'

Then as quickly as the matter had been brought up it seemed to be forgotten and Rhodri started to fry the sausages, turning them over in the pan with a stout twig so that they cooked evenly. Katy watched him as the fire flickered across his face, illuminating the dark bristle of facial hair that hugged his upper lip and crept along his jaw. His features were rugged and weathered from spending his life outdoors, battling on regardless of the rain or sun. But the muscular body and the handsomely strong face were a mask it seemed. There was a sadness to him; a darkness in his eyes that came from a hurt that hadn't quite healed. What was it he had said? *I wish everyone was more like you. The world would be a much happier place.* Those weren't the kind of words you said unless someone had made you truly unhappy.

Suddenly one of the sausages burst, spitting out a small shower of fat that scolded Rhodri's hand. He recoiled from the pan and let out a yelp that interrupted her thoughts and caused her to jump up and check he was all right. She had his hand cupped in hers and was rubbing gently at the pink-flushed skin before she realised what she was doing.

'Sorry,' she said.

He didn't reply and so she looked up and found herself face to face with him. He was staring at her, eyes wide and glistening in the firelight. His brow was furrowed in concentration and for the first time she noticed a tiny scar there. It was just above his left eyebrow; a small 'y' shaped blemish that had faded and stretched with the passing years. Her eyes fell onto his lips, which hovered only an inch from hers. They were slightly parted and it would have been so easy to lean forward and to kiss him. It was then that she realised it wasn't Rhodri's restraint she had to worry about, it was her own, and that was a far more difficult prospect to manage.

Chapter Sixteen

It was beginning to grow dark by the time they pulled up outside Katy's apartment. The journey home had been a little strange on account of the barrier of green needles separating them where the tree poked in between the front seats. A small part of Katy was grateful for it though, she didn't fully trust herself when she looked at Rhodri. Whenever she did she found herself imagining what his lips would taste like kissing hers, how his beard would feel like nuzzling against her cheek and how long she could stare into the dark pools of his eyes before she lost herself in them.

If it hadn't been for the oil nearly catching in the heat of the pan she wasn't sure she would have made it out of the woods unscathed. As it was, her body was still tingling with the warmth of his touch where he had helped her in to the car. Until she knew where things were with David she would just have to be extra careful around Rhodri.

As they struggled up the staircase Katy consoled herself with the knowledge that for the following ten minutes at least there would be 5ft 10 inches of pine tree keeping them apart. It meant that all she had to worry about was trying not to damage the paintwork in the hallway or colliding with any of her neighbours' front doors. As for what followed, she would have to deal with that when it came to it.

'You never said you lived on the top floor,' Rhodri grumbled, 'If you had I would have told you to pick a smaller tree!'

'What?' Katy called back, unable to hear him behind the dense wall of pine.

Rhodri was about six steps ahead of her and considerably further up the hallway.

'Never mind!'

Eventually they made it to Katy's front door, where she found Rhodri leaning against the wall panting.

Getting it in to the flat was just as difficult and Katy was a little worried that some of the decorations she had put up might not survive the process. However with some careful manoeuvring Rhodri managed to get the tree upright and in position in front of the large bay window opposite the sofa. He secured the stand and then took a seat whilst she cut away at the netting with a large pair of kitchen scissors.

Once all the branches had sprung satisfyingly back in to place, Katy took a step back to admire it. The tree was just as beautiful as when they had first cut it down, if a little bare – but that could soon be rectified.

'Blimey Katy,' Rhodri exclaimed. 'Where's all your stuff?'

'What do you mean?'

'Well, where is everything?'

Katy looked round the apartment again with a stranger's eyes and she could see what he meant. There were the basics in terms of furniture, some books and a television set, and a whole heap of Christmas decorations, but nothing else.

'I had to get rid of everything before I went travelling. Mum and Dad took some stuff and I ended up leaving most of our joint stuff to David. In the end I only had a few boxes in storage when I came back.'

'Wow, it's going to be a pretty bare tree then.'

Katy laughed and disappeared in to the bedroom. She returned with two large cardboard boxes with *Christmas decorations* scrawled in black marker pen on the sides.

'Christmas I have covered.'

'You really are a remarkable woman Katy Winters, you don't have a toaster, or even curtains for that matter, but you kept two whole boxes of decorations!'

'Three actually, these are just the tree decorations, the rest are already out.'

Decorating the tree was something David and Katy had always done together. It was an activity that she loved and looked forward to every year. David was generally less excited by the whole thing, but Katy normally managed to persuade him to get involved with the help of an eggnog or two to keep him happy. It felt strange sharing the moment with somebody else, especially a man she had met only just over a week before. But Katy couldn't help feeling that decorating a tree on her own would be incredibly depressing, and so, odd as it was, she gratefully accepted Rhodri's offer to stay and help.

Rhodri got quite in to the spirit of decorating, even without the aid of alcohol. He sang along to the Christmas songs, even some of the less well known ones and to Katy's relief he left the more personal decorations in the box for her to deal with while he arranged the tinsel and lights.

As large as the tree was, it was no match for Katy's decorations and by the end there was very little green still showing. She took the empty boxes from the living room and returned a moment later carrying one final decoration. It was the one David had given her at the weekend and she hung it in the centre near the top – the final piece of the puzzle.

'It looks great,' Rhodri said and he gently put his arm around her and gave her shoulder a small squeeze.

'Do you think your mum would like it?' Katy asked.

'I think she'd love it. She's a proper Christmas nut too.'

Katy playfully slapped him on the shoulder and shrugged away his arm.

'Well at least someone in your family has good sense.'

Katy made them both a hot chocolate and they sat on either side of the sofa admiring the tree. She knew it was over the top and she had too many decorations, but she loved all of them and each one held a special memory for her. She was glad Rhodri hadn't made fun of any of them, even the slightly ropey looking ones she and her brother had made when they were children.

'I best be off then,' Rhodri said a little time later, just as he came to the end of his drink.

'Thanks again for everything, I've had a lovely day, and the tree really is perfect.'

She walked him down to the front door and out on to the pavement. Although it was dark it was still early and there were plenty of people around. Some were only just returning home from work, whilst others were making their way in to town for the evening. Katy had thought it safer to say goodbye outside. She felt more in control with other people nearby than she would have in her own flat, where the twinkling lights of the Christmas tree leant a certain magic to the room.

'Goodbye then,' she said, pushing her hands in to her pockets so she wasn't tempted to grab hold of Rhodri and pull him in for a kiss.

'I'll see you at the weekend then?'

'Yes, holly wreathing day three! I'm looking forward to it already.'

'Me too.'

There was an awkward moment of silence. The two of them had said all that was to be said and the only route left to them was to embark on a parting marked by lingering hugs and tentative kisses. But that was a path Katy wanted to avoid and so sensing Rhodri's hesitation, she took the lead and began to wander back to her front door, leaving him standing by the car. When she had passed through the little iron gate that marked out her front yard she pushed it closed and stood behind it to wave him off, congratulating herself that once again she had resisted a kiss.

Chapter Seventeen

Saturday came around quicker than Katy expected and she was beginning to wonder how she would ever have time to fit in work. Between job applications, catching up with a year's worth of lapsed paperwork and Christmas Club she had been rushed off her feet since moving back. Then there was the increasingly time consuming matter of fending off the advances of two men, both of whom she liked. The return to real life was proving a lot more difficult than she had hoped.

At 8:40am the doorbell went and Katy was still nowhere near ready, but at least it would only be Tom and he had seen her looking far worse. Even so, the prospect of answering the door in her pyjamas with her hair tangled and her face puffy from sleep didn't exactly appeal.

When Katy opened the door and found David on her doorstep, she wanted the ground to swallow her up. Of course he had seen her in various stages of undress over the years – but that was before – and she was hoping to maintain some dignity as they renegotiated their relationship with one another.

'David! I wasn't expecting you.'

'Who were you expecting? Cos I'm kind of jealous if they get to see you like this.'

'Tom.'

'Gay guys really do get all the luck don't they, he gets to come over and you're in your pyjamas and then you'll probably have a shower while he's here and then you'll be wandering around in a ridiculously small towel.'

'Idiot,' Katy chided, but she couldn't help smiling as she said so.

'I'm just saying – it sounds pretty hot, I can't help feeling I'm missing out…maybe I'm gay.'

'No, you're a perve; there's a big difference. See Tom *is* gay, so he has no interest in seeing me shower. You're not gay, so you'd be pretending to be gay just to see me shower. Which is kind of messed up.'

'OK, you got me. I would be doing it just for the perving.'

'So was there anything else you wanted?' Katy asked, starting to enjoy herself. 'Or are you just going door to door creeping out young women?'

'Well I was, but I think all the young one's are too hungover to answer their door and I just seem to keep striking out on these cranky 30-something pyjama types.'

'Well good luck in your search then,' Katy said and started to close the door very slowly.

'OK, OK I give in. I came to give you this.'

David brought his right hand from behind his back and in it he was holding what looked like a giant cone of magazines.

'What's that?' Katy asked, genuinely intrigued.

'It's a TV guide bouquet,' he announced proudly.

'A what?'

'But it's not just any TV guide bouquet. This is a *Christmas* TV guide bouquet. Four different magazine's crammed full of festive viewing. Handpicked for you this morning.'

Katy took the magazines from David with a little giggle. He had rolled the four magazines together so that they resembled a giant ice-cream cone and then tied them loosely with a ribbon.

'Four *different* magazines?' Katy asked.

'Yep.'

'Even though you always say it's a waste of money buying four because –'

'Because they all have exactly the same listings. Yep, and they do, I mean I'm completely right on that. What you have there is four sets of repeated information.'

'But...' she prompted, testing him.

'But...' and then he mimed air-quotes: 'they have different features and suggestions.'

'Exactly!'

'Which you can spend hours reading over and highlighting, only to complain that there isn't really anything on and you'll end up watching a DVD instead.'

'Probably,' Katy conceded. 'But it'll be a well-informed choice.'

'Well that's good to know. I hope you like it anyway; I know you don't really get flowers.'

'It's great – thank you.'

He was right as well; she appreciated a gesture like the TV guides, which probably cost him less than a fiver far more than she would a

£20 bouquet of real flowers, which within a week would be a depressing mess of dried stems and wilted petals. The TV guides were personal and it was sweet of him to think of it.

'I'm really sorry David, but Tom really is on his way over, and I'm running really late.'

'Hey it's okay. I have to…well actually I have nowhere to be, which is why I came over to see if you fancied going for a walk. But you have plans, so maybe another time?'

'Yes, definitely,' Katy said apologetically.

'Okay, well I'll see you soon.'

He leant in and kissed her gently on her lips. It was a tender moment and though it was most unlike their last kiss, it was just as intimate.

Katy stayed on the doorstep long enough to watch David walk through the gate and disappear down the street. Part of her wanted to cancel holly wreathing and skip after him, pyjamas and all. But instead she decided on the more sensible option of heading back upstairs and getting ready.

The doorbell went for the second time just as she was getting out of the shower. Luckily it really was Tom on this occasion, which was a good job seeing as she answered the door in just a towel.

'Shouldn't you be ready by now?' Tom asked.

'Helpful.'

Katy rushed back up the stairs leaving Tom to follow at a more moderate pace behind. Once back in the flat she headed to the bedroom and started to change, whilst Tom stood just outside so they could talk through the doorway.

'David was just round.'

'Really?' Tom asked, sounding interested. 'As in just leaving after staying the night?'

'No! As in just popping round to see if I was free. It was really cute actually; he bought me a TV guide bouquet.'

'A what?'

'It doesn't matter; I'll show you in a minute. But isn't it nice that he thought of that. You know I really think he's changed. He's putting a lot of effort in, and he seems to have reigned himself in as well. In the past if he'd turned up like that and I had plans I think he'd have expected me to cancel them, or for him to come along as well. But instead he just went along with it and said he'd see me soon.'

'So it's David then?'

'What do you mean?' Katy asked as she struggled to put her socks on.

'Well in the big David-Rhodri love triangle. It's David you're going for?'

Katy appeared at the door, she was dressed but her hair was still a mess and she hadn't cleaned her teeth yet.

'There's no love triangle Tom. There's no anything. Rhodri and I are friends. David and I are friends. It's as simple as that.'

'Really?' he asked sceptically

Katy hesitated to answer, reluctant to prove him right: 'Well no, David and I kissed the other night...and it definitely wasn't a friendship kind of a kiss.'

'So I was right it's David all the way?'

'Um, well not exactly. Rhodri's made it pretty clear he likes me. In fact he's basically said that if David screws up then he'll be waiting to step in.'

'Bloody hell Katy, you've got a man and a back-up too?'

'No, I don't have anyone, there are just two men and David and I have more history. Really Tom, don't go making this out to be a bigger thing than it already is, I'm doing that enough for two people already.'

'Okay.'

Katy hoped that was the end of it, but before she had even made it to the bathroom Tom had picked the conversation up again.

'So which one do you think's hotter? I mean David's always been okay looking, not like stunning, but I always sort of saw the appeal. But now he's like running magazine hot, all toned abs and pert bum...and I'm loving the stubble. It makes him look a bit bad-boy, which he totally never was before. But then you have Rhodri...and he's like a *proper* man, the kind who could make a fire with one hand and throw you over his shoulder with the other...and those eyes!'

'Thanks for that little insight Tom. I'm sure Owen would love to know you're such a hornbag.'

'Oh, he knows. And the only reason I haven't been able to discuss this with Owen is that he hasn't met either of them yet. I think Owen would like Rhodri, I kind of imagine them wrestling and getting all physical together – now that would be hot!'

'Enough now, he's going to be here in five minutes! Give it a rest.'

'Spoilsport,' Tom sulked.

As much as Katy had wanted to avoid the conversation there was a lot of truth in what Tom had said. She was incredibly attracted to both men, and in different ways. And it wasn't just about looks either; David was kind and caring, a little domineering maybe, but most of that came from a good place. He was ambitious and clever, and funny, and they liked a lot of the same things; going on walks, enjoying the same books and the same films. She was comfortable with him and that was no bad thing.

She knew much less about Rhodri of course, but she had still seen a lot she liked. Rhodri went out of his way to help people; he was generous with his time, he clearly helped Cerys with things she couldn't manage and he had dutifully ferried Sophia and Katy to and from the farm without a single grumble. He was thoughtful too; the way he had left the personal tree ornaments to Katy to put up, the way he picked up how upset she was with him when she found out he was married and never criticised her for going off on one when it was her that was at fault. And for all his physical strength there was a real softness to him, a vulnerability that left you wanting to look out for him.

Katy finished getting ready just in time for Rhodri's arrival and as she answered the door for the third time that morning she realised how lucky she was that things were working out so well for her. She had been a little apprehensive about returning after a year away, worried that all her friends would have moved on and that she would have been forgotten. She couldn't really have blamed people either, it had been a year and it was her choice to leave. But if anything her social life was busier than it had ever been before.

For once Rhodri had managed to find a parking space and Katy was touched that he helped not only her in to the 4x4, but Tom as well. The atmosphere was different in the car with Tom there. When it was just Katy and Rhodri the conversation often ended up a little flirty. Instead they talked about Tom's job and Rhodri seemed genuinely interested in his work as an artist. Tom mainly did small commission pieces; family portraits and some local landscapes for a few gift shops, but what really interested him was sculpture and larger scale pieces that combined painting with other mediums. Katy was surprised at how knowledgeable Rhodri was on the subject and he seemed to know a lot of the artists Tom raved about, many of whom Katy had never heard of.

Sophia and Jenny were already there by the time they arrived and Cerys was bringing Jenny up to speed on the tasks that needed doing. When Katy saw the huge pile of materials still waiting to be transformed in to wreaths the enormity of what they planned to do that day hit her all over again. She was glad that Tom and Jenny were there to help – they were going to need every spare pair of hands they could get.

They started much the same as before with Rhodri bending the wire in to shapes and Sophia and Katy covering them in moss, whilst Cerys added the holly and the ribbon. Tom joined Rhodri on the wire bending, clearly not wanting to be outdone by the only other man in the group and Jenny joined Sophia and Katy plugging the wire frame with moss.

Jenny took a while to get the hang of it and her first few looked a little raggedy with clumps of moss falling out before they even reached Cerys. Sophia was great at helping her however and patiently showed her how to wrap the outer wire round to secure the moss.

Tom was having equal trouble with the wire and though Katy was sure Rhodri would have helped if he asked; she knew Tom was too proud to do so. She tried to help Tom as best as she could, but given how difficult she had found the task herself she doubted she was much use.

By lunchtime however the newcomers were as adept as the old hands and had tried out each part of the process. And when Cerys produced her usual trays of delicious pastries and cakes Tom's eyes lit up as if it was Christmas Day itself. All in all the day was going well and when they stopped to chat over lunch, Katy was surprised to learn that Cerys had already sold some of the wreaths they had made the week before. Cerys even said that people in the village had said they were the best ever, but Katy suspected that was more Cerys being generous than a reflection on their work.

'It's kind of sad really,' Katy said thoughtfully. 'In a few hours we'll be finished and it feels like we're all only just getting to know each other.'

'Oh, but this isn't going to be the end is it?' asked Sophia, sounding disappointed.

'Well I don't really know what else we could do, if it wasn't for Cerys we wouldn't even have had this,' Katy replied.

'Of course this isn't the end,' said Cerys cheerfully. 'You must all come along to the village Christmas party. We'll be selling the rest of the wreaths and there'll be carols and mince pies. The whole evening's lovely isn't it Rhodri?'

'It's quite something. And Mrs Stillwater's industrial strength mulled wine guarantees that everyone will be in high spirits. You should definitely all come.'

Although he was addressing everyone Katy couldn't help but notice that Rhodri looked directly at her as he was speaking.

'That sounds great fun,' said Tom. 'Could we bring our other halves?'

'Of course, I didn't realise you were married Tom. I'd love to meet your wife!' Cerys boomed.

'So would I,' Katy replied cheekily and the rest of the room fell about laughing.

'Cerys,' Rhodri said kindly; 'Tom's gay, he'll be bringing along his boyfriend, Owen wasn't it?'

'Yes.'

'Oh well that's lovely too dear,' Cerys replied quickly. 'Is Owen gay as well?'

At that point all thoughts of work completely disappeared and the entire room descended in to hysterical laughter around the slightly mystified Cerys. It took some minutes before anyone could say anything and then when Tom did speak he barely managed to contain himself.

'You know what Cerys, I think he might be.'

Just as he finished speaking Tom and the rest of the room lost it again and it was a good five minutes before anyone picked up a sprig of holly or a clump of moss again.

They finally finished a little after 4pm, and though they were all nursing a few scratches and cradling aching fingers, the group were all in high spirits. Every inch of Cerys' table and much of the floor and worktop space was covered in piles of wreaths. Cerys was a little tearful at the sight of it and Katy was first in line to give her a big hug.

The whole experience had been absolutely wonderful, meeting new people, doing something creative and practical and of course the mountains of pastries and cakes they had consumed in the process. Starting Christmas Club had turned out to be the best mistake Katy had ever made, and she was eternally grateful to

Cerys. Not only had she come up with the cause that united them all in the first place, but she had also come up with a reason for them to meet up again once it was over.

Just as they were all getting in to their cars Cerys came running out of the house with a row of wreaths lined up along her arm as if she were a target in an enormous game of hoopla.

'I nearly forgot, I made sure we made enough for everyone to have one,' Cerys boomed.

Cerys handed Jenny and Sophia a wreath and then headed over to Rhodri's car. First she handed Tom a wreath that had been finished off with a flourish of rainbow ribbon and Katy smiled at the touch, though she imagined Rhodri was probably as much responsible for it as Cerys. Finally Cerys came to Katy and handed her a beautiful wreath, decorated with a rich velvety red ribbon. As she did so she leaned in to give Katy a hug.

'I saved the best one for you.'

Katy felt her eyes pricking with emotion as she placed her arms around the older woman's neck and whispered a *thank-you* in to her ear.

Katy could still feel the tears building up and threatening to spill on to her cheeks as they turned the corner on to the muddy lane. A little lump had formed in her throat and when Rhodri asked her if she was okay she struggled to answer him clearly.

'It's meant a lot to Cerys, you all helping out,' he said as he gently rested his hand on Katy's knee to comfort her. 'And she's really taken a shine to you Katy; I think you've made a friend there if you want to.'

'Of course, I don't want this to be goodbye for any of us.'

'Neither do I,' he replied sincerely.

All three of them were a little subdued as they drove out of the countryside and back towards Cardiff. Even Tom, who had only spent a short time in everyone's company, seemed disappointed to be leaving, and he said more than once that he wished he'd been able to join them on some of the other days.

'Actually,' Tom said as they were nearing the city centre, 'could we take a little detour. I'd like to show you what I've been working on.'

Tom directed Rhodri away from Katy's flat and they headed towards the main shopping centre. The city was starting to empty its cargo of Christmas shoppers and day trippers back in to their cars and they found a parking space without too much difficulty. They walked along St Mary's Street and then turned right on to Caroline Street - affectionately called "Chippy Alley" by the city's residents – on account of the large number of late night takeaways there. When they came out on to The Hayes; a wide open section of street in front of the city library, Katy's eyes were drawn to an enormous wooden box-like structure that hadn't been there a week before.

'Here it is,' said Tom proudly.

'You built this?' asked Rhodri, sounding impressed.

'Not built no, Owen did most of that. But come look what I've been doing.'

Tom led them round to the front where they saw that the box was in fact an outdoor stage. There was a large wooden plinth with a covered roof and then the two sides opened out into a wide façade on either edge. The whole thing was elaborately painted so that the outer sides looked like giant three-dimensional curtains that had been drawn to reveal the stage. The detail on them was incredible, using countless shades of purple blended seamlessly to give the impression of shadow and depth. On the inside of the curtains there was a barnyard scene with an ox on one side and a donkey on the other. Inside the box the stage was bordered by a starry sky that was so lifelike it looked as if they were staring directly at the heavens. Around this Tom had recreated the rest of the stable, with two small sheep and a lamb and piles of hay bales, each strand of straw carefully painted and brought to life.

'Tom, it's beautiful! You did all of this?' Katy gushed.

'Yeh, it's been a lot of work. Hence not being able to help you guys out more. But hopefully it'll all be worth it.'

'Mate, it looks bloody fantastic,' added Rhodri. 'You should be dead proud.'

At that moment Owen arrived, he gave Katy a kiss on the cheek and shook hands with Rhodri before putting an arm affectionately around Tom.

'He's amazing isn't he?' said Owen, and no one was going to argue with him.

'What's it for?' asked Rhodri.

'The kids in my year are putting on a nativity play, they do it every year but normally it's just in the school hall. I wanted to do something different this year and bring it out in to the community. But this – this is all Tom's idea.'

Katy felt her chest filling with love and pride for her friend and she could only imagine how Owen felt. The whole thing was simply phenomenal and really showed how talented an artist Tom was.

'When's the play?' Katy asked.

'The week after next,' Owen replied. 'We've still got a lot to do before then, but I'm hoping we'll get there. You should come, both of you.'

Katy promised she would be there, and of course she would, she wouldn't miss it for anything. What worried her a little was Rhodri's reply. It was nice that he said he'd come, but she couldn't help but worry that things were going to get awkward. There was no way that David would miss the play – he was friends with Tom too and it would be odd for her not to invite him. She just didn't relish the prospect of having the two of them there at the same time.

'He's a clever one your friend Tom,' said Rhodri on their way back to the car afterwards.

'He is and I've always known it. But I've never seen him take on anything quite as big before. I think it even surprised me just what he's capable of.'

'We should tell the rest of the club about the play, it could be fun to do something like that all together.'

Katy didn't answer straight away, unsure of what to say. But when she saw the hurt look on Rhodri's face she instantly regretted that she hadn't thought of something positive to reply.

'Ah,' he said. 'You'll be going with David won't you? I should have thought – I don't know why I didn't.'

'He's Tom's friend too, well most of the time. And our other friends will be there too; Anne and Matt and…' Katy tailed off feeling incredibly bad about what she was saying.

'I guess it's going to be harder than I thought, being your friend but nothing more,' Rhodri said sadly.

'Please don't say that. I want you there, I really do, and the others. I'm just not quite sure how it'll work yet. But I'm sure we can figure it out.'

'It's OK. Hey, I said I wouldn't make this more difficult for you than it already is, and I stand by that. It's just I like you Katy, I like you a lot and I feel like I'm only just getting to know you and it really sucks having to share that with someone else. Especially when he's the one you have all this history with and shared friendships. I guess it's just tough being *the other guy*.'

'I feel so bad about this, really I do.'

'I know,' Rhodri replied. 'But please try not to. Not unless you feel guilty enough to ditch that chump for good and come for dinner with me?'

There was an awkward silence before Rhodri laughed and drew her in to a bear hug.

'I'm only joking, just stop beating yourself up about it.'

She knew he was trying to cheer her up, but if anything the hug only made things worse. It was torture being so close to him and not being able to act on it. She wanted to throw her arms around him and nuzzle in to his chest and never let go. But more than that she wanted to kiss him, to part his thick fuzz-lined lips with hers and kiss him as if there would be no tomorrow.

But she couldn't…she wouldn't.

'Can I give you a lift home?' Rhodri asked hopefully.

'I think I'm going to walk back actually, if that's OK?' Katy said, trying to put some ground between her and six-foot of burly temptation.

'Of course,' he said, sounding thoroughly disappointed. 'Katy – it feels like you're doing more than just walking home. It feels like you're walking away from me. I am going to see you again aren't I?'

'Yes, I promise. I just never thought this would happen to me – having feelings for two men at the same time.'

'So you do then? Have feelings for me?' he asked.

'Yes,' Katy finally admitted, both to herself and to Rhodri. 'I like you, I like you a lot and I want to get to know you more. I want to see where this could lead. But I also have all this history with David…and some of the things I thought had gone away with him, well it turns out they haven't.'

Katy could feel the situation becoming overwhelming, she thought she might cry, or give in to what they both wanted and kiss him. The problem was even she didn't know which she might do if she gave in to her emotions, and she didn't want to mess Rhodri around any more than she already was.

'To be honest I'm a little relieved,' Rhodri said finally.

'Relieved?' Katy responded with surprise.

'Yes. At least now I know I'm not going crazy, and that there is something between us. I don't normally get like this and thinking that it's all in my head has been driving me mad.'

'Well it's definitely not,' said Katy, failing to see how it made things any better for either of them.

'Then I'm going to leave you to walk home and for now we'll just have to make the best of it. I'll see you on Wednesday at the village Christmas fair and then we can worry about the play later. But for God's sake Katy don't beat yourself up about this. You can't help how you feel, and you're making this far harder on yourself than it is for either David or me, so please promise me you'll go easier on yourself.'

Katy agreed, but even as she was saying it she knew she was lying to him. Katy felt terrible. Her indecision was tormenting Rhodri and she was deceiving David and what was worse was she knew both men had been hurt before. There was no way she wasn't going to beat herself up over this, no matter what Rhodri said.

Chapter Eighteen

The following day Katy found herself sat on the sofa staring at her phone. For nearly an hour she had been trying to find the right words to say to David. Twice she had started to load his contact details up ready to call, only to bottle out at the last moment. As far as she knew there was no correct etiquette for telling the man whose heart you'd already trampled over that ever since you'd walked back in to his life you were falling for another man.

Eventually she just picked up the phone and called. There was never going to be a right way to tell him, but she had to say something, she owed him that.

'David, it's Katy.'

'Hey, I'm really glad you called. How was your date with Tom yesterday?'

'It was good thanks, actually I was kind of hoping to talk to you about that.'

'And how are the TV guides?' David asked, seemingly ignoring what she had just said.

'Erm good,' Katy lied, having not actually had the chance to look at them yet. 'David I really do want to talk to you about something.'

'Okay' he replied, sounding a little unsure this time.

'When I first got back I guess I was struggling a little bit with the whole thing – not really knowing what to do next with my life; missing travelling and having to think about work and so on.'

'Yeah,' David interjected, 'I guess that must have been hard.'

'Yes it was, well still is really. But that's not what I wanted to say. I got horribly ridiculously drunk.'

'Like Oxford drunk, or Oregon drunk?'

'What?' Katy asked, growing a little frustrated at the interruptions when she had something so important to say.

'Well are we talking drunk like when you threw up in that park in Oxford that time, or Oregon drunk, where you were so drunk you lost like a day and a half?' David asked, chuckling at his own take on the occasions, neither of which Katy really wished to relive.

'Let's just leave it at really, really drunk. David I did something stupid – well actually it turned out pretty great. But at the time I thought it was incredibly stupid. I posted an ad about starting a Christmas club.'

There was silence on the other side of the line, and Katy wondered if he had heard her or whether he was trying not to laugh. But seeing as David had finally stopped interrupting her she decided to carry on.

'I was hoping no one would turn up and then they did, and it was all a bit awkward at first, but then we ended up helping out this woman – Cerys. Every year she makes all these holly wreaths for her village and this year she was struggling. So we – Tom, me and these two women Sophia and Jenny, and Cerys' neighbour Rhodri – all got together a few times and we made over 200 wreaths for Cerys to sell and raise money for the village and a local charity.'

'That's fantastic Katy! Why didn't you tell me about this the other day? I'm so proud of you!'

Katy hesitated, unsure of what to say next. The longer she left it the worse it would be, but she hated the thought of hurting David all over again.

'Katy. Are you still there?' David asked.

'Yes,' she replied quietly.

'What's up?'

'I'm sorry David, I wanted to tell you the other night but we were having such a good time I didn't want to ruin things.'

'Okay...' he prompted, sounding increasingly worried.

'This man Rhodri – Cerys' neighbour, we've been spending quite a bit of time together. Nothing's happened, I wouldn't have done that to you. But I like him and he likes me too.'

'Bloody hell Katy. You're telling me you're seeing someone? Even after that kiss the other night?'

'I'm not seeing him and I never planned on that kiss.'

'But you didn't do anything to stop it either.'

'No,' Katy agreed.

'So that's it then? It's over between us before you've even given us another chance?' David replied angrily.

Katy could feel herself getting upset and even more confused than she was before.

'No. I...I don't know David. How was I to know you'd be here when I got back? Last I knew you were in London. I never expected us to give things another try. And I never expected to meet Rhodri either. And I certainly didn't want to give either of you the impression that I wanted to start something up. It all just kind of happened.'

'So what has happened between you?' he asked, still sounding cross.

'Nothing. We've talked, he's flirted a little and that's it. I told him from the start that I'm not willing to get involved until I know where things are with you.'

'Well at least you've been straight with one of us,' he retorted.

'I'm sorry David. I don't know what else to say.'

The phone went quiet for the longest time and Katy was worried that she had lost David all over again. For four years they had been a couple, but beneath the sex and the intimacy they were friends. She liked his company and it had been hard not having him in her life. She really hoped that she hadn't jeopardised that friendship irreversibly.

'So what next?' David said eventually.

'I don't know, that depends on you really,' Katy said truthfully.

'I knew that there would have been other people while you were away, there were bound to be. And it's not like I haven't been on dates in the last year. I guess I just thought that when you came home single that was how it was. I didn't really expect you to meet someone at the same time as we were getting back in touch.'

David's voice was calmer this time, a little sad, but the anger had definitely subsided.

'Do you think maybe we've just been trying too hard to go right back to how things were before though David? I mean just now is the first time that you've told me you saw people while I was away. And don't get me wrong I'm glad you did, the last thing I want is to think you've just been sat around waiting for me to come back. But if we are going to be in each other's lives again then we both need to start telling each other the difficult stuff as well as the good things. I should have told you about Rhodri, and I'm sorry I didn't. But I was just so worried about ruining things. And part of the problem is that you seem to have come back this perfect guy. You're not angry with me, you're not bitter and until two minutes ago I wasn't even sure if you'd been with anyone else since.'

'What do you want me to say Katy? Do you want to hear that I was pissed at you? Because yeh I was, I was absolutely furious. I felt you gave up way too easily and that you buggered off round the world rather than facing up to problems that if you'd stuck around we probably could have solved. And yeh I went off the rails a bit and slept around when I first got to London. But I've put all that behind me because giving us another shot is more important to me.'

David had told her exactly what she asked to hear but the truth still smarted. She hated that he had been so angry and so hurt by what had happened. And she found herself feeling an unwarranted pang of jealous torment at the thought of him sleeping with other women. But as much as it hurt, it was a relief to finally get some of it out in the open and she felt they stood a better chance by being honest with each other than pretending everything was fine.

'I think I needed to hear that. I am sorry you know, sorry for ending things and for leaving so soon after. But we just weren't the people we used to be anymore,' Katy said sadly.

'I know, and when I stopped being mad at you I realised that. And I'm trying really hard to put things right there.'

'I know, just maybe you don't need to try quite so hard.'

'Are you still happy to see how things go for now then or –'

Yes,' Katy interrupted, not wanting him to think for even a moment that she had given up on him a second time.

'And what about this Rhodri guy?'

'The club's going to meet at this village fair on Wednesday. He'll be there, but so will Tom and the others. It's not like it's a date or anything.'

'I guess I can live with that,' he said. Although Katy could tell his pride had taken a little dent. 'Let's do something before that though,' he added. 'How about ice-skating tonight?'

Katy was a little stunned at the sudden turn around, but she was relieved that David seemed to have handled the situation and was still happy to see her.

'That'd be nice. How about seven o'clock?

'Okay, I'll meet you there.'

-

An hour before Katy was due to meet David at the ice rink she had a sudden bout of nerves. She felt better for being honest with him; it had been the right thing to do and though he had been mad at first he seemed to have settled down by the time they had finished talking. However the closer it got to their date the more unsettled she became. It wasn't just the phone call either. The last time they had been out had been perfect; the conversation had flowed, they'd watched a beautiful sunset together and enjoyed a lovely romantic meal and it was all followed by the most spectacular, explosive kiss. Suddenly that seemed like a lot of pressure and expectation to put on their second date, especially after the intensity of their conversation on the phone. Katy was worried there was only one possible outcome given all those factors: a second date that failed to excite and one that might even derail the rekindling of their relationship; whether that was friendship or something more.

Panicking she picked up the phone and dialled quickly, tapping her foot impatiently whilst she waited for the person on the other end to answer.

'Tom? What are you doing tonight? I've got a massive favour to ask…'

Chapter Nineteen

Katy could hear the thud of music and the excited squeals of the skaters long before she saw the rink. All around her there was an air of anticipation. Excited children ran ahead only to look back in frustration at their dawdling parents a moment later, urging them to hurry up. Even Katy found herself falling under the spell, quickening her pace to match the beat of the music and feeling its rhythm pulse through her body. The closer she got, the louder the music became and the more the energy of the people around her seemed to grow. Then as she stepped into the fenced off park, everything exploded in a cacophony of light and sound.

Towering above everything else was an enormous Ferris wheel; vibrant and white like a giant Catherine wheel blazing through the night sky. At the other end of the park was a helter-skelter, a vision in bright pink and yellow candy stripes. It stood out like a lighthouse, but instead of a spinning bulb at the top there was an endless downward spiral of whoops and cheers from the riders.

Katy wandered through the stalls, where teenage boys vied with one another over shooting ranges and tin can alleys, as their female classmates watched on in mock disinterest. Amongst these, food stalls clamoured for Katy's attention, each one smelling more delicious than the last as the perfumed sweetness of candyfloss blended in to the warm bready cinnamon smell of frying doughnuts.

Then, right in the centre of it all was the enormous ice rink, shining a beautiful icy blue under the tinted floodlights. Katy could feel the chill coming off it as she walked around the edge, her feet squelching slightly on the damp carpet surrounds. She looked around to see if David was already there but when she couldn't see him she headed over to the base of the big wheel where she had arranged to meet Tom and Owen. After a few minutes she felt a tap on her shoulder and turned round to see Owen standing there with a pair of ice skates slung around his neck.

'Hey, it's good to see you,' Katy said. 'Have you already got the skates then?'

'No, I brought my own,' he replied.

'Wow, Tom never said you were a pro!'

'Hardly, but I spent a few years in Canada, so I'm pretty nifty on the ice.'

'Well you'll have to help me out; I'm hopeless,' said Katy a little nervously.

'Ah you'll be fine; anyway I'm sure David will be only too happy to look after you.'

Katy didn't say anything, but she had a feeling Owen was probably right. David was remarkably competitive; from board games to sports he liked to be the best in everything and based on previous trips skating was no exception. He'd be happy to help her, but he'd also want to be zipping round in the middle of the rink, whereas she'd feel much more comfortable pootling around at the sides with the rest of the novices.

'What's Tom like at skating?' asked Owen. 'He wouldn't say.'

Katy wondered what the polite way of telling someone that their boyfriend was about as steady on ice as a giraffe on roller skates.

'Um, well – maybe Tom and I should keep each other company on the sides, whilst you and David race.'

'That good then?' Owen chuckled.

'He's not the best.'

'Well, I guess you can't be good at *everything*.'

A moment later Tom came bouncing over to them excitedly, proving that enthusiasm was definitely something he excelled at.

'Have you seen this place? I swear it gets more awesome every year! They've got ice sculptures and guys on stilts and mulled wine and hot dogs!'

Owen and Katy laughed as Tom struggled to regain his breath. He looked as if he was at distinct risk of becoming the first person over the age of 30 ever to overload themselves on Christmas cheer.

Just as Tom started to calm down, Owen nudged Katy and pointed in the direction of the rink: 'I think you've got an admirer.'

Katy looked up to see David heading towards them. He was wearing a thick knitted jumper and a light grey jacket, with the same scarf he had worn when they went for a walk in the bay. In his hand he had a long stemmed rose, which he held low by his side as if he was a little embarrassed to be seen holding it.

David's face was a mask of disappointment and he carried himself like a puppy that had just been shouted at and dragged outside.

Katy felt horribly guilty for being the cause of his dejection by ambushing their date. She had invited Tom and Owen in the hope that it would take some of the pressure off and to give her and David the space to relax in one another's company – but it had clearly had the opposite effect.

As soon as he realised he had been spotted David picked up his pace, swopping the rose from his right to his left hand as he joined them. David gave Katy a quick peck on the cheek and then proceeded to give Tom a hug, but he seemed antsy and agitated. Tom started speaking, but David ignored him and stepped aside, turning his back on Tom in the process. To Katy's surprise David positioned himself confrontationally in front of Owen, standing much closer than necessary before thrusting his right hand out.

'I'm David. I don't think we've met before, who are you?' he said gruffly.

'David!' Katy said loudly. 'Don't be so rude, apologise right away.'

'It's okay Katy,' Owen said calmly as he put out his own hand to firmly shake David's. 'I'm Owen, Tom's boyfriend.'

Suddenly David's demeanour completely changed. His shoulders dropped back to their normal position and he instantly took a step back, giving Owen some space.

'I'm sorry,' he said meekly, 'I thought you were someone else.'

Katy was about to ask David what on earth he was thinking when she suddenly realised what had happened. David must have thought she'd brought Rhodri along to their date, with Tom along to umpire the sparring.

'Let's get our skates,' Katy said quickly, hoping to take a little of the heat out of the situation. She put her arm through David's and swiftly led him away, hoping that Tom would guess what had happened and explain it all to Owen.

As soon as they were a few feet ahead David started talking rapidly. 'I'm sorry Katy, I thought–'

'I know,' she interrupted. 'David I would never do that to you. I just thought it would be nice to have Tom and Owen along.'

'It's okay, I overreacted. It was stupid.'

David sounded genuinely upset and embarrassed about the whole thing. Katy dropped her arm and took his hand in hers, interlocking their fingers. Two thick layers of gloves meant that it wasn't a very intimate gesture, but Katy hoped it would help make David feel a little better.

When they got to the skate hire area, David handed Katy the tickets and suggested she and Tom go and get their skates and that he would follow them up in a minute. As they were leaving Katy watched David take a seat on the bench by Owen as he started putting on his own skates.

'I'm so sorry Tom,' Katy said. 'I can tell David's really embarrassed. He mistook Owen for Rhodri. I think he's gone over to apologise now.'

'It's okay,' Tom said, clearly unfazed. 'I told Owen as much. Mind you, he said David gave him one hell of a handshake, practically tried to crush Owen's knuckles.'

'Oh God, I'll have a word with Owen and apologise too.'

Tom laughed, 'Owen can give as good as he gets. From what he said he gave David a pretty rough response. Anyway it'll take a lot more than a handshake off David to ruffle him!'

Tom's comment really annoyed Katy – it was bad enough that David was going all alpha-male on her, without Owen making it worse by joining in. And Tom being competitive over whose boyfriend was the strongest was the kind of thing she thought she'd left behind in secondary school.

'Well I hope he apologises to David as well then. At least David had a reason for behaving like a stupid boy, what's Owen's excuse?' Katy said snappily.

'Don't blame Owen for this mess. Anyway it was you that wanted us here.' Tom replied, his voice escalating a little higher than necessary.

'Clearly that was a stupid idea – thinking that you might actually want to help rather than going out of your way to make things worse!'

'Fine, we'll go home then,' said Tom almost shouting. 'You know we have all managed to get on with our lives without you this past year. It's not as if we don't have other things we could be doing right now.'

'Just go then,' Katy snapped back, aware that people were staring at the two of them.

Before she had even finished speaking Tom was walking away, leaving Katy standing on her own in the queue, confused and upset.

Within moments David was by her side, putting his arm around her and gently pressing his lips to her forehead.

'Hey, what's wrong?' he asked. 'Tom's just stormed over and said that they're leaving.'

'We got in a stupid fight and it's not even Tom I'm angry with.'

'Who are you angry at then?' David asked

'Me. I'm angry at me, for all of this…this mess. Tom just got in the way.'

'Hey, you don't need to be upset. I shouldn't have had a go at you on the phone earlier, or acted like such an idiot when I arrived. I'm sorry.'

David gently fussed her hair and pulled her in closer so that her face was nestled in to the nape of his neck. Katy felt safe there, as if a bubble of calm had closed around her. Huddled in his arms, surrounded by the comfortably familiar smell of his skin, Katy was reminded of the countless times he had soothed her stresses after a long day at work, or cradled her through some passing fever or cold. It was like her body wanted him, needed him at some base chemical level to feel okay again. She missed him; his kindness, the gentleness of his touch, the ease of being around him.

'Do you think Tom is okay?' Katy asked.

'I'm, sure he'll live. Are you okay?'

'Yes, I'm sorry. Let me go and talk to Tom – I don't want them to go.'

Katy reluctantly extricated herself from the warmth of David's body and made her way over to Tom. Before either of them could say anything she gave Tom a massive hug, pulling Owen in to join them with her left arm.

'I'm sorry, please don't go, I'd hate that. I really appreciate you both coming and I was just being stupid. Please say you'll stay.'

'Off course we'll stay. And I'm sorry for being stroppy; I didn't mean what I said. I just missed you Katy, I missed having you around and it was hard last year – before I met Owen.'

'I know, I'm sorry Tom. God there were so many times when I was away I just wanted to fly home and see you. I missed you terribly. But it was something I needed to do.'

'So are we actually going to go skating now then?' asked David as he headed towards them with a big pair of blue boots in his hands, each one sporting a sharpened blade.

With all the drama that had unfolded, their booked session was already well under way and David's suggestion was met with universal agreement. Owen and David confidently stepped out on to the ice first and then each of them moved back enough to let Tom and Katy on to the rink. Katy placed one tentative skate out and grabbed hold of David's arm with her left hand whilst still clinging on to the thick wooden barrier with her right. As she was struggling to even commit to putting both feet on the ice a girl who couldn't have been more than six or seven whooshed past and launched herself fearlessly in to the speeding inner circle of skaters.

'I won't let go of you, I promise,' David said reassuringly, taking hold of both her hands. Katy brought her second foot forward to join the first and instantly felt like she was losing control.

'It's okay...I've got you.' David said and he gently skated backwards pulling them away from the entrance.

Katy was too terrified to turn round but she could hear Owen and Tom going through a similar process behind them.

'Try and at least smile Katy,' David said, his eyes fixed on hers. Katy marvelled how he could skate backwards without worrying where he was going. Occasionally he would take a quick glance over his shoulder, but for the most part his eyes stayed trained on Katy.

They slowly drifted round the rink in a clockwise direction, inhabiting the middle ground between the rapidly revolving skaters in the centre who were doing laps in less than a minute and the ones slowly pulling themselves round the edge hugging the barrier for safety. After they were around a third of the way round Owen and Tom caught them up. Tom had his hands firmly latched on to Owen's sides so that he was being towed around like a railway carriage.

'Fancy a race then?' Owen asked playfully.

Tom's protests came out even more quickly than Katy's. In the end the four of them settled on a steady pace around the rink with Owen and David doing all the work and Tom and Katy hanging on in fear. Katy was a little worried that when she did let go David's hands would be bruised beyond recognition and she decided it was a good job he was a GP rather than a surgeon as he was likely to be very sore the following day.

They managed three or four laps before Tom asked to be dropped off back at the entrance. Katy gratefully joined him, relieved to have an excuse to get off the ice. Both David and Owen put up enough resistance to maintain at least an air of chivalry. But when it became clear that their partners were happy to be sitting out they both disappeared at a phenomenal pace, kicking up a small spray of slush as they did so.

'He's been desperate to do that ever since we got here,' Katy said, pointing at David. Finally facing forward he was able to move freely on the ice, weaving in and out of the other skaters and lapping them with ease.

'God, he's fearless isn't he?' Tom said in awe.

'But look at Owen, he's amazing. I've never seen anyone jump around like that and not fall over.'

Tom quietly took her hand in his and gave it a squeeze and the two friends watched David and Owen racing around the rink. Katy smiled, content in Tom's company and feeling much happier now that they were complementing one another's partners rather than competitively comparing them.

'I'm sorry about earlier,' Tom said quietly. 'We had a bit of an argument before we came out. Sunday evening's are really busy for Owen preparing lessons for the week.'

'Oh, I'm sorry Tom, you should have said if you couldn't come.'

'It's okay, it's not like it was a big argument. He just works so hard, it's tough sometimes.'

'I know, it can be hard balancing it all.' Katy replied sympathetically.

'I'm not really used to this bit – I never normally get this far,' Tom said.

'But that's good isn't it?'

'I love him Katy.'

'That's brilliant Tom,' Katy said excitedly.

'I haven't told him yet though, He's said it to me. But I haven't said it back yet,' Tom said in a near whisper.

'Why not?' Katy asked softly, putting her arm around him.

'Because I'm scared. I've never been in love before and I wasn't really expecting it to happen. I mean I always hoped it would one day, but I thought maybe it would be when I was older, or that I'd decide it was the right time. But with Owen, it just kind of crept up on me, well more like collided with me head on I suppose. But now that it's happened I can't stand the thought of losing him. What if he changes his mind, or cheats on me, or decides I'm not good enough or something?'

Katy gave her friend a fierce hug: 'How could anyone stop loving you Tom. You're the sweetest, most wonderful man – the best man I know.'

'But you're biased Katy, you've put up with me for years. Six months ago Owen and I hadn't even met. Who's to say how he'll feel in another six months.'

'I think he'll still adore you just as much as he clearly does now. But if he doesn't – will whether you've said you love him or not make a difference?'

'What do you mean?' asked Tom.

'You'll still love him all the same. You can tell him and make him as happy as he's making you, or you can keep it from him to try and protect yourself. But it won't do you any good. Whatever you do or don't say you feel it and it'll hurt just as bad if you don't tell him as if you do.'

'So you think I should tell him?'

'Absolutely. I think you have far more to lose by not telling him than you do by being honest with him.'

'God Katy, when did we become so grown up?'

'Katy laughed: 'I've been grown up for years, it just took you a little longer to catch up.'

As Katy rested her head on Tom's shoulder Owen zipped by waving, closely followed by David.

'You know I feel the same don't you, I love you Katy. You're the only woman I'll ever love, that makes you pretty special! And you know I just want you to be happy. I don't care whether that's with David, or Rhodri, or…or this guy,' he said, pointing at a stranger in his late thirties stumbling on his skates towards the side of the rink.

'Well,' Katy said, trying to adopt Tom's relaxed attitude to the problem. 'This guy's not my type, even if skating wise we might be a better match. But I'm not sure that's enough grounds for a relationship.'

'And the other two?' Tom pushed. 'Anne told me about your late night phone calls with David and the text marathons with Rhodri – are they still going on?'

'Yes,' Katy said sheepishly. We've been for drinks too.'

'Who? You and David, or you and Rhodri.'

'Both,' Katy said, instantly feeling guilty. 'I keep telling myself that I won't do it, not to them, or to me. But the truth is I love spending time with them: both of them. I know getting back with David makes perfect sense, it feels like everyone expects it of me and he's made his thoughts on it all perfectly clear.'

'He's certainly come up fighting for you.'

'He has, and I wish I could be as sure as he is. But I'm not. I love David and I'm having to try really hard not to just run back to him and give us a try all over again.'

'But why are you fighting it?'

'Because it didn't work before and because it feels like if I go back one day it'll just stop working all over again, but then it will be a hundred times worse for both of us,' Katy said sadly. 'And I can't ignore how I feel about Rhodri, if things were really meant to be with David then surely I wouldn't be feeling like this – so conflicted.'

'But isn't this just what you were telling me, to be brave and give myself to it fully?'

'No, it's different when you've already been together and you've split up. It was such a massive thing leaving David. It was the hardest thing I've ever done, and I agonised over it for months – you know that. But I did it because I thought it was the right thing to do, and then we both spent a year getting over each other.'

'But I don't think David did get over you did he? The moment he knew you were coming home he moved back.'

'No, I don't think it really worked for either of us in truth. But that's not the same as thinking we should give it a second try.'

'Hold that thought,' Tom said swiftly.

Katy looked up to see Owen and David come to a dramatic stop just in front of the barrier.

'Time to get you both back on the ice,' David said.

Katy cautiously walked back towards the entranceway holding out her hand for David to help her. To her surprise though it was Owen who returned her grip.

'We thought we'd swap,' Owen said grinning.

Katy copied Tom, putting her arms around Owen's waist and moving her hand to steady herself against his back when needed.

'And you're with me,' David said, holding out both hands for Tom to hold.

Katy felt her heart grow a little as she saw David taking the same care with Tom as he had with her. He was skating backwards again, holding Tom with both hands. There was something incredibly touching about the way David handled the situation, not even flinching when a group of lads wolf-whistled mockingly from the bar as they skated past. And Katy was far more impressed with that than any of the macho posturing that had happened earlier.

'You okay?' Owen called back to her.

'Yes, I was just watching David and Tom.'

'Feeling jealous?' Owen chuckled.

'No!'

'Just me then,' Owen said, sounding as if he might mean it.

'Don't be silly, Tom adores you.'

'David's a good looking man though…'

'He is.'

'But…?'

Katy risked her grasp on Owen's waist long enough to give him a playful nudge and tell him off for teasing her. She couldn't believe she had walked – or rather skated – right in to that one.

They looped around the rink a few more times, with Owen going a little faster than Katy would have liked. Then when it started to quieten down with people leaving the ice, they swapped back and David towed her round at a gentler pace.

'Thank you, I was beginning to get a little dizzy hanging on to Owen,' Katy yelled over the music.

'It's okay, I've been waiting to swap back for ages, wanting to do this….'

Suddenly David pulled her towards him, letting go of her hands so she softly collided with his chest. Just as she felt her legs begin to wobble and her balance deserting her, David scooped his arms round her, with one hand braced across her back and the other cheekily cupping her bum. Before she could protest, or tell him off for making her lose control he was kissing her, his tongue darting between her lips as his stubble tickled below her nose. Katy felt his grip on her body tighten and the firm sweep of his torso pressing against her chest. She was entirely dependent on him, unable to even stand without his support. Suddenly he moved his left arm, the one that had been supporting her back and dropped it to join his other hand at the top of her thigh. Without warning he lifted her clean off the ice, causing her upper body to tilt even further into him so she didn't fall backwards. Involuntarily she broke away from the kiss, letting out a little squeal of fear.

'I've got you,' he said. 'Just relax.' He flashed his perfect white teeth at her in a cheesy grin long enough to put her at ease and start kissing her again.

Katy closed her eyes, lost in the warmth of his lips on hers and his urgent, excited exploration of her mouth. She had never been kissed like that before: not by David, not even when they had first started going out, nor anyone else before or since him for that matter. She felt like she was his entire world and nothing else mattered but her and the moment. She was so engrossed in the pleasure of his affections that she didn't even realise they were moving. It was only when Katy heard a big whoop behind her that she opened her eyes to find that not only was there a whole world still out there, but it was standing only a few feet away cheering her on. Suddenly she realised that David must have skated nearly the whole length of the ice rink carrying her in his arms, the two of them lost in the most breath-taking kiss as the crowd around them watched. Katy pulled her lips away, still tingling and moist, and buried her head in David's neck so she didn't have to look at any of the assembled watchers. Clearly sensing her embarrassment David carried Katy past the whistling and cheering throng to a quieter spot away from the entrance before setting her down on the bench. As mortified as Katy was she couldn't help but stare at David in wonder. He had lifted her on to his chest as if she were weightless, not even working up a sweat. Straddling his torso she had felt the strength in his body, the firm line of his abs and the defined sweep of his pectorals. And that didn't even cover his arms, which felt twice the size she remembered. Each one sported a sloping mound of muscle that stretched the fabric of his jumper at his biceps. Katy couldn't believe that all the time he had been passionately kissing her, he had been skating as well. She had barely been able to breathe the kiss was so intense. It seemed the old stereotypes of men not being able to multi-task needed a rethink.

David kneeled down to help her off with her skates, running his hand along her leg as he did so. 'You okay?' he asked.

'More than,' Katy smiled, still not quite able to believe how quickly the evening had turned from disaster to dream.

Chapter Twenty

Having a 'proper' boyfriend for the first time had brought many things to Tom's life, lots of them exciting and new. One of the more unexpected changes however had been adapting to Owen's school night routine. Left to his own devices Tom would stay up until one or two o'clock in the morning, finally getting up sometime around ten the following day.

Since university Tom had never had a job that required him to work to structured hours. If he had to meet someone about a commission or exhibition then he would do so in the afternoon over coffee, or perhaps at the end of the day over a glass of wine. It wasn't that Tom didn't work hard, he did; but he worked at times that suited him. The structures of working weeks and to some extent day or night were irrelevant to his work, and many of his best pieces were conceived in the night and finished in the dawn. The concept of having to be up at a set time for work was totally alien to him and it had taken Tom a while to accept the rigidity of Owen's term-time life. To begin with Tom had tested the boundaries frequently; complaining at having to leave dinners and parties earlier than others and encouraging Owen to join him on spontaneous movie marathons or late night bar crawls. To all such temptations Owen had held firm; Tom was welcome to stay out, but he had to go home. Eventually Tom stopped trying to change Owen. Ultimately he found that spending time together was what mattered; the exact schedule was an area he could be flexible on. Between them they developed a comfortable compromise where at weekends and holidays they adapted to Tom's body clock, whilst on school nights they lived by Owen's.

After six months there were fewer and fewer times when the inflexibility of Owen's work life still bothered Tom. But leaving David and Katy in the bar to head home for 11pm was one of those occasions. And even though Owen had reminded Tom that he could have stayed out without him, the look on David's face made it clear that he was more than ready for Tom to go too. An early night might have been a disappointment, but a later one as the third wheel in a couple's night out was far worse.

'You okay?' Owen asked a little way in to their walk home. 'You've been quiet ever since we left?'

'Yes,' Tom said, trying to sound convincing.

'You're not still upset about the fight with Katy are you?'

'No, I think in a funny way it needed to happen. Before she left to go travelling everything was about the break-up; and since she's been back her head's been all over the place. I guess I just needed to let off some steam at her. I know it's selfish and silly and childish – it's not like we were together, not like her and David. And I've no real right to feel like this, but a part of me feels she left me behind too last year and we've never really dealt with that. I suppose I was mad at her, and tonight helped get some of that out in the open. Does that sound awful?'

'Of course not, you're her best friend. You're bound to have been a little put out that she went away like that, and I know how much you missed her. But you're okay now right?'

'Yes, much better, I feel like we cleared the air – that we can go back to being us again.'

'What is it then? Something's bothering you,' Owen said.

'David said something to me earlier tonight when it was just the two of us in the toilets. I'm not really sure what to do about it.'

'Do I need to rush back and defend your honour?' Owen said jokingly.

'No,' replied Tom, threading his fingers through Owen's. 'The funny thing is that's kind of what he was asking me to do.'

'What do you mean?'

'David asked me to speak to Rhodri. Well, warn him off really. He wanted me to tell Rhodri that Katy and him had a chance to be happy and he should back off.'

'Wow, that's pretty intense, what did you say?'

'I told him I didn't really know Rhodri that well. But that only seemed to make it worse. He said that my loyalty should be clear then – that we've been friends for years and I should have no trouble telling him nicely but firmly that Katy was spoken for.'

'And what did you say?'

'That was the strange thing,' said Tom. 'He didn't really give me a chance to reply. It was just like he expected it to happen because he'd asked.'

'When was this? Was he drunk?'

'No, I don't think so; it was quite near the start of the evening. And he didn't mention it again – at least not out right. But there was a point later at the bar when we were talking and he was laying it on a bit thick about us being friends. And it's not that I don't like David. We get on fine, but in my head I've always been Katy's friend and he's just been a part of that package. I mean I wouldn't go for a drink with him without her being there or anything.'

'Maybe he was just trying to make sure he had you in his camp.'

'Maybe,' agreed Tom, not wanting to worry Owen. But as much as he tried to dismiss it, he couldn't help feeling that there was a veiled threat to David's words. Or not a threat perhaps – that was too strong a word – but an assertion of power. David was laying out his territory for sure, and Tom couldn't help but wonder what would happen if he didn't help him out. Tom and Katy would always be friends, but David could certainly make that more difficult if he really wanted to. In the past David had rarely challenged the amount of time Katy spent with Tom. He was happy for Tom to stay over at the house and Tom and Katy had been away on weekends together. In fact barely a few days went by without some kind of lunch or dinner date. But if David chose to (and on one or two occasions he had), he could make Katy feel really guilty about the time she spent with Tom and make him feel more and more unwelcome in their home.

'You sure you're okay?' Owen asked again.

'Yes, I'm sorry, I'm being paranoid. Imagining things in my head that's all,' Tom said, wondering if perhaps he was a little tipsier than he thought.

'What are you going to do?'

'Nothing I think. I'm not going to speak to Rhodri, it's not my place. And from what Katy's said he's giving her space anyway.'

'You could tell Katy.'

'No. I don't want to worry her; she's been beating herself up about all this anyway. I don't want to make things worse.'

'You think she should give David another chance don't you?' Owen said, suddenly changing tact.

Tom thought about the question, wondering whether the events of that night had changed his view at all.

'Yes, I think she should.'

'Why?' Owen asked, sounding genuinely curious.

'Because of everything he's done for her – moving back to Cardiff, all the effort he's making on their dates and not giving her too hard a time about travelling. And let's face it, the guy must have put himself through hell in the gym this past year. That takes dedication – you must *really* want something to work that hard.'

'I suppose so.'

'You don't sound convinced?'

'I don't think you should go back. I mean there are exceptions, especially if you've got kids together, or it's a heat of the moment thing. But generally you break-up for a reason. And you can move across the country and give yourself a six-pack, but unless you fix whatever those reasons were you're just going to break-up all over again.'

'That's kind of bleak,' Tom said a little glumly. 'What if we split up – that's it?'

'Well, I guess it depends why we broke-up and if I could forgive you,' Owen said seriously.

'Me?' Tom said incredulously. 'What makes you think we'd be breaking-up because of me?'

'Well I'm not going anywhere,' said Owen, 'so if we're breaking-up it must be down to you, because I'm in this for the long haul Thomas Matheson. I still plan on loving you when you're in your eighties, so get used to it.'

'Oh,' said Tom blushing. He felt his stomach somersault and his mouth widen in to the biggest grin. In that one moment Owen had shown him a picture of his future; an image unfolding that he had never imagined, but wanted more than anything to come true. It was like seeing an incredible painting in a gallery and being so captured by its beauty that you had to have it and then not believing that it was actually yours when you bought it. Especially as so many other people had walked by it and not seen it for what it really was and because of that it was yours to cherish forever.

'It's probably a really rubbish time to say this for the first time. The first time ever actually, not just with you, but with anyone – but I love you Owen.'

Tom had a fairly good idea that Owen was happy with the news when he kissed him passionately in the street. It was a liberty of affection that the two of them rarely felt comfortable with in public. A moment later though it was confirmed when Owen whispered in to Tom's ear that it was in fact the perfect moment to tell him. And that Tom had made him the happiest man alive.

Tom was stunned; overwhelmed that he had met someone that made him feel that way and in awe of Owen and his confidence in their future. As Owen lifted Tom off his feet and put him over his shoulder in a fireman's lift, Tom felt his head spin. But it wasn't the height, or the bumpiness of being carried on someone's back at the age of 31, but the giddiness of love. And as they headed home towards Owen's flat, Tom felt sure that despite Owen's usual routine, neither of them was going to be going to sleep any time soon.

Chapter Twenty-One

As she opened the oven door Katy was met with such a wave of heat that she instantly leapt back and banged her head on the cupboard behind. It was hard trying to be a domestic goddess in a kitchen that was smaller than some of the desks she'd sat at in work. When the cloud of steam cleared she risked a peek inside the oven and was pleased to see the pastry on the steak and ale pie was turning a satisfying golden colour on top. Meanwhile two pans of water were simmering on the hobs. One contained a small army of somersaulting potatoes and the other an assortment of winter greens.

Reassured that there were no signs of an imminent kitchen disaster, Katy slipped in to the bedroom to change for the evening. She picked a long cobalt blue dress with a silver chain belt and put on some silver crescent moon earrings to match. For a moment she toyed with the idea of letting down her hair but she had grown used to wearing it up and wasn't sure she had the time to ensure it was sufficiently tangle free. Instead she decided to leave it in a tousled bun. But to give the appearance of having made an effort she fetched a pair of painted chopsticks from the kitchen and pushed them in to the knot in an 'x' formation. When she had finished Katy took a step back to admire her handiwork. The dress looked perfect and all in all she was happy with what she saw in the mirror.

After a quick check on the pans, Katy laid the table and lit some candles. Finally she put on some music and turned the lights on the Christmas tree on. Everything was as ready as it could be and all that was left to do was to wait for David to arrive.

The dinner had been a spontaneous decision but when Katy texted David mid-afternoon he seemed happy with the idea. Despite its rocky start, the date at the ice rink had gone so well that it seemed silly to wait until later in the week to see each other again. And after ambushing David with the appearance of Tom and Owen on their last date, Katy wanted to show him that she was happy to spend time together one-on-one as well.

David arrived just as Katy was mashing the potatoes and she popped down to the front door with the pan still in hand. He was wearing a pale blue suit and an aubergine shirt with no tie. It was a bold look – but a good one and the tailored suit seemed to hug his body in all the right places. In his right hand he held a bottle of red wine and hooked over his left arm was a black umbrella with a wooden handle. Over his shoulder was a small cloth satchel that Katy recognised as David's work bag – a kind of canvas record bag that he stuffed with everything from changes of clothes to stethoscopes.

They greeted each other a little shyly, kissing on the lips but briefly and with closed mouths. Katy led David up the stairs and into the apartment, taking his umbrella and the bottle of wine from him as he removed his shoes by the door.

'It's a nice place,' David said as he walked in to the living room.

'Thanks. It's a little small, but after a year sharing dorms with ten other people it feels like a palace most of the time!'

'Yeh I guess it must,' said David.

He sounded thoughtful and she wondered if like her, he was thinking of their old home together. It had been a beautiful and spacious two-bed apartment within walking distance of Roath Park. In the summer they would go for picnics and feed the ducks and in the winter they would walk around the boating lake, warming their hands on takeaway coffees. Katy missed those days; she missed the apartment of course – something she could never afford on her own – but most of all she missed those times with David when they had been truly contented together. Standing in her bijou one-bed flat and knowing that David was living alone nearby in a similarly empty apartment it seemed incredibly sad how things had changed. The life they had built together was gone, David had rented out their apartment when he moved away, and their belongings were divided up between them, the two of them dispatched to smaller, separate flats.

'Hey, you put up the decoration,' David said interrupting her thoughts.

Katy looked up to see him holding the disc with *Nadolig Llawen* written on it that he had brought to their first date.

'Of course,' Katy said, before adding 'in pride of place.'

'I can see, I'm glad. It's a beautiful tree by the way. Where did you get it.'

Katy hesitated a moment before she answered. 'It came from Rhodri's farm, we were all down there working on the wreaths when he showed us some trees and he said I could have one.'

David let the decoration fall from his hand and it swung gently back in to position on the tree before coming to a stop.

'Wow, I get you a decoration and he gets you a whole tree.'

'It's not a competition David.'

'It kind of is though Katy.'

Katy smarted a little at his comment, which made her sound something like a prize bull at an auction. But as uncomfortable as it was there was some truth in it. She liked them both but ultimately she couldn't date the two of them. At some point she would have to choose and somebody would be disappointed as a result.

To her relief Katy was able to avoid discussing the tree any further by turning her attention to dinner. Using a folded over tea towel she pulled the steaming pie from the oven and breathed in deeply, savouring the delicious waft of meat and gravy as it filled the room. She cut out two large slices and placed them on the waiting plates. Using a spoon she then scooped up the bits of filling left in the tray and poured the gravy over the top of the pie. She then used the same spoon to heap a generous mound of potato alongside it and finished the plate off with the vegetables.

Whilst Katy was dishing up David poured the wine and then took a seat at the table. It was strange but despite four years of living together they had rarely eaten meals at the table and Katy felt there was a certain formality to the evening as a result.

'Makes a change from being sat on the sofa with a DVD doesn't it?' joked David, seemingly reading her mind.

'Yes. Would you rather that? I could put a film on.'

'No, this is nice, thank you,' David said and he reached out his hand to hold hers across the table.

The pie was a huge success and had turned out much better than Katy had expected. The meat was tender and soft, the gravy thick and luxurious and the pastry flaky and delicious. Katy couldn't help but wolf it down, enjoying the warmth and homeliness of it. There was something incredibly comforting about eating a pie in winter that no amount of salad or cous cous was ever going to match.

'Is it okay?' Katy asked, when she noticed David hadn't eaten nearly as much as she had.

'It's lovely, thanks,' he said unconvincingly.

'Are you sure?'

Katy couldn't figure out what was wrong; steak and ale pie was one of David's favourites and in the whole time they had been together she had never known him to eat slower than she did.

'Um, I haven't eaten meat in a while – well a year actually. It's great really, it's just taking me a little longer than normal.'

'You're a vegetarian! Why didn't you say anything?' Katy asked, feeling mortified.

'Well there wasn't much time. When you texted I'd figured you'd probably already been shopping and I didn't want to panic you by throwing it out there at the last minute. I wasn't going to say anything – it's just a diet thing, not an ethics choice or anything, so please don't feel bad.'

'I thought it was odd you didn't have a steak at the restaurant, I just figured you fancied having fish for a change.'

'It's okay really,' David said smiling; 'I just don't eat red meat anymore, or pastry…or potatoes often.'

'So pretty much the only thing I've cooked that you can eat is the beans and the kale?'

'Well there's mushroom in the pie too, and onion – they're both fine,' David said, stifling a giggle.

'So I'm guessing the double chocolate mousse for dessert was a bad idea too?'

'It's fine – I'll just spend from now until next week at the gym. It'll be okay. I'll phone work and tell them that I can't come in because I'm working off the biggest slice of pie ever. I'm sure it'll be okay…I mean there's a small chance that someone will get misdiagnosed or die or something while I'm not there. But it's more the pie's fault than yours and you really shouldn't feel bad.'

'You're an idiot,' Katy said affectionately.

After a smaller than planned portion of dessert, David disappeared to the bathroom whilst Katy piled everything haphazardly into the dishwasher. By the time he returned she had lined up a movie on the television and taken a place on the sofa. He sat beside her and gently pulled her body towards his, wrapping his arm around her as he did so.

'Comfy?'

'Very,' replied Katy as she nestled her head against the warmth of his firm chest.

'Me too. I've missed this – incredibly bad romantic comedies just aren't the same without you.'

'Shut it,' Katy said and playfully tapped his leg with the remote control as she pressed play. The television exploded in a noisy carnival of colour and sound announcing the start of the movie and Katy settled herself in to enjoy the film.

It was a movie Katy had seen countless times and there were moments when she found she was laughing before a line was even spoken in expectation. Whilst David didn't seem quite so engrossed in the film he seemed happy enough and he took regular advantage of the film's soppier moments to sneak a kiss on to her lips.

After about an hour Katy excused herself to use the bathroom, picking a moment where she knew nothing exciting would happen in her absence. As Katy turned on the light something felt a little out of place but she couldn't figure out what it was until she washed her hands. As she stood in front of the mirror, her eyes rested just above the bathroom shelf. It was a small glass ledge and on it stood a bottle of mouthwash, a tube of toothpaste and a chunky glass tumbler – containing two toothbrushes! Katy stared at the newly-arrived second toothbrush sitting alongside her own for a moment, and then aware she was taking a long time turned off the light and exited the room.

Katy walked out in to the corridor still reeling from the surprise and almost tripped over David's bag in the darkness. She turned on the hallway light and then seeing the door to the living room was closed decided to take a quick peak in to the bag. Katy knew she shouldn't be prying but the toothbrush had thrown her and she wondered what other surprises David had in store. She gently lifted the lid on the satchel – convincing herself that if David had been worried about her having a look he would have buckled it properly shut. Inside was a change of underwear and a shirt, a few toiletries and a small brown paper bag. It was the last of these items that sent the biggest ripple of panic through Katy. She knew exactly what was in the bag, David got them through work and they had been a fairly regular sight when they first started dating. The nurses at the practice would package up the bags and each doctor would have a supply for handing out to anyone that wanted them – usually teenagers and young couples attending the weekly family planning surgery. It was one of the jokes David always made about his job;

there were few perks but an unlimited supply of condoms was one of them and there was a whole bag of them sitting in her hallway.

Katy returned to the living room with her mind racing. Clearly David was expecting a lot more from the evening than a meal and a movie. She tried to relax and enjoy the rest of the film but the whole time questions barrelled back and forth in her head. *Was she ready? Would it be awkward? Was he going to stay the night?*

Katy managed to keep her worries to herself long enough for the film to end but as soon as it did David seemed to step his advances up a notch. The kisses grew longer and his hands seemed to grow braver in their explorations. What little space there had been between them on the sofa had completely disappeared. Katy should have been enjoying the moment – she was enjoying it – but all the time she was worrying where it would lead. She wanted to relax in to the pleasure of his touch on her body, but she had had an insight in to where his mind was headed for the evening and she couldn't forget it. 'I found your toothbrush,' Katy suddenly blurted out, the words muffled by the attentive press of David's lips.

'What?' he asked in confusion.

'I found your toothbrush in my bathroom.'

'Oh yeah,' said David and then he returned to kissing her, running his hands along the side of her leg as he did so.

'It freaked me out a bit.'

'What?' he asked again.

'So I looked in your bag and I know I shouldn't have but I found the bag of condoms and the change of clothes and –'

'You went through my bag?'

Katy could hear the annoyance in his voice. She had wanted to cool things down and she had definitely succeeded.

'I'm sorry, I know I shouldn't have. I just panicked.'

'Why are you panicking Katy?' he asked, speaking a little more softly.

'You know – staying over. I wasn't expecting it.'

'Really?'

He sounded surprised and Katy suddenly worried she'd been incredibly naïve. Somehow she'd just assumed that because she wasn't ready he wouldn't be either.

'It's our third date in less than a fortnight Katy. And it's not as if we haven't done it all before – a lot,' David grinned. 'So when you invited me over for dinner I thought I should come prepared.'

'I'm really sorry David – I really did just mean dinner and a movie. Things are going great, I've loved every one of our dates and I don't want to ruin that by rushing things.'

'We spent four years together Katy – I hardly think we're rushing in to it.'

'I know,' Katy said softly. She could feel David withdrawing from her and wished there was a way she could make him see it the way she did. She wanted to sleep with him, of course she did, but that didn't mean they should, not yet anyway.

'Look, we've had a great night and I don't want that to be ruined. How about you just stay over but we leave the rest for now.'

'So stay over but don't have sex?' David said a little bluntly.

'Well, yes – I guess. It doesn't mean we can't cuddle and kiss and –'

David cut off her words with a hug, gently kissing her forehead as he did so.

'I'm sorry,' she continued.

'You don't need to be sorry Katy. You're not ready – that's fine.'

'You seem annoyed.'

'Not at all – I mean I'm kind of gutted you don't feel the same but I'm not annoyed.'

'I'm not saying I don't feel the same, just that it's too soon.'

'It's fine really, I should go anyway. It's getting late and I've got open surgery from 8:30 – that always knackers me out.'

'You're not staying?' Katy said, the disappointment clear in her voice.

David gently held her hand and looked at her with a thin smile.

'No, because as much as you're not ready for the next step, I am, and the thought of lying next to you all night when we're not on the same page – I just don't think I can do that to myself. I love you Katy – there it is, I've said it. I miss you and I want you back – I want *us* back together and I really hope you come to that same conclusion. But until then maybe we should hold off on the friendly sleepovers.'

Katy started to apologise but David wasn't having any of it. He hugged her and held her tight, soothing her hair until she felt a little less guilty about the whole thing. Eventually he said goodnight, fetching his bag and letting himself out the front door.

Suddenly Katy felt enormously drained, she cast a cursory eye over the living room but once she saw the television was off and that all the candles were out she decided to head to bed. She stepped out of the dress letting it fall to a crumpled pile on the floor and then headed to the bathroom. The moment she saw the two toothbrushes in the tumbler the tears sprang to her eyes and they didn't fully stop until she fell asleep some time later.

Chapter Twenty-Two

The following day Katy received a phone call from Cerys offering to give her a lift to the farm. Katy was a little surprised. As Rhodri had always picked her up Katy had assumed that perhaps Cerys didn't drive. But sure enough by mid afternoon Cerys was standing on her doorstep whilst an old estate car sat in the middle of Katy's street with the engine running. Seeing the chaos that was ensuing, Katy quickly dashed towards the car and chivvied an oblivious Cerys to move on before her furious neighbours lynched them both.

Driving with Cerys was distinctly less pleasurable than Katy's journeys with Rhodri. It wasn't that Cerys was bad company – far from it – but she paid little or no attention to the road and as a result pedestrians, other cars and kerbside trees were all at high risk at different points of the journey. Katy wasn't sure exactly how old Cerys was, but she drove as if she had learned to drive in an era when traffic wasn't really a problem and a high probability of death made the journey more invigorating.

It wasn't until after they left Cardiff behind and the roads grew quieter that Katy managed to release her grip on the seat enough to return the colour to her knuckles. When it finally seemed like the risk of veering in to a hedge had dropped below impending certainty, Katy unclenched her teeth and tried to breathe normally again.

'No Rhodri today?' Katy managed. She hoped a conversation would keep her mind occupied and had long resigned herself to the fact that distracting Cerys was unlikely to make much difference to her driving.

'No, he's setting up in the village. He always helps with the stalls. He and Claire used to organise a lot of the village events.'

'Claire?' Katy asked.

'His ex-wife. He said he'd mentioned her to you.'

'Yes, he did. He just didn't say her name.'

'He told you because he likes you. You know that don't you?'

'Yes,' Katy said, a little reluctantly, 'I like him too, but it's a little more complicated than that.'

Cerys sighed, 'I could tell the first night we met that he liked you. You see Rhodri was never going to help out with the wreaths this year. He said he was too busy. I only asked him to take me to the meeting at the last-minute, as I wasn't really feeling up to driving. But the moment he saw you suddenly that all changed and he was volunteering to help out and drive you to and from the farm. I was worried and so I tried to keep the two of you apart that first day holly-wreathing.'

It was hard not to be hurt by what Cerys said. Katy knew that she and Rhodri were close, but to be told so bluntly that Cerys wanted to stop her seeing him was hard to hear.

'I thought maybe I was imagining it,' Katy said eventually.

'No, but it wasn't for the reason you might think. Rhodri's wife Claire cheated on him. She'd been seeing this man Ben for months and he was one of Rhodri's best friends from school. When Rhodri found out, Claire emptied all their savings accounts and left the country with Ben. His wife and his best friend betrayed him. It completely tore Rhodri apart and he nearly lost the farm on top of it.'

'My God, that's awful. Who would do such a thing?' Katy asked, horrified.

'My daughter,' Cerys replied sadly. 'So you see, I'm very protective of Rhodri. I couldn't bear to see him hurt again. I wouldn't want him falling for someone who wasn't sure of her feelings...'

'Cerys I'd never do that to Rhodri. To anyone! I couldn't.'

'There was always something about Claire. As a mother you don't want to see the bad in your child, but it was there. She was selfish – she always put herself first. She saw something she liked in Ben and she went after it. She probably never gave Rhodri a second thought. I know you're not like that Katy. I hope you know that I think you're a lovely young woman – kind and thoughtful. It's hard to admit it but I'd go as far as to say you're everything that Claire wasn't. I wish she had been more like you, and then Rhodri would never have gone through what he has. But I think perhaps there is one thing you have in common...'

Katy felt like she knew what was coming already, but she waited, wanting to hear Cerys say it herself to see what she really thought of Katy.

'I think you're not sure what you want,' Cerys continued. 'And how could you be? When I was your age women didn't have a choice, I went from my father's house to my husband's and though I loved them both dearly it wasn't until my husband died that I realised I had never had the time to figure out who I was. Your generation has had everything, every choice we never had thrust upon you all at once, with no one before you to show you the way. And then we wonder why that freedom drives you all a little crazy.'

Katy blushed, despite the seriousness of what Cerys was saying. It was true though, ever since she had come back from travelling Katy had been acting crazy – that was exactly the word for it. She didn't know where her life was going, whether she should return to her old career or start afresh, or what she really wanted. And how was she supposed to make a decision that affected two other people's lives when she couldn't even figure out her own?

'I feel like everything's a mess. I've tried to be honest with Rhodri from the start. But I just don't know what to do about any of it. The day after I met you and Rhodri I bumped in to my ex-boyfriend. He moved back to Cardiff when he found out I was coming home from travelling. And ever since both Rhodri and David have been so kind and attentive and…romantic. And I just don't have the first clue what to tell either of them. But I've not – I haven't *done* anything with either of them – I wouldn't do that. I mean there's been some kissing, but nothing more and –'

Cerys put a hand on Katy's and gave it a gentle squeeze. 'Only you can know what's right dear. I think it's too late to stop Rhodri falling for you, and I imagine the same is true for David. Just don't make either of them wait too long to find out.'

'No,' Katy promised, feeling the pressure of the situation increasing. She was already worried about hurting David, but hearing about Claire only added to her guilt over Rhodri.

Chapter Twenty-Three

Cerys' house felt strangely empty without the bustle of the other club members, or the hum of music from the stereo. Katy suddenly realised how big the place was and how it must feel to rattle around in there with no one else about. It wasn't just Rhodri's life that had changed when Claire walked out on him, but Cerys' also. Once upon a time the house was probably a hive of activity, with Rhodri and Claire coming over for dinner, or popping in for cups of tea. Cerys must have imagined her later years being filled with the excited squeals of muddy-booted children running next door to see their grandmother. But all of that had disappeared; a lost future that would never be recovered.

Katy looked around the kitchen and recalled her last trip when she had had to walk through the lounge to reach the bathroom. There had been no photographs or postcards, no sign at all that Cerys had ever had a daughter, Maybe Cerys wasn't sentimental, but Katy suspected there was more to it than that. Cerys was a proud woman and Claire's actions would have brought shame as well as sadness in to her life. That Cerys and Rhodri had rebuilt a relationship in the wake of Claire's departure was testimony to both of their good natures. But Katy wondered if ultimately Cerys had paid the price of estrangement with her own daughter for reconciliation with her son-in-law.

Katy promised herself that holly wreathing wouldn't be the end. Whatever else happened, and even after her time was carved up between work and boyfriends, housework and holidays – she would make time to visit Cerys.

'Have you always lived next to Rhodri's family?' Katy asked, the topic still playing on her mind.

'Yes,' Cerys replied as she carefully piled a stack of wreaths into Katy's waiting arms. 'I remember him being born, a right barrel of a baby he was – all tummy and toes. From the moment he could walk on his own he was in and out of my kitchen twenty times a day and always bringing half the farm in on his boots. And he adored Claire – right from the start. She was three years older than him and in his head she could do no wrong. The number of times he covered for her, taking the wrap for everything from pilfered biscuits to broken vases. I think he decided he was going to marry her before he even turned ten. There was never anyone else for him. I think he spent his life waiting for the day she would notice him. When it finally happened he was 19 and she was 22. Claire had just finished university and she came back to find the boy she left behind was a man and not so easily brushed aside.'

Katy noticed tears had appeared in the corner of Cerys' eyes. She wished she could reach out and give Cerys a hug, but her arms were full. 'I'm sorry Cerys – it must have been very hard for you when it ended.'

'Yes, but not as hard as it was for Rhodri. She destroyed him, I couldn't bring myself to speak to her for months afterwards and even now it's not the same as it was. I'm not sure I'll ever fully forgive her, but we've made our peace at least.'

As Cerys took the wreaths from Katy and carefully piled them in to the back of the car it became clear that the discussion was over. Her usual demeanour crept back out from the shadow of her memories and she started fussing over the positioning of individual leaves whilst organising Katy in and out of the kitchen with military efficiency. Only Cerys' eyes, which were still glassy with tears, betrayed how much the foray in to the past had affected her.

It took more than ten trips for Katy to finally get all the wreaths from the kitchen to the car. It seemed impossible that they would all fit, but Cerys was determined. Gradually the pile of waiting wreaths on the driveway grew smaller and the car started to look more and more like a sculpted hedgerow. When the parcel shelf started to fill and the rear window became obscured from the front cabin by a wall of green, Katy's nerves about the onward journey started to grow.

'Perhaps we should do two trips?'

'Nonsense! I've had twice this number in here before with no problem.'

Katy looked into the bulging boot and wondered if that was even possible – but if anyone could make it happen, it was probably Cerys.

When the car was completely full and every wreath had been loaded in Cerys and Katy climbed in to the front. Katy felt a prickly sting against her ankle and looked down to see that even the footwells had been stashed with wreaths. She only hoped that Cerys had left her own free so that the brake and accelerator pedals could be easily reached.

They set off down the lane at a refreshingly gentle pace and Katy hoped that the cargo of wreaths was enough to curb Cerys' speed. It was a twisting, winding road in to the village, with plenty of potholes and overhanging branches to contend with. Katy noticed that as Cerys swerved to avoid each of these she overcorrected a little too much each time, so that the car strayed in to the middle of the road. Once Katy had spotted it she found it harder to ignore and each time she spied an obstacle in the road ahead her eyes drifted to the steering wheel. Cerys' grip seemed to waver, drifting up and down the wheel and the tremor that Katy had noticed the first time they had met was clearly visible.

As the car turned a corner the road narrowed and the hedges closed in on both sides of them. Somewhere up ahead Katy could hear the rumble of an oncoming vehicle. She shifted nervously in her seat expecting Cerys to tuck the car in tighter to the hedgerow to leave as much room as possible on the other side for the vehicle to pass. But the car didn't budge and Cerys kept the car centred in the middle of the road. Katy cried out just as the van roared in to view, and braced herself for the lurching swerve, but none came. The two vehicles were on a collision course but Cerys didn't seem to be moving at all. The van beeped its horn in warning but didn't seem to be slowing down. Katy pumped her foot impotently against the floor in an involuntary mimic of braking, but of course it made no difference.

Just as the two vehicles seemed destined to collide with one another Cerys suddenly sprang in to life, jerkily steering the car to the left. They veered in to the hedge; twigs and branches scratching and clawing at the paintwork like skeletal fingers. The front wheel jumped a little as it drifted up the bank and planted itself firmly in the mud. On their right side the van flew by in a blur of beeping horns and clipped their wing mirror in the process.

Cerys was visibly shaking and her knuckles were firmly anchored on the wheel, even though the car was no longer moving and the engine had cut out.

'Are you okay Cerys?'

'Yes, I think so. I'm sorry. I didn't see him coming. I'm sorry.'

Her words came out quickly, tumbling over one another in their rush to get out. Her breaths were shallow and noisy and Katy worried that she was going to go in to shock.

'It's okay, nobody's hurt. Can you pull the car out though as we can't really stop here?'

Cerys restarted the engine by way of an answer and the car spluttered back in to life. They edged their way out of the hedge and back on to the road with a small skid as the front wheel spun in the mud. Katy turned round to look in the back and was surprised to see that most of the wreaths were still in place. Luckily they were so crammed in that only a few had been dislodged in the bump. All in all they had got off fairly lightly and Katy only hoped that neither the side of the car nor Cerys would be scarred by what had happened.

The rest of the journey was blissfully uneventful and they pulled in to the car park at the village hall with no further mishap. There were already plenty of other cars and people around and Cerys' arrival was greeted by enthusiastic waves and smiles through the windscreen. Katy reached across and gave Cerys' hand a squeeze.

As Katy got out of the passenger side of the car she had a quick look at the panelling. Other than a few minor scratches to the paintwork there was little evidence of the collision. On the other side of the car a buzz of eager villagers had already surrounded Cerys with offers to help unload the wreaths and set up the stall. Katy wished that the two of them had had a moment to talk first, but that chance had passed as soon as the car doors opened.

Katy started ferrying holly wreaths to a long table in the hall that was covered by a purple tablecloth. There a waiting army of middle-aged women gladly took them from her and arranged them in to piles ready for sale. Katy noticed that some of the choice ones with the more unusual ribbons never even made it to the table. Instead they were snatched up instantly, with wads of £10 notes being hurriedly pushed in to Cerys' hands.

Once the car was unloaded Katy wandered around the hall whilst Cerys finished setting up. It was a fairly large building and reminded Katy of school assemblies. Enormous radiators hung from each wall, noisily creaking as they battled to keep the drafts from the open doors at bay. At the back of the room was a small kitchen peppered with giant silver urns and piles of red gingham tea towels. Some rather tired Christmas decorations hung from the rafters. They were the metallic foil type that unfolded into snowflake-esque designs in gaudy shades of red, green, purple and yellow-gold.

Around the room and running in a central line down the middle were rows of stalls selling everything from bonsai's to jigsaw puzzles and many other things in between. Lots of it was clearly locally produced handicrafts; tree decorations made from thinly cut logs, beaded jewellery, leather-bound books and watercolour canvases of the surrounding area.

From the back of the hall came an enticing aroma of baked goods. Frosted cream cupcakes and enormous Victoria sponges nestled alongside jams, chutneys and homemade pork pies.

Katy had just finished eating a delicious warmed sausage roll when Cerys arrived and suggested they walk in to the village centre. The hall was on the edge and together they walked along stall-lined streets lit with hanging lanterns until they reached the main square. Gathered around a central bandstand were a sizeable number of people, their faces lit by the jewelled glow of fairy lights and the warm light of candles as the day surrendered to the night and darkness settled on the village.

'You made it!' cried a familiar voice. Rhodri scooped first Cerys and then Katy in to a big bear hug. He kissed Katy on the cheek and she giggled at the spicy warmth of mulled wine on his breath.

'It all looks wonderful Rhodri,' said Cerys.

As if on cue a spotlight swept across the crowd before landing on the bandstand, illuminating the musicians as they readied themselves under a shiny web of paper chains. A few minutes later and the low hum of a trombone heralded in the first notes of *While Shepherds Watched*.

'Quite some party you have here.'

'You haven't seen anything yet!' Rhodri said, gently taking Katy's hand and leading her away from the throng of people.

They stopped at a stall on the edge of the square where a man in a wax bushman style hat handed them each a steaming cup of mulled wine. Katy went to fetch her purse from her bag but before it was even out the man at the stall had waved them both on with a friendly clap across Rhodri's back and an exaggerated nod of his head in her direction.

'Shouldn't we have paid for these?' Katy asked worriedly.

'Organiser's perk. Just stick with me and you'll be fine.'

Rhodri led them away from the main square and down a side street. The village was beautiful, with slate roofed houses and brightly coloured front doors. A scattering of houses even had one of their wreaths hanging proudly from a brass doorknocker, or silver handle.

At the end of the road Katy could see another group of people gathered, many of them cheering and whooping loudly. They joined the huddle, tacking on to the back row, but Katy struggled to see over the heads of the people in front. She craned her neck and shuffled side to side but found she still wasn't tall enough. Before she could protest Rhodri had ducked down and lifted her on to his back, hoisting her up towards his shoulders. Katy gave a little squeal at the sudden movement, but any fear was soon forgotten when she saw the view.

The crowd were standing behind a five-bar wooden gate that led in to a field. Beyond, ten or so fully-grown men were energetically bouncing through the mud in enormous sacks that covered them to the armpits. And all of them were wearing some form of Christmassy headgear; from Santa hats to reindeer antlers, all completely at odds with the intense masks of concentration and steely competitive glares beneath.

'Who's that in the lead?' Katy asked, calling down to Rhodri.

'That's Max, the butcher's eldest son. And right behind him is Howard, he's a distant cousin of Cerys' and then in third is Sam – he's won the sack race the past three years, but he turned his ankle over last week the stupid git. I had twenty quid on him to win.'

'Damn! Is there a women's race too?'

'Of course and they're twice as competitive as this lot. Last year there was practically a fight when they called it a tie for first.'

'Perhaps I should join in? I was a mean sack racer in primary school – maybe I've still got it in me.' Katy said.

'A last minute add-in just before the race? You'd be lynched and so would I probably, just for bringing you here. Nope we're going to have to get you away from here before you have any more crazy ideas.'

With that Rhodri gently set her down on the ground and the two of them meandered away from the field, taking a different street than they had arrived on. The second street ran at right angles to the first and led them back up the hill in the direction of the village hall. Suddenly it felt very quiet after the excited cheers of the sack race and Katy felt the thing that had been playing on her mind all evening fighting its way to the fore.

'Rhodri,' she started tentatively, 'there's something I've been wanting to say but I don't really know how to.'

'Really? Because I've been thinking exactly the same. But you first.'

'Oh, OK,' said Katy, a little flustered at the idea of Rhodri also having something to say.

'Well – it was in the car on the way over with Cerys. It wasn't that we had an accident as such, but there was a van coming towards us and she didn't move until the last second. We ended up hitting the hedge – only a little – but…but I've seen that her hands shake at times and I noticed it again in the car. I'm sorry, I know it must be hard for you.'

Katy suddenly stopped talking. She felt bad enough telling Rhodri what had happened in the car. But she worried that her final remark had betrayed Cerys' trust a second time; by letting slip to Rhodri that she knew about Claire. Katy studied his face for some sign of annoyance, but instead she saw only sadness and his glum expression was accompanied by a deep sigh.

'She shouldn't really be driving. We've talked about it a lot. But she's stubborn – you know that by now. She only drives round the village and the lanes – it's quiet there and most of the locals recognise her car. It's not that she can't drive, but like you say her reactions are a little slow and the shake – well it's got worse this winter. It's the reason she hasn't been able to do the wreaths. It's why I drove her to Cardiff that first night we all met. The doctor checks in on her regularly and there are plenty of us in the village looking out for her. But I'll have a word and check she's okay.'

Katy swallowed hard, already hating herself for what she was about to say. 'She came and picked me up from Cardiff.'

'She drove to Cardiff and back?' Rhodri roared, his voice spiking loudly.

'I didn't know. I'd never have asked her to – she offered,' Katy said weakly.

Rhodri stayed silent and Katy couldn't tell if he was mad with Cerys, or her, or just plain worried. Either way he had started to race up the hill at such a speed that Katy struggled to keep up with him.

There was a warm glow of light coming from the hall, making it look even bigger than Katy knew the building to be. Since she had left a little earlier lanterns had been lit all around the outside. The car park was even busier and vehicles had been abandoned all around the hedgerows and into the lane on either side of the entrance. Rhodri pushed his way through the cars and towards the front door, which he opened with a little more force than necessary, causing it to bang against the pebbledash wall with a loud thud.

Once in the hall Rhodri headed straight to the table of holly wreaths and steered Cerys away to the cloakroom area off to the right. Katy wondered what he was going to say to her and hoped he wouldn't be too hard.

Katy felt a little lost without Rhodri, but she didn't want to make the conversation any more awkward than it already was by hovering around them waiting for it to finish. She meandered slowly around the hall, walking close to the wreaths stall to see how they were selling. The table was still fairly full but some gaps had started to appear and the piles that had been stacked on the floor were gone. Katy recognised a few of the women on the stall as the same ones who had collected the wreaths from her when they arrived, but she didn't feel able to stop and chat with any of them. Just as she was wondering what else she could do to fill the time Katy felt a tap on her shoulder. She turned round to see Jenny, Sophia and Chris all wrapped up warm in winter coats.

'Katy!' Jenny said excitedly. 'It's so good to see you!'

Katy hugged the two women and then gave Chris a little wave. To her surprise he leant in to give her a kiss on the cheek. He seemed to be in a better mood than Katy could ever remember and as the four of them walked around the room catching up he even joined in the conversation where he could. Jenny was practically beaming at her husband's new-found affability and Sophia seemed equally high-spirited.

'Where's Tom?' Sophia asked as they left the hall and headed towards the village.

'I don't know actually, they should have been here by now.'

Katy checked her phone and was concerned to see that she had five missed calls and a voicemail – all from Tom. She tried to dial in to her voicemail but she had no reception.

'Damn it,' Katy said loudly, still holding the phone to her ear. 'There's no signal. I hope they're okay.'

'Probably stopped for a pint or two en route,' Chris said. 'That's what we did,'

Katy smiled, momentarily forgetting her worries over Cerys and the whereabouts of Tom and Owen. It was funny – at that moment there were probably women all over the world putting hours of thought and care in to what to buy their husbands or boyfriends for Christmas. But for most of them Katy reasoned – if you just sent them to the pub with a twenty-pound note in their hand they'd think it was the best day ever.

'Perhaps they're in the village,' Katy reasoned

There was no sign of Tom's car in the car park but that didn't mean they weren't there. They could have come in Owen's car and Katy could have been stood right by it and not known. She decided to lead the others down the hill, following the sound of the brass band, which was just finishing a rousing rendition of *O Come All Ye Faithful*.

There were crowds of people everywhere, many holding lanterns or torches, even though the streets were well lit. Katy looked around but she couldn't see Tom or Owen anywhere. Even amongst the sea of black and brown winter coats Katy imagined that Owen would stand out given his build.

They reached the bandstand and Katy checked her phone again but there was still no reception. She chatted with Sophia absentmindedly whilst Chris and Jenny went off in search of some mulled wine. She tried to focus on what Sophia was saying – something about upcoming exams for the end of the year – but all she could think about was Cerys and Tom – her mind flitting between them, hoping they were both alright. The evening had started off so enjoyably; it was a shame how quickly it had turned to anxiety.

'So?' Sophia prompted.

'Sorry, I didn't quite catch what you said.' Katy said, unconvincingly.

'You know – you and Rhodri. What's happening?' Sophia asked impatiently.

It seemed a big jump to go from mock exam papers to men, but Katy rationalised that maybe she had missed more of the conversation than imagined.

'Oh we're just friends – you know how it is.'

'Friends! Nonsense, I don't look at *any* of my *friends* the way you two stare at each other.'

At that moment Jenny and Chris returned, but instead of it bringing the subject to a close Sophia seemed to take the opportunity to expand it.

'Katy is pretending that there's nothing happening with Rhodri. We've all seen it haven't we Jenny – we were only just talking about it in the car.'

Katy felt her face turn the same shade of red as the mulled wine that Jenny passed to her. She caught Jenny's eye and saw a similar flush of embarrassment.

'Well,' Jenny said, playing for time, 'there's definitely a spark there. But of course it's never quite that simple is it.'

'No,' Katy said sharply. 'It's not. We really are just friends.'

Katy was tempted to walk away to put a definite stop on the conversation, but it seemed a little churlish to do so. She knew Sophia was well intentioned – and as Katy reminded herself – still incredibly young, but she didn't want any more of a fuss being made about it than there already was. It was bad enough that Tom would be speculating about it when he arrived, she hadn't expected it from Sophia and Jenny too. It seemed all the members of Christmas Club wanted her and Rhodri together.

'Tom's here by the way and is it Owen – his boyfriend?' Jenny asked.

'Yes,' replied Katy, grateful for the conversation change,

'They're on the way over now; they were just behind us in the queue for mulled wine. And someone else was with them too but I can't remember his name I'm afraid.'

'That's okay – it's probably just Simon one of our other university friends. He did say he might come along.'

'Simon, is he young and handsome your friend?' Sophia asked playfully.

'He is,' Katy replied enjoying herself 'and he has a lovely boyfriend.'

'Oh Katy, all your friends are gay – it's no help at all.' Sophia laughed.

'You must have men falling over you at university, you don't need me to set you up with anyone!'

'Well, I was hoping you might know someone older and sophisticated…and straight!'

'I'm afraid you lost me after older,' Katy replied. 'That's pretty much all I can offer.'

Katy was glad that the thorny subject of Rhodri had passed and that she was enjoying herself again. Tom and Owen were on their way and hopefully Rhodri could sort things with Cerys without any upset. She took a large sip of mulled wine and returned her gaze to the band. She had barely been watching a few minutes before the world suddenly went black.

A gloved hand covered her eyes just as a shouted chorus of 'mistletoe!' broke out from those around her. Katy smiled – it was something Tom did every year – he would always surprise her with mistletoe and she would kiss him on the lips in a grown up game of chicken. They would both carry on kissing, daring the other one to continue until one of them gave in and pulled away. And it was always Tom who lost. He could never manage more than a few seconds before descending in to a giggle or pulling away squeamishly rubbing his lips.

She closed her eyes and spun round, allowing Tom to initiate the kiss. As soon as his lips found hers she kissed him back with faux passion, darting her tongue between his lips and squeezing his shoulders. A cheer broke out around them but Katy could tell something wasn't right. The lips were too bristly, the shoulders too wide and the kiss reciprocated too fiercely.

Her eyes opened in horror to see Rhodri's face pressed against hers, his eyes closed as his tongue flickered inside her mouth. Her head was screaming for her to pull away but her body wouldn't allow her to follow, she wanted it too much. She closed her eyes, promising herself that she could stop – that she would. But she didn't. The whooping continued and then suddenly the tone changed, there was shouting in amongst the cheering and she couldn't understand why.

Katy felt Rhodri spinning away from her and opened her eyes just in time to see the fist colliding with the left side of his face, falling squarely on his jaw. The punch landed with a sickening thud and David recoiled instantly, shaking his fist out in to an open hand. For a moment Rhodri stood in stunned silence, a small rose of blood forming at the corner of his nose. Katy saw the sprig of mistletoe drop from Rhodri's hand and fall on to the pavement before he lurched forward. He raised his right arm behind him but his gloved fingers remained outstretched and his palm open. Sophia cried out for him to stop but Rhodri carried on, his hand thudding in to David's chest just below the right collarbone and shoving him back a step.

'Who the hell are you?' Rhodri yelled?'

'Me?' David said. 'Who the hell are you – kissing my girlfriend?'

There was a collective pause as everyone, Katy included, mentally stumbled over the word girlfriend, seemingly wondering why they were the last to find out. In the temporary lull Katy saw Owen's massive figure break through the crowd. He wrapped his arms around David in a standing rugby tackle and pivoted him away from the fight, placing himself between the two men.

David was still yelling angrily as Owen manoeuvred him away, leaving Katy to face Rhodri. She was worried that he would go after David. He was physically bristling with anger, his fingers clenching and unclenching and his breath coming in short violent bursts. The trickle of blood had reached his chin and she only hoped his nose wasn't broken.

Katy rummaged through her pockets and found a clean tissue, which she handed to Rhodri as she begged him to calm down. He brushed the offer of help aside and stared at her intently, his usually hazel eyes were ablaze with the fury of autumnal fires.

'Girlfriend?' he finally asked accusatorily.

'No!' Katy responded. 'You know that. But what were you doing kissing me? What happened to backing off?'

Before he had time to answer Tom had appeared at their side. 'Everyone okay?' he asked.

'I'll live.' Rhodri replied moodily.

'Someone should take a look at that.'

The voice came from behind Katy. She turned round slowly, her heart sinking as she already knew who she would see. Cerys pushed her way through the crowd and took Rhodri's head in her hands, gently tilting it back to stem the bleeding.

'Cerys I'm-' Katy faltered.

'I think you should leave,' Cerys said sternly, 'You've done enough already.'

Katy felt her words keenly, each one like an icy blade. But as she looked around she knew Cerys was right. The evening they had all worked so hard for was ruined, Rhodri had a bloodied nose, David was hurt and lashing out and Cerys was furious. And the worst of it all was that they all had reason to be angry with her. They were right, and she was in the wrong.

She blurted out an apology and then started to walk hurriedly away. By the time she had reached the edge of the square she was running, hot shameful tears streaming down her face. All around people were calling out to her, confused and concerned over her distress, but she didn't stop. It wasn't until she reached the car park that it dawned on her that she was stuck. It was too late for a bus and her phone had been without signal since she arrived.

The door to the village hall kept opening and closing, spilling out warm light and laughter. But Katy couldn't face going in alone to ask for a phone. For one brief and ridiculous moment she thought about walking, but there was no way she would find the way and even in her distraught state she could see the foolishness in the idea.

'I'm sorry.'

Katy looked round to see Tom standing in the car park a few feet away from her looking terrible.

'David bumped in to us in town – we were working on the stage and he invited us to go for a drink. I ended up telling him we had plans and he asked if he could come along. I didn't know what to say. I tried to phone you all the way over here but I couldn't get through.'

'It's okay; he's your friend too. There's nothing you could have done differently. How is everyone? They must all hate me.'

'Of course not. Owen has taken David for a walk to cool down and Rhodri's fine. When I left he was polishing off a huge glass of mulled wine and looked to be quite enjoying everyone fussing over him.'

'And Cerys?'

'A little worried about Rhodri, but she'll soon see he's fine. But it's *you* I'm worried about. I've come to take you home, then I'll come back for David and Owen.'

Katy didn't have the energy to protest, she just stepped silently in to the car and watched as the hall fell in to a blurry haze behind the misted screen of the window. They pulled out of the car park and the hedgerows sprang in to life under the beam of the headlights, just as the first flakes of snow started to fall.

Chapter Twenty-Four

David rarely took a lunch break; there was hardly ever the time. In theory the practice booked them all a forty-five minute break somewhere between 12 and 2, but appointments overran and lunch was always the first casualty. So at 1pm when David announced to the receptionist that he was heading out he triggered a flurry of panic. It started with a chain reaction of raised eyebrows across the front desk that rapidly escalated in to a chorus of frustrated sighs and grumbles from the waiting patients. He knew that going out would only pile additional work on to his already overstretched colleagues. But for once he made an exception – he had to escape.

David's morning had consisted of a seemingly endless procession of sniffles and seasonal skivers. The latter he could spot a mile off – they were all nursing the tail end of a cold (or flu as they had all decided to themselves) and were hoping a runny nose and slight cough would be enough to get them signed off for the last week of work. Normally he would have handled them all with cheery sympathy but today their trivial complaints grated on him. The knuckles on his right hand smarted with a restless ache and the more he listened to them all the more he felt like an explosion was building inside him. It was like all the emotions and angers he had ever suppressed in his lifetime suddenly wanted to make themselves heard and threatened to burst from his lips in screamed rebellion. By the time lunchtime came around a break wasn't an option…it was a necessity.

The surgery door closed behind him with the small jangle of a bell and he found himself standing in a quiet suburban street of the city. Parked cars lined the road on either side and the checkerboard pattern of the pavement was interrupted only by the occasional planted tree, each one in a neat square of earth. Only faint traces of slushy snowmelt were visible from the small smattering of flakes that had fallen the night before and it wasn't enough to spoil the overall look of order. It was a reassuringly calm scene, quite at odds with the chaotic mess of his troubled mind. The truth was for only the second time since his childhood David was utterly lost.

From a young age David had felt disconnected from his parents. At play parks he had looked longingly on as other parents picked up their children to soothe grazed knees and calm furrowed brows. At the end of the school day his friends would race to the gates to their waiting families who fussed and tousled over them in competitive displays of affection. In contrast David would walk calmly over to his mum and he would let her take his hand coolly in hers and lead him home.

As David grew older the gap widened. As a young boy he had at least been entertaining and a source of unintended humour as he naïvely negotiated the world. But as he entered his early teenage years what few charms David possessed seemed to fall out of favour. Suddenly childishness became a nuisance and clumsiness a curse and David increasingly felt like an unwanted guest in his own home. He started to retreat in to himself, spending hours alone in his room poring over books. At first he read fiction, identifying with the ragtag collection of orphans and child malcontents that became his heroes. But after a while he grew frustrated, because there was nothing else for him, no worlds through wardrobes or lands beyond dreams. All he knew was the four walls of his bedroom and a family that was slowly drifting away from him. Tired of stories, he turned his attention to school textbooks and his dad's dusty collection of reference books.

The extra hours of study soon started to pay dividends. David started to excel in school and as his grades improved and his teachers became more glowing in their feedback something miraculous happened. David noticed his parents' interest piquing again. For the first time in years they started to ask him about his day when he came home from school and to his surprise they listened. A few weeks later and he overhead his mum talking about him in a supermarket and for once it wasn't to grumble about the cost of uniforms or the state of his bedroom, but with something that sounded a little like pride. Fuelled by the attention, David ploughed more and more time in to his schoolwork. Whilst his school friends read comics or played computer games, David learnt about photosynthesis and studied the elements of the periodic table.

He developed a greed for knowledge that his parents were only too happy to feed, and science was at the epicentre of that. It was where David seemed to excel the most and the area his dad placed the most importance on. Christmases and birthdays became lavish affairs again with presents of microscopes and textbooks piling up and David's parents beaming proudly as he gratefully lapped up each one with enthusiasm.

David finished secondary school with a string of A's and his pick of universities. And as his parents proudly crowed over his accomplishments as if they were their own, he never once corrected them. If anything he agreed that they were partly responsible for his achievements. Not because they had encouraged or supported him, even though they had in their way done exactly that. But what his childhood had taught David was that you could learn to make people love you, or if not love then a facsimile of it that ultimately produced the same results. He had become the son his parents wanted and in return they had loved him. He had finally come to understand that you made your own happiness and that all you had to do was figure out what those around you wanted and give it to them.

David enrolled in medical school at UCL, moving in to a small room in a shared house near Kings Cross. The course was challenging, but David already had a head start on most of his fellow students. He understood the sacrifices needed to succeed and he was prepared to make them.

Outside of lectures the lessons of his childhood were just as readily applied. David made friends easily, surprising everyone with his knack of remembering their drink orders, the dates of their birthdays, their favourite films, and simply knowing when to talk and when it was best just to listen. And more than one of his female classmates made the transition from confidante to lover, swept along by the seemingly perfect blue-eyed boy who always knew exactly what was wanted from him. David understood that love was a simple contract and as long as you kept to the terms everyone was happy – or so he thought.

David graduated from UCL with a first class degree and a job offer swiftly followed. He ended his relationship of six months with Jessica gently and amicably and moved to Cardiff the next week. It was there that David truly began to shine; the patients and staff loved him and he never begrudged squeezing in an extra appointment or staying another hour.

For over five years David excelled at being exactly what he believed everyone wanted him to be. Girlfriends adored him almost as much as their mothers did and when relationships ended it was down to distant job offers or moves abroad rather than any fault with David. Then, at age 27 everything changed.

David met Katy at a local theatre production of Macbeth. A colleague of David's from the surgery had a small part in the play. In total he later estimated she couldn't have been on stage for more than a few minutes. But dutifully he had volunteered to support her and had taken his seat in a rather empty and drab theatre with something approaching dread. He wasn't really one for the theatre at the best of times, but everything from the home printed A4 programmes to the distinct lack of an audience was signalling a truly dire evening lay ahead. Just before the curtains lifted the lights went out and David resigned himself to being one of a very select group of people that would ever see the performance. And then something unexpected happened. From a few rows ahead and to the left a crumpled ball of paper came soaring over the seats and landed in David's lap. At first he thought it was just kids but he couldn't remember seeing any children in the foyer, nor when he had taken his seat. He took a closer look and unfurled it as noiselessly as possible. There was some writing on it. It was still dark but as the performance hadn't started he risked switching on his phone to cast some light on to the paper.

HELP – Please rescue me, fearing boredom, awful accents and a distinct possibility of falling asleep.
E7

David couldn't help but smile at the note, which had managed to capture his mood completely. It was a Thursday night near the end of a very long week. The theatre was the last place he wanted to be and nodding off was a definite risk. He craned his neck to try and catch sight of the person who had thrown it but the seat backs were too high. He hesitated for a moment and then just as the curtains lifted and the stage flooded the auditorium with light he made a dash for it. He flumped down in to his new seat just as the first of the three witches announced her presence with a melodramatic cackle.

'I wasn't sure you were coming,' the woman in the seat next to him whispered. As she spoke she cocked her head so that her long brown hair fell on to her shoulders like tumbling soft caramel. She smelt incredible; her perfume dashing over him like the first hit of spring after the longest winter.

'I'm Katy,' she said, and then in an embarrassed garble she added; 'The moment I threw that note I had a terrible thought, that there are so few people here you must be with one of the cast and there I was saying it would be awful.'

David chuckled, feeling a guilty spike of pleasure as he whispered conspiratorially in the hallowed quiet of the theatre.

'Just a work colleague, and I'm not overly hopeful either,' he said.

'That's good then.'

'What?' David asked.

'Well that you're not here supporting your boyfriend or something,' Katy replied.

'Boyfriend?' David retorted a little louder than intended.

Katy laughed but even after David had explained himself he felt he was still missing the joke.

It wasn't until after the performance when David met Tom, Simon and Adam – all of whom had been in the play that David finally understood.

Once he had congratulated his colleague on what was at best a mediocre appearance David followed Katy and the others to a bar. It seemed the joke was continuing as David quickly realised that Katy was the only woman there, though not the only person to be wearing a dress.

'Do you mind?' she asked.

'Of course not, I've been here before actually,' he lied.

Katy studied him for a moment; 'No you haven't.'

'Okay well maybe I haven't, but-'

Suddenly she laughed a rich bubbling laugh that sounded like the most genuine and beautiful noise David had ever heard. 'You've *never* been to a gay bar have you?'

'No,' David said honestly.

It seemed to be all the ammunition Katy needed to drag him gleefully in the direction of the stage, ushering him on to the podium in front of everyone. What followed was possibly the most embarrassing, but also the most exhilarating night of David's life. And when he finally stumbled home drunk at 3am he knew one thing more surely than anything before; that he had to see Katy again.

What David could never have predicted was just how much Katy would change his world. The challenge at the bar when Katy had caught him in his lie hadn't been a one-off. David quickly learnt that she wasn't impressed with any of his attempts to please or impress her. For the first time in his life David had met someone that he couldn't logically anticipate what to do to make her happy. But instead of being frightened by this he found it exhilarating. It was real. Suddenly he understood that all his previous relationships; from his parents right through to his most recent girlfriend were a sham. They were pale imitations of love that he had manipulated in to being through tireless self-sacrifice. And not one of the recipients of his attention had ever stopped to ask what *he wanted*; what mattered to him and what made him happy. Until Katy.

She wanted to know everything, from what made him laugh to what made him cry. She asked what type of tea he drunk in the morning and smiled as she discovered the taste of his lips when he crawled in to bed beside her at the end of a long day. She wanted him, and it was only through opening up to her that David started to understand himself, and more than that to appreciate himself as his own man.

Then one day, it all went wrong. Somehow the man who had spent his life pleasing other people suddenly stopped making the woman he loved happy. He had stopped trying hard enough and had lost his way. Katy left, and the year that followed was long and full of bitter disappointments. Time and time again he tried to pick himself up and start over, confident that he could find someone else that he would love the way he loved Katy. But there was no one.

So when David heard she was coming back – that Katy was returning from travelling, single and unattached, he seized the opportunity to try and win her back. For a few weeks it had seemed like it was working, and then it all fell away from him a second time. David was lost all over again.

He picked his way through the busy streets with his head cast low to the floor. The last thing he wanted was to bump in to someone he knew or a patient who would doubtless stop and ask him about some new ache or ailment. What he really wanted was to go back and stop it all going wrong in the first place, or if he couldn't do that, then at least to go back to the previous day. Maybe that would be enough. Maybe if he hadn't been so stupid as to punch Rhodri then perhaps he would still stand a chance.

It was as David was at his lowest – when he thought that he had lost all hope of ever winning Katy back – that something miraculous seemed to happen. A sudden gust of wind picked up and scattered the contents of an overflowing bin in to the street. The heavy items; the cardboard cups and plastic food cartons fell to the floor, but one crumpled piece of paper flew out and landed on David's foot. He tried to kick it away but the wind had pinned it against his leg. He picked it up and walked back towards the bin. Just as he was about to throw it away he cast a quick glance at the sheet and did a double take. It was a leaflet for a university theatre production of Macbeth.

    David stopped where he was and lifted his eyes from the floor for the first time since leaving the surgery. He was stood directly in front of a dress shop. It was one of the places that had opened while he was in London and mostly it seemed to cater to the current demand for secondary school prom-dresses. But there were a few other items too; bridesmaids' dresses, flower-girl outfits, and right in the centre a shimmering silver ball gown inlaid with gold thread snowflakes. David walked in to the shop, still clutching the Macbeth flyer and went straight over to the woman at the counter. He wasn't ready to give up just yet.

Chapter Twenty-Five

Katy put the phone back in its cradle and settled herself in to the cosy armchair near the window. It was a battered old thing, with faded coffee mug rings on the arms and a dent in the cushion stuffing that no amount of fluffing or rearranging could shift – but Katy loved it. When she had gone travelling she had argued with her mum for hours to convince her to store it while she was away. Her mum had thought it a waste of space and Katy was sure she would return to find it had been taken to the tip in her absence. But when her parents had arrived in her dad's old sedan with the scant boxes of her belongings the chair was waiting for her, as tatty and loved as ever.

The chair reminded her of home and in particular the small room over the garage where it had spent the first fifteen years of its life. In that room Katy had had sleepovers, watched movies and nursed heartbreaks and hangovers with mugs of tea and mountains of ice cream; both lovingly delivered by her mum. The chair connected her to all that history, and even in her one-bed apartment in Cardiff it still reminded her of home and the big blue house brimming with memories.

Often she wished she could go back to those days, when there was little that couldn't be soothed away by a well-timed hug from her dad or a heart-to-heart with her mum. It was a time when life was simple. Not that the problems had changed much since she was sixteen; the boys were a little hairier, the deadlines less flexible and the bills a fair bit higher. But it was the consequences that had changed, back then mistakes were forgotten in a week and even the worst heartbreaks faded away in time. Now at thirty-one she was only too aware that it wasn't always so easy. And that was the moment in the phone call when much to her surprise Katy's mum had burst in to a rich honeyed laugh.

'Oh darling, it doesn't get any easier by sixty-five, believe me. You will always make mistakes, and men will always cause you heartbreak – just as you will them. That's just life, sure as fire burns and bees sting. Everyone

gets hurt at times and everybody heals. All you can do is what feels right at the time and hope for the best.'

'That's it?' Katy asked, a little disappointed.

'That's it,' her mum replied.

'So your motherly advice, built up over sixty years – is to hope for the best?'

Katy's mum laughed again. *'There's no magic answer Katy. But what I can say is that some of my favourite memories are my mistakes.'*

'Well that's really helpful mum,' Katy said, a little scathingly.

'Oh Katy, look I know this feels a big deal now and it is and I'm here for you. But please try not to be so serious. Ever since you've been back you've been beating yourself up over this and to what end? Are any of the three of you any better off for it?'

'No,' Katy reluctantly agreed.

'Well then, lighten up for goodness sake. Just wait till you've been married forty years and then you'll look back on two men fighting over you and wish you'd enjoyed it more.'

'Mum!'

'You have to admit it must have been at least a little exhilarating.'

'No! David could have really hurt Rhodri.'

'Oh come on Katy.'

Katy paused for a moment. 'Well I'll admit it is a little flattering. But that doesn't change the fact that it shouldn't be happening.'

'But it is and so you can make the best of it and get on with things or you can mope about them.'

'So what would you do?' Katy asked, still hoping for something more helpful.

'You're asking me who I'd pick?'

'I guess so.'

'Whichever one makes you happier.'

Katy may have groaned at her mum's continued evasion, but she didn't mean it. Her mum had helped and by the time they had finished speaking Katy felt considerably better about the whole situation. So much so that she decided to give herself the day off – not just from feeling guilty but from everything; job hunting, chores and even the smaller tasks that she normally enjoyed, like wrapping presents and pinning up Christmas cards. Instead she fetched an enormous bag of popcorn from on top of the kitchen cupboard, made herself a flask of tea and returned to the armchair, book in hand.

Katy became so engrossed in the story that she lost all track of time and it was only when she had to switch on the lights to continue reading that she realised how late it was. As soon as she stood up her stomach griped at her like a grumbling bear stirring from hibernation. She hadn't eaten since breakfast (if popcorn and chocolate even counted as breakfast) and her body was starting to rebel. She emptied a can of soup in to a saucepan and slowly heated it up whilst buttering two thick slices of bread. Katy then poured the steaming liquid into a large bowl and grabbed a spoon before returning to her seat. Just as the first mouthful passed her lips the doorbell went. She eyed her long overdue lunch longingly before placing the bowl on the windowsill and walking downstairs to the front door.

'David,' Katy announced, a little surprised.

'Hi, look I know you probably don't want to see me but-'

'Don't be silly David; I'll always want to see you. You know that, come on in.'

'Really?'

'Of course. Look I think we've all been acting a little crazy since I got back.'

She started walking up the stairs and David trailed gratefully behind, a clear look of relief on his face.

'How's your hand?' Katy asked.

'A bit sore, but no more than I deserve. Do you know how…?'

'Owen said he was fine. But probably best to lay off the fisticuffs from now on.'

It was the closest Katy got to telling David off. She wasn't sure if it was her mum's nonchalance rubbing off on her, or the remorseful expression on David's face when she had opened the door. But she didn't see the point in making him feel any worse than he clearly already did.

Once in the flat Katy busied herself making David a coffee. The kettle was still warm so it didn't take long to boil. She added a generous spoonful of coffee and a small splash of milk – just the way David liked it and then gave the mug a stir.

'Sorry – I didn't mean to disturb your meal.'

Katy followed David's gaze to the windowsill where a small cloud of condensation had formed on the glass above the bowl.

'Oh, don't worry I can reheat it later.'

Katy passed him the coffee and took a sip of her own tea, whilst she waited for him to speak. She had always been able to tell when something was on David's mind and she knew from experience it was best just to give him the space to talk when he was ready.

'I'm sorry,' he said eventually. 'You don't know how bad I feel about last night. I should never have come, it was stupid and I wish I could undo it.'

'Really, it's ok. And I'm sorry too; I had no idea he was going to kiss me. I thought it was just Tom messing about. And then, well you know –'

'I never thought it would be like this,' David said quietly.

Katy looked over at David and recognised the regret in his eyes. 'No,' she said, 'nor me.'

'We were pretty good weren't we? Most of the time I mean.'

'We were,' Katy agreed.

'And all I want is for us to go back to that. I know I didn't make enough effort come the end. But ever since you came back I've been trying, and if you'll just give me one more chance I know I can be the guy you want.'

Katy put her cup down and walked over to the sofa where David sat. She sat down beside him and put her arm round his shoulders giving him a gentle squeeze.

'David, I never want you to be anyone but you. Don't ever think that.'

'But, you do. I mean if that were the case we'd still be together,' he replied.

'There are lots of reasons why it ended, some of them down to me, some you, some that neither of us could have helped and some that don't even matter anymore. But either way it happened and we both need to stop blaming ourselves.'

'Okay,' David said unconvincingly.

'And as my mum helpfully told me this morning apparently mistakes are good.'

'Really?'

'Well, I'm paraphrasing, but the general message was that we should all be making less of a fuss. Apparently it only gets worse as you get older.'

'Shit. It get's worse?'

'Apparently,' Katy chuckled.

'I have to say I was expecting to have to work a bit harder to win you over today.'

'You can thank mum for that.'

'Okay, well there was another reason I came over – besides all the planned begging for forgiveness. The Doctor's Ball, I wanted to ask if you'd go with me. It doesn't have to be a date, just think of it as an apology for all the years you wanted to go and we never did.'

David's invitation took Katy completely by surprise. The Doctor's Ball was an annual gala dinner and dance held every Christmas. The invitation was much wider than the name suggested and covered GPs, surgeons, nurses, nutritionists; anyone really that worked in healthcare, and of course their partners. In the four years they had been together David had never once considered attending, despite Katy's enthusiasm for the idea. It was – he had said – the worst type of social event, with stuffy outfits and awkward conversations and not even the prospect of getting drunk as an escape. The last year they were together Katy hadn't even asked when the invite arrived in the post, she just tossed it straight in to the bin unopened.

'You really want to go?'

'Yes. It'll be dreadful of course…but then sometimes the evenings you really dread turn out to be the best.'

'Macbeth,' Katy said fondly.

'Yes, best worst night ever,' David said, taking her hand in his.

'Okay, let's do it. And I expect the full works from you Mr Barratt – tuxedo, bow tie and one of those silly silk coloured belt things.'

'A cummerbund?' David asked.

Katy stifled a laugh. 'Is that what they're called?'

'Yep, and there's no way I'm wearing one.'

'Then I'm afraid you'll have to find another date. There's absolutely no way I'm turning up to The Doctor's Ball with a man not wearing a cummerbund.'

'Okay, I will wear the ridiculous man sash if you promise to wear something for me.'

David stuck out his hand to secure a deal. Warily Katy shook it, figuring that there was very little he could use to embarrass her, a corsage or tiara perhaps, but both were easily removed as the night went on.

'Deal,' Katy confirmed.

'Good,' David said, sounding pleased. 'Then I want you to wear the dress I bought you. I'll bring it round before the ball.'

Katy could tell immediately that the dress wasn't going to be an embarrassment.

'David, you shouldn't have.'

'Hey, I figured I owed you one for all the times we should have gone before. Besides I really don't think I'd look half as good in it as you would, so you should definitely have it.'

'Thank you,' Katy said, sensing it was hopeless to argue. She kissed him on the cheek and thanked him again, still not quite believing that they were finally going.

Chapter Twenty-Six

The week leading up to the ball seemed to fly by in a blur, not least because everyone around Katy seemed intent on turning it in to a major occasion. On the Tuesday, (the day following David's invitation) Tom arranged to meet David for lunch and immediately after took Katy shoe shopping to ensure she had a pair that matched the dress. On Wednesday it was Anne's turn to lead her round the shops; this time in search of new underwear. They finally decided on a matching set in purple lace, decorated with lilac flowers. It was far skimpier than anything that Katy would normally wear and far nicer than anything David had ever seen her in. Neither of which seemed to matter to Anne. And Katy's protestations that they were unlikely to be seen by anyone but her went completely unheeded.

On Thursday there was a brief respite as she attended a job interview in the morning and in the afternoon she helped Tom with some of the final paintwork on the nativity stage.

After two days of being fussed over and dressed up in various accessories she was grateful for the chance to throw on an old shirt and get covered in paint. By the end of the afternoon Katy figured she had managed to get twice as much paint on herself as she had the wooden surrounds of the stage – but it was better that way. Tom had produced a masterpiece and there was no hope of her improving it. She knew he had only asked her to join him so that they could chat whilst he worked and she was happy with that level of contribution.

The following day Katy met up with David for lunch and he handed over the dress. When she had first asked he had been a little reluctant – hoping instead that she would see the gown for the first time on the day of the ball. However Katy was anxious to make sure that no alterations were needed. She had lost 20lb since David had last bought her anything to wear and even then he had never been the best at getting her size right. But once she got the dress home and placed it, still in it's protective jacket, on the arm of the sofa she couldn't help but picture the disappointment in David's face.

Resisting the temptation to take a peek she picked up the phone and dialled Tom's number.

It was tricky but between the two of them they managed to get Katy in to the dress without her seeing it. Once on she was able to check it quickly over with her hands to check that it fitted well in all the right places and that there wasn't an excess of material. The rest she left to Tom. To his credit he gave nothing away, only confirming that it fitted perfectly. But when the dress was off and packed away and Katy finally opened her eyes she could tell that he was emotional.

'Hey, what's up?' she asked, worried that the dress was terrible and he wasn't sure how to tell her.

'I know I'm not supposed to say anything, but you looked incredible Katy. He's certainly outdone himself. I don't think there could be a more perfect dress.'

'I didn't look silly?'

'No,' he said quietly, his eyes glistening with moisture. 'You looked beautiful.'

Seeing her friend so affected brought a wobble to Katy's voice and sparked tightness in her throat. They hugged, Tom's warmth spreading to her like water from a hot spring.

'I was going to wait till tomorrow to say something but Owen and I booked you in to a salon for Saturday morning. And before you start protesting we wanted to do it. Just think of it as an early Christmas present. Believe me, once you've seen the dress you'll thank us for making a fuss.'

'God, what are you all going to be like when I get married?' Katy asked, a little overwhelmed by all the attention.

'Relieved,' Tom said drily.

Chapter Twenty-Seven

Despite all the preparations the ball seemed to creep up on Katy far quicker than she expected. She left the hairdressers with less than two hours to spare before David was due to pick her up. Although it was dry she ordered a taxi to take her from door to door, fearing that the slightest gust of wind or passing double-decker bus might disturb the fragile beauty of her new hairstyle.

To save time she phoned her mum from the taxi. The call satisfied her mum's need to gush with excitement and gave Katy five minutes to fret over every eventuality with someone who wouldn't judge her too harshly.

The journey was painfully slow, as long snakes of cars poured out of the teeming car parks and slowly wriggled their way home through the crowds of Christmas shoppers. All Katy could do was stare hopelessly at the meter and watch as time and money slipped away from her until they finally arrived home.

Once inside Katy sat in front of the mirror and rummaged through her make-up bag. She didn't have a dressing table; instead she sat cross-legged in the corridor with a white-framed mirror propped up against the wall. It took her twice as long to do her make-up as normal, partly because she was being extra careful, but mainly because every few minutes she had to stop and stare at the unfamiliar creature looking back at her. In the year she had been travelling Katy's hair had been frequently neglected, it had coped with sand, sun, mud and more sea-water than imaginable. She had come to accept that every photo of that year would show her smiling back from beneath a bedraggled and tangled mop. So seeing her hair freshly washed, coloured and styled was an unfamiliar sight and one that would undoubtedly remain a continual fascination until the glamour faded away under the stress of routine.

When she had finished, Katy finally unwrapped the dress in full for the first time. That morning she had allowed herself a small peek to be sure of the colour, but it was the first time she had seen it properly. As the silky material splayed out on to the bed and brushed against her knees Katy gave a sharp intake of breath. She was running late but she couldn't help but pick up her phone and text David. *It's beautiful. I love it. Thank you. X*

Tom was right – David had excelled himself, so much so that it was almost hard to believe he had picked it himself. The dress was exquisite and undoubtedly expensive; a realisation that sent a flicker of guilt racing down Katy's spine. It was the kind of dress she normally admired on other women but would never dare to wear for herself. But somehow, between the long-awaited occasion and the newly discovered comfort in her appearance, Katy felt not only ready to wear the dress but excited to do so. She carefully stepped in to the gown and pulled the straps over her shoulders. It was a little bit of a stretch to reach the zip at the back, but once she had got a proper grip it followed her hand willingly, bringing the material to a snug close.

Katy stepped back in to the corridor and lifted the mirror from its place on the floor. She then carried it into the lounge and rested it on the sofa angled up slightly, before taking a step back. The ball gown was phenomenal; a silvery sweep of silk and lace that seemed to shimmer like moonlight. Katy twirled around exactly as she had done as a child when trying on a new dress. As she moved the material seemed to change colour, with glacial blue shadows dancing across the surface like clouds. Around the waist and just below the neckline small golden snowflakes hung as if trapped in a lacy spider's web of pure snow white.

The wintery look was completed with soft blue eyeshadow and the slightest hint of platinum in her rich brown hair, which had been coiffed in to soft waves that tumbled gracefully down to her shoulders. Katy felt like she was looking at a movie star; a taller, more slender, more beautiful version of herself that she had never seen before. She knew it was only fleeting and that her hair would tangle, her make-up fade and the following day she would be back in jeans and a t-shirt – but for that moment, everything was perfect.

When the doorbell rang Katy fetched her purse and keys and placed them in a small silver clutch along with her phone. She grabbed a long black coat from the hall and placed it over her arm so as not to ruin the illusion of the outfit for David. Gingerly she walked down the stairway and opened the front door.

Katy felt the sudden escape of breath from her chest like a punch. Her own transformation was nothing compared to David's. Gone were the sports clothes and baggy hoodies and in their place was an immaculate black tuxedo with dark panel lapels. He had shaved, but not since the morning, so a fine dusting of black stubble lined his jaw and top lip, framing his piercing blue eyes and tight-lipped smile. His hair was styled in a chocolate brown wave of tussocked peaks that she wanted to tousle and fuss with her fingers. He had accented the tuxedo with a light periwinkle blue bow tie and matching pocket square. And, as promised, a cummerbund sash encircled his waist, bridging the gap between his crisp white shirt and the black trousers that clung invitingly to his toned thighs.

'David,' Katy said, as if she didn't quite believe it herself.

'Were you expecting someone else?'

'No, no – it's just you look fantastic.'

He laughed modestly and shuffled his feet slightly. 'Katy, there won't be a single person looking at me when we walk in.'

Katy blushed but she could see in David's eyes that he believed it and she wished she could hold on to that moment forever, him looking at her as if she was the most beautiful woman alive.

Chapter Twenty-Eight

The ball was taking place at a large hotel in the centre of the city. The whole building had been hired out, with many of the people from outlying towns booking rooms so that they could stay the night. Katy and David arrived to a champagne reception in a white marble lobby decorated with giant silver and purple baubles. In the corner of the room stood an enormous pine tree sparkling with star-shaped fairy lights and long ribbons of shiny tinsel and beads.

All around them were men in smart black tuxedos offset by the occasional suit in crisp granite grey or pinstripe charcoal. Ties, pocket handkerchiefs and in one or two cases a bold tartan kilt provided a splash of colour, but for the most part they were an orderly array of blacks, greys and silvers. The women however came dressed in colours as varied as the rainbow. From long flowing ball gowns like Katy's, to short cocktail dresses and slinky figure-hugging outfits, every colour was on show and a lot more besides. Katy was amazed to see that many of the women had braved the Welsh winter in every kind of strapless, backless and low cut dress imaginable.

'People have really gone all out haven't they?' Katy remarked.

'Yeh, who knew everyone could scrub up so well,' David said, sounding genuinely surprised. 'Woah,' he suddenly added. 'Let's go through here.'

'What was that about?' Katy asked as they shuffled through the corridor.

'Giles Thornborough. Possibly the most boring man you could ever meet. He's a dermatologist at the hospital. The man genuinely believes that skin conditions are a cornerstone of most people's conversations.'

'Oh I'm sure he's not that bad.'

'You can go back and chat to him if you want to learn all about contact dermatitis?'

Katy was thinking up a retort when they stepped in to the main ballroom and suddenly whatever joke she was about to make disappeared completely from her mind. The room was dressed in thick black drape curtains decorated with bold silver snowflakes. A fine net of bright white LEDs lit the ceiling, so it felt as if you were walking out in to the night under a carpet of stars.

Spinning out like satellites from every gleaming white table were eight beautiful white linen-covered chairs, each decorated with a black bow. Silver inked name cards announced each guest's seat and every place setting was framed by a crystal champagne glass and shiny cutlery. In the middle of every table was a collection of candles. They were the large church-style ones, arranged in circles of varying sizes so they looked a little like miniature trees sporting tiny leaves of fire.

'Oh David, it's beautiful.'

Katy took David's hand and kissed him softly on the cheek.

'It is pretty amazing,' he agreed. 'What would you like to do? I think there are photographers in the hall – we could go get our picture taken, or they have some kind of casino somewhere and some wandering magicians.'

'Everything.' Katy beamed.

'Okay – everything it is.' David said. 'But first, let's get another drink.'

Katy and David moved from room to room in their own private world of wonder. They pulled silly faces as they posed for photos, bet against one another on blackjack and drunk copious glasses of sparkling wine. David introduced Katy to his new colleagues and they caught up with old friends they hadn't seen since their return. At times it felt not only as if they hadn't split up, but as if they had never drifted apart at all. The evening was a reminder of how they could be at their best; David was relaxed and in good humour, whilst Katy practically glowed in the warmth of his attention. She moved from one group of David's friends to another, seamlessly bringing outliers in to the conversation and helping everyone feel at ease.

When, after dinner, David asked Katy to dance, she didn't hesitate and immediately followed him on to the shiny wooden floor. There they stayed for the rest of the night, dancing in carefree abandon and totally absorbed in the smiles on one another's faces. Slowly the number of groups dancing around them dwindled away and as the lights dipped and only couples were left on the dance floor David pulled Katy towards him, resting his hand gently upon her hip. He kissed her with lips sweet with wine and fuzzy with stubble. Katy giggled as she kissed him back and felt her body relaxing in to his, her chest sinking in to the familiar nook of his torso and her arms cradling his back. They slow-danced until the music stopped and the hotel staff started to hover awkwardly at the edge of the dance floor, keen to start clearing tables and make their way home.

Taking their cue to leave David went and fetched Katy's coat from the cloakroom and gently enveloped her arms in its warm sleeves. She sighed and then when she saw David's face dip in anxiety she stood on tiptoes to kiss his warm lips.

'I just didn't want the evening to end, it's been magical,' she said,

'It doesn't have to end yet.' David replied, speaking each word breathlessly between kisses.

In the hotel lobby a slightly dishevelled group of revellers stood loudly making plans for taxi shares and nightclub venues. Outside yet more people from the ball lingered over seasonal goodbyes, wishing one another Merry Christmases and Happy New Year's. David waved to a few of them and then seeing that there was no queue they quickly jumped in to a taxi. When the driver asked them where they wanted to go neither of them answered immediately and instead gave each other a slightly awkward look until Katy gave her address and the car drove off in to the night.

David held Katy's hand the whole way home in the taxi and didn't let go until they pulled up outside her flat and he started fumbling for money in his wallet.

'Here,' Katy said, as she held out a slightly crumpled ten-pound note and passed it through the small gap in the window between the cabin and the front seat. 'Keep the change.'

In her efforts to open the front door as quietly as possible, Katy ended up dropping her keys, and the two of them had to search through the flowerbed to find them. They eventually found them tucked against the underside of an open takeaway box overflowing with chips. 'Downstairs neighbour,' Katy explained. 'It's the same every Friday and Saturday night – takeaway never makes it past the front garden.'

They walked up to the top floor stifling giggles and trying to tread as softly as the creaking wooden floorboards allowed until they were safely in Katy's flat. There they practically collapsed in fits of laughter, stumbling in to the lounge as their fingers competed to remove one another's coats.

Kisses merged so that it was no longer possible to tell where one ended and another began until their lips were locked in an unbroken struggle of exploration. Suddenly Katy felt David's arms slope down her back and scoop along the line of her hips until he had one hand under each thigh and he was lifting her in to the air and on to his chest. She held on tightly as the thick muscles in his arm tensed and coiled under her body. Then breathlessly she heard David whisper quietly in her ear; 'I don't have to stay…unless-'

And before he could finish she was interrupting him, telling him to stay and showering his taut neck with kisses. David carried her in to the bedroom and gently laid her on the bed before pouncing more energetically down beside her and rolling in to her open arms.

'Mind the dress,' she whimpered half-heartedly, as his tongue raced down her chest and towards the embroidered snowflakes that sat at her breast. Without a word he skilfully lifted her left shoulder from the duvet and slid a long-fingered hand around her back to the zip. Once undone the dress fell away with ease, revealing the lacy bra Katy had bought for the occasion.

'Wow,' David said, gently tugging down the rest of the dress to reveal the matching knickers. With almost visible effort he broke his gaze long enough to place the dress safely on a nearby chair and then returned to her body, peppering her navel with soft stubbly kisses that traced a line ever downwards.

'David,' Katy interrupted softly.

'Yeh,' he answered distractedly, his voice muffled by her abdomen.

'We're a bit unevenly dressed.'

David's head bobbed upwards and Katy watched as the realisation slowly dawned on him that whilst she was in her underwear he was still fully dressed, right down to the bowtie, cufflinks and ridiculous cummerbund.

'Oh, yeh – sorry,' he said with embarrassment. 'I kind of got a bit carried away.'

It was a long time since he had been so lost in her, and she was flattered by the ferocity of his desire. 'It's okay,' she added, as she reached up to loosen the tie at his neck. 'I liked it.'

David hurriedly tossed his jacket to the floor at the same time as Katy carefully placed his bow tie on the bedside table. Seeing how the other acted they both laughed and two sets of hands reached furtively for the top button on his shirt. The buttons parted to reveal a firm chest with a short fuzzy down of hair tracing a line between his recently acquired abs.

'Wow,' Katy said, echoing David's earlier enthusiasm.

David removed his shirt to reveal two dark circular nipples standing firm and erect from the muscular plates of his pectorals. The cummerbund was cast aside to reveal the taut indent of his belly button and the sloping top of a v-shaped ridge that led a trail beneath the waistband of his underwear on either side. He removed his belt and wriggled free from his trousers until only his boxer shorts remained. They were a crisp tight black pair that hugged his form tightly and drew Katy's eyes to the growing bulge.

A moment later and David's hands were at her breasts and his lips at her neck. She reached out and her fingers pulled at his boxer shorts, lowering them over the firm mound of his buttocks and down his long muscular legs. Katy breathed a deep contented sigh as she inhaled the familiar scent of him and felt her body meld ecstatically with his.

Chapter Twenty-Nine

In the warm haze of morning, somewhere between sleeping and waking, Katy arched her body in to a long luxurious stretch that sent a ripple of contentment from her toes right up to her slightly fuzzy head. It was only when her back met the hot firm resistance of another body that she remembered what had happened. She rolled over gently and opened one eye to see the softly slumbering form of David lying next to her. She felt the soft breeze of his breath tickle at her nose and listened happily to the familiar low rumble of sleep from his chest.

Katy unfurled an arm and brought it to rest in the muscular crook of David's waist, her fingers straying on to the firm rise at the base of his back. He murmured slightly but didn't wake, so Katy nuzzled in to the u-shaped hollow between his head and his shoulder and contentedly closed her eyes.

Katy woke a second time to find her neck tingling with stubbly kisses. In slumber their bodies had shifted so that Katy was lying spooned in David's embrace, their legs intertwined and his muscular chest pressed tight against her back. 'Morning,' he whispered a little sleepily.

'Hey,' Katy replied as a big grin spread across her face. 'Did you sleep well?'

'Yeh, you?'

'Very.'

Katy craned her head round and with eyes still closed she found David's lips with her own and melted in to his kiss. His body was warm like the glowing morning sun and she arched her legs so that the soles of her feet rested against his lower legs. David gave a sharp intake of breath at the coldness of her skin, but he didn't move or pull away and she felt the heat slowly transfer to her heels.

'This is nice,' David whispered, 'I mean it's all been fantastic, every minute – and last night was amazing, but this – it just feels –'

'Right,' Katy finished for him.

'Yes.'

They kissed again and when Katy's feet were finally warm she shuffled round to face David properly. In the lowlight of the room his glacial blue eyes stared back at her lovingly and Katy couldn't resist running her hand through the wave of his hair again.

'I like the stubble,' she said eventually, as if she had been giving the matter great thought.

'You do?'

'Yes, it makes you look kind of…rugged, I guess.'

'Well I suppose I better keep it then.'

'But don't get too bristly,' Katy added quickly.

'Yes ma'am.' David replied cheekily.

Katy laughed and kissed him again before he could tease her further.

'Mmm,' he murmured. 'Just hold that thought a moment if you can.'

David slid out from the bed and skipped through the cold air of the bedroom in the direction of the hallway. Katy giggled as his firm bum bounced past her, his body briefly illuminated by the light from the corridor. Luckily being on the top floor the flat wasn't overlooked and so Katy left the curtains in most of the rooms open at all times.

A few minutes later Katy heard the bathroom tap singing noisily. As the water bubbled through the old building it triggered a crank from the plumbing system that reverberated through the flat. The pipes were still complaining when David returned to the bedroom, a towel wrapped around his waist and a faint trace of self-consciousness beneath his smile. He clambered on to the bed, removing the towel and letting it fall to the floor as he slid under the duvet.

'Your hands are cold!' Katy squealed as his fingers landed on her hips.

'Sorry,' he said and promptly withdrew them and tucked them under his arms to warm them up.

'So what do you want to do today?' Katy asked, 'It's Sunday – we could go for breakfast then maybe go for a walk in the park?'

'You're not going anywhere for at least the next hour Winters,' David said firmly and then proceeded to pull the duvet up over their heads, his warmed hands returning enthusiastically to her body.

Chapter Thirty

Katy pottered around the kitchen frying bacon and mushrooms in a large pan whilst David showered. It had started raining heavily and so they decided to have breakfast in, rather than braving the downpour. She opened each of the cupboards in search of further food and soon added a pan of beans to the hob and four slices of bread to the toaster.

Once the toast appeared above the parapet Katy snatched it away, she shook her fingers at the heat and quickly tossed them on to two waiting plates. She then loaded each slice with butter and spooned on a generous heap of mushrooms, leaving the bacon in the pan to crisp up. David appeared just as she was spooning the last of the beans on to the plate and she presented the delicious offering to him with pride. He seemed a little hesitant in taking the plate and Katy couldn't work out why.

He was wearing her dressing gown, given that a tuxedo was a little formal for breakfast, so she wondered if he felt uncomfortable. After all it did look a little small on him; the fabric rode high on his legs and finished just below his bum, barely concealing his modesty.

'Damn,' she suddenly exclaimed. 'I've done it again haven't I? You don't eat meat anymore. It's just I'm so used to –'

'It's okay really, it looks fantastic,' he said kindly.

Katy leant over and grabbed the two rashers of bacon from his plate. They were a dark rusty brown and near rigid in their crispiness. She quickly dropped one piece of bacon on to her plate and bit the tip of the other one, holding it in her left hand as she carried her breakfast over to the table with the other.

'Problem sorted,' she said.

'Thanks,' he said, and as he sat beside her he gently rested his hand on hers and smiled warmly.

They ate in silence for a few minutes, both of them hungry after the ball and the activities of both the night before and that morning.

'God I don't know how you could give up bacon,' Katy said between mouthfuls. 'You know when I was in Australia they had this really odd bacon, it was really thick and like a foot long. It was the first thing I asked mum to make when she picked me up from the airport; a proper British bacon sandwich.'

'You went all round the world, experiencing all sorts of things, and you're complaining about the bacon?'

'Yep, and fish and chips – proper chip shop chips, you can't get them anywhere else.'

'You're unbelievable Winters, you really are.'

As David finished speaking he picked up something from the windowsill that was just out of Katy's eye-line. He lifted it over his plate and idly turned it over as he chewed his breakfast.

'What's this? Are you thinking of doing some evening classes?'

Katy felt a flicker of embarrassment as David eyed the college prospectus she had picked up the week before.

'Yes, well no – day classes I guess. I'm thinking about going back to college part-time.'

It was the first time Katy had told anyone. Not even her mum or Tom knew she was considering it. But she had been for a while now, and it wasn't one of those passing ideas that came in the night and disappeared in the light of a new morning. The snowballing conviction had been growing in her for months, starting even before she came home. But it had only really crystallised in to being once she began looking for work again.

'Wow, really? That's kind of a big step.'

'That's not exactly the reaction I was hoping for,' Katy said disappointedly.

'I'm just surprised. I mean you have – well had – a good job. I assumed you'd just pick that up again.'

'I know, and it's there if I need to come back to it. But I want to do something more creative. While I was away I was writing, quite often really, about places I visited mainly, but stories too. And you know I always wished I'd studied English at university. Well maybe it's not too late. I want to write about things that interest me, not just writing dull copy to get offices to buy a new printer.'

'But it's not like you'd be going back to work at the same place.'

'No, but the theory will be the same, I'll be trying to make something very ordinary and average sound exciting to make people part with their money. And if it's not office supplies it'll be phones, or furniture, or cars, or I don't know what. But I'm just not sure I want to do it anymore.'

'But haven't we been through all this already?'

'What do you mean?' Katy asked, growing a little irritated.

'Well isn't that what the last year was all about, getting that out of your system? I mean no one wants to go to work everyday and I'm sure it must be one hell of a come down after a year off. But that's just life isn't it?'

'So I should just hunker down and make the best of it?'

'Well I'd like to think it wouldn't be as bleak as all that,' David said softly, taking her hand again. 'Come on Katy, you know I want to be with you. I'm kind of hoping last night means you want to be with me too. A year or two in your old job and you'd probably be on maternity leave anyway. Then you can go back part-time without having to retrain, and on a lot more money.'

Katy felt her appetite instantly drop away and a little ball of frustration knotted in her stomach. It was exactly the kind of conversation she hated having with David – the type that made her feel as if all the decisions of her life were being made for her and she was nothing more than a passive bystander in it.

'Maternity?' Katy managed incredulously.

'Don't Katy, please, let's not spoil what's been an incredible time together. I'm just saying you should think it over, and think about what you'd be giving up. Not just the money, but the time also. You've had an amazing year and it's clearly worked for you – you've got your spark back and that's great to see. But as fantastic a year as you had, mine was pretty crap and I feel like I'm only just getting you back and there's so much I want us to do together. Like buy a house, have kids, and I know that stuff freaks you out and that's okay because I can handle the stresses. But we've lost enough time already. I want to be with you, I want to move on with our lives together and not always be waiting for them to start.'

Katy fell silent. She knew David would never understand, they had been over it too many times before for her to think otherwise. And maybe he was right; maybe it was her that didn't make sense. David was gorgeous and funny and intelligent. He had a good job and more importantly a good heart. He loved her unfalteringly and all he wanted was to build a future together. Why was she fighting that? Why did that make her feel so trapped? It was after all what every woman wanted supposedly. So why did it send her in to this knotted fury?

But she knew why.

It was because the choices were never hers. She wanted everything David wanted; a family, a nice house and a settled future. But she wanted to be allowed to come to them in her own time and not to have them laid out for her based on some schedule that she was the last to hear about.

'Let's not do this now David. Like you say we had a wonderful night.'

'Okay, but this kind of feels like it did the first time you walked out on me,' he replied sadly. 'And I really don't know how much more space someone can need Katy. I mean you put a whole world between us for goodness sake. And I waited for you – which before you say anything, I know you never asked me to do. But I did, even when it turned out you really were going to be away for a year. I waited because I want to be with you, but if you want to be with me too you've really got to start showing it soon.'

'What do you mean – *even* when it turned out I was going to be away for a year?'

'Oh come on Katy, nobody thought you were going to last the year, not your mum, nor Tom, nor any of our other friends. They all thought we'd be back together within a few months, so I waited it out. It was only after four months when it started to look like we were all wrong that I decided to move to London.'

'You were all talking about me behind my back? Expecting me to fail?'

'Bloody hell Katy – you always do this. You see the worst in everything. We were all worried about you, we wanted you back safe and back to normal.'

'With you?'

'Yes, okay – I wanted us to get back together, you know that.'

'And everyone else?'

'Yes, all right? Your mum called me every now and then. She was worried about me and she wanted to let me know you were okay. I bumped in to Tom and Simon now and then and at first we all thought it was just something you needed to do to get out of you system. But we were wrong. I can see that now.'

Katy couldn't believe what she was hearing. She was cross with David for waiting, and for assuming he knew better than her what she was feeling and what she needed. But she was furious with her mum and Tom, and all the others who had clearly spent the first few months of her trip waiting for her to come home with her tail between her legs.

'So you think this is just another fanciful idea?' Katy asked, picking the college prospectus up and slamming it down on the table.

'No. I'm quite sure you'd do this for a few years and then they'll be something else – some new venture to immerse yourself in and something else after that too. And you know what Katy? You're always saying that I never include you in planning for our future; well you might want to take a look at yourself. Because I'm perfectly clear that I want you in my future. You on the other hand don't seem to have factored me in at all.'

David pushed the half eaten plate of food away from him and walked back into the bedroom, leaving Katy sat at the table alone. She heard him moving swiftly around before reappearing in the shirt and trousers he had worn the night before. His jacket was slung over his shoulder and the bow tie and cummerbund hung from his hand, swinging wildly in the storm of his footsteps. She stood up, but he walked past her without stopping and he ignored her pleas to stay and talk.

A moment later she heard the front door slamming shut, sealing her in the cold emptiness of the apartment. It was heart-breaking how quickly things had soured and how soon their insecurities had poisoned the magic of the night before. And yet Katy knew there was something there; a rotten apple at the heart of much of their unhappiness.

She had come so close to saying something, but she had shied away from it at the last moment. She knew David loved her, and she loved him. She had never doubted either of those things. But from the moment they had met he had put her on a pedestal. At first she was flattered, but it had been going on so long, and she couldn't stand the height anymore. The weight of his expectation was breaking them both in two. She worried David loved the idea of her more than the reality.

David had always had a plan for his life, something Katy had never had. And when they met it soon became clear to both of them that David had never known love before. Suddenly the weight of all his hopes and dreams for the world transferred on to Katy, as rigid as steel and as unchanging as granite. Where most couples forged their futures together, theirs was written entirely by David in an effort to pin down some distant dream and make it concrete. And as much as Katy was a cornerstone of his future, she worried she was only there by chance and that had someone else come along first that same future would have belonged to them.

Chapter Thirty-One

David didn't call, or text, or even email, and neither did Katy. Three or four times she picked up her phone and contemplated sending an angry text to her mum, or Tom, or Simon. But she wasn't really annoyed with any of them. She had never expected to last the year, any more than they had thought she would. That travelling had suited her so well and turned out to be the best time she had ever had was as unexpected to Katy as it was to her friends and family, and she had no reason to bear them a grudge over that.

In truth Katy had never expected any of the big things that had happened in her life. She could never have predicted when at eighteen she took a boy to a club in freshers' week that he would turn out to be her best friend, or that she would fall in love with David and him in love with her. Just as she could never have anticipated that somewhere along the line she would fall out of love with him. And then there was travelling and all the many confusing things that had happened since, and the strange realisation that her former life was closed to her. There was no way she could just walk back in to her old job, or pick up her relationship with David just as it had been before, however much David hoped she could.

The real question was where she would go next. As difficult as everything was, Katy couldn't escape the feeling that new paths awaited her. Maybe those paths would lead her to a different career, maybe a new love like Rhodri, or maybe somehow she would find her way back to David. Whatever path she took she knew she would have to make that decision soon. There was too much at stake and too many people waiting on her to delay. But the decision had to be hers and hers alone.

When the phone finally rang it was Tom. His voice was broken and cracked and Katy could tell he had been crying. Holding the phone in the crook of her neck she hurriedly dressed as she listened and her heart slowly sank towards her stomach. She swapped her pyjama bottoms for jeans and hurried out in to the corridor, still wearing her old sweater that never normally left the apartment.

Once outside Katy looked around for a taxi, but there were none in sight and she didn't want to hang up on Tom. It was too late for a regular bus service; well past 10pm on a Sunday evening, and so Katy started to run in the direction of the city centre. Before she had reached the end of her street a fire engine sped by, sirens screaming and lights flashing. Katy quickened her pace, turning the corner on to the main road just as a police car joined the chase.

'I'll be there as soon as I can Tom,' Katy panted.

It was a cold night and Katy could feel the freezing air clawing at her lungs as she ran. Every hurried footstep threw up large puddles of muddy water that spattered her trousers and caked her shoes. Twice she was splashed by cars straying too close to the pavement as they careered through rain-filled potholes at speed.

Katy came to the end of the street and headed towards the castle and it was there that she first saw the plume of grey smoke billowing in to the sky. Another street and the sky had taken on a reddish orange tinge, which soon became a glow. People were stopping and staring and others were already beginning to talk about the blaze, sharing the news with anyone that would listen.

Katy got as far as St David's Hall before the way forward was blocked by a thick line of police tape and a host of uniformed officers. But it was close enough. From there she could feel the heat of the fire and watch as the furious tongues of orange and yellow flame tore through the stage that Owen and Tom had been working on for weeks. Katy heard a voice and it seemed to echo and it took her a while to realise that Tom was not only on the phone but also standing only a few feet away. She turned round to see Owen and Tom standing together, both clearly upset. She put the phone down and ran towards them, flinging her arms around the two men and hugging them fiercely.

'I'm sorry,' she said, 'I'm so sorry.'

It was gone midnight by the time the blaze was finally extinguished and Owen was allowed close enough to inspect the damage. His face when he returned confirmed what Katy and Tom already feared – there was nothing left. The wooden stage and surrounds were gone and all of Tom's artwork had been destroyed. It would take a few days for the fire service's report to come back but Katy could already imagine what it would say – the fire was probably started by drunks on a night out, too far-gone to think about what they were doing.

'How am I going to tell the kids?' Owen asked quietly, as much to himself as to Katy or Tom.

Tom hugged him and promised they would think of something, but Katy could hear the doubt in his voice. It was the early hours of Monday morning and the nativity was on Wednesday afternoon. There was no way they would be able to rebuild the stage in time, even if the school could somehow find the money for the materials.

Dejected, the three of them returned to Tom's one bedroom flat where Katy made them all hot mugs of tea to nurse their limbs back to warmth. She watched Tom with deep affection as he put aside his own sadness at the loss of his work and focused his energy on consoling Owen. She only wished there was something she could do, a way to be more helpful than dishing out cups of tea and sympathy.

Owen eventually went to bed a little before 2am. Of the three of them he was the only one who would have to be up for work in the morning, though Katy imagined he was unlikely to sleep much that night.

'Will you stay?' Tom asked. 'It's late to be heading home. I have blankets and a spare pillow.'

'Of course,' Katy replied.

'I'm sorry, with everything that's happened I never asked how last night went?'

'Oh Tom, don't be silly. That doesn't matter now. What matters is you and Owen.'

'I think he'll be okay; it's just the kids he'll be worrying about. It will devastate him having to tell them the nativity's not going to go ahead.'

'Could they do it at the school instead?'

'There's no room, the hall's being refurbished and none of the classrooms are big enough. It's one of the reasons he decided on the outdoor stage in the first place.'

'Is there somewhere else then?' Katy asked

'A week before Christmas? Everywhere will be booked up.'

They were both silent for a moment before Katy said; 'And how are you Tom?'

'What do you mean?'

'I know you're worried about Owen, but you worked on that stage for weeks. It's okay to be upset.'

'I need to stay strong for him, Katy.'

'Then be strong tomorrow. But for now you don't have to be. Let me be the strong one tonight.'

Katy pulled Tom towards her and wrapped her arms around him tightly until she felt his body gently relax in to a sob.

It felt like Katy had only been asleep for five minutes when Tom gently woke her. He was wearing a crumpled plain t-shirt and giant woven boxer shorts that she assumed belonged to Owen.

'What time is it?' Katy asked.

'Half past five. I'm sorry – I know it's early.'

Katy had to physically stop herself from groaning. It hadn't been five minutes, but it hadn't been a lot more either. Tom had finally gone to bed about 3am and so Katy had been asleep for less than three hours.

'Can we do it?'

'What?' Katy asked sleepily.

'Christmas Club – if we all worked together do you think we could do it?' Tom asked excitedly.

'Do what?' Katy asked, still struggling to understand what was being said.

'Rebuild the stage. I know it's a huge task. But look at what we achieved on the wreaths, I never thought we'd be able to do them and we did.'

Katy prised herself up by her elbows and looked at Tom through bleary eyes. 'Rebuild it?' she asked. 'But how, I mean, where would we even start?'

'I don't know, but I've been lying awake since we went to bed trying to think of a way and it's the only thing I think might stand a chance. Owen will be up in an hour, and I can't let him go to school like this; having to tell the kids it's cancelled.'

Katy didn't know what to say. She wasn't sure if Rhodri or Cerys would even speak to her after what had happened at the winter carnival, let alone help them out. But when Katy looked at the desperation in Tom's face she knew that didn't matter. He was right – there was a chance, and as slim as it was she would do everything she could to make it happen, no matter how humiliating it was, or how many people might hate her. What mattered were Tom and Owen and the kids in his class.

'We'll give it our best shot,' Katy said as enthusiastically as she could.

Tom practically leapt on Katy and though he whispered so as not to wake Owen, there was no doubting his gratitude or relief. When he had finally calmed down sufficiently Katy sent him back to bed so he could tell Owen the good news as soon as he woke.

Katy looked at the clock, it was 6am and she wondered if there was any chance she would be able to get back to sleep. Her mind started to race as she worked through what she would say to Rhodri and to Cerys. As much as she was dreading both conversations she had a feeling that Cerys would be the harder of the two to win over, and for that reason she knew she had to speak to her first. Only then, if Cerys agreed, would she ask for Rhodri's help.

Chapter Thirty-Two

At 7:15am Katy heard the chirp of an alarm clock from the room next door and she resigned herself to the fact that she wasn't going to get any more sleep. Not only that, but if they were going to succeed she wasn't going to be getting much rest at all until after Wednesday. She folded Tom's blankets away and quietly padded to the bathroom where she splashed copious amounts of cold water on her face in an effort to try and make herself feel a little more human.

From the bedroom Katy could hear the rapid exchange of voices. Despite everyone's tiredness there was an unmistakeable excitement to Tom's tone that seemed to be steadily transferring to Owen. Five minutes later the two of them emerged, both looking exhausted and sporting hooded eyes and thickly stubbled chins. But there was an undeniable undercurrent of optimism that hadn't been there the night before.

'Do you really think it's possible?' Owen asked hopefully.

'We'll try, but yes I think there's a chance,' Katy said as positively as she could, although secretly she was becoming more and more anxious.

'Thank you,' Owen roared as he scooped Katy up in to a bear hug.

Whilst she appreciated Owen's gratitude, Katy wasn't quite sure where to look or place her hands. There was quite a lot of Owen to be squeezed in to a tiny night vest and incredibly short boxer shorts.

'Of course Owen,' Katy replied, gently extricating herself from the muscular 6ft 2 man-mountain. 'But can we just rebuild the stage? I mean will they let us?'

'Owen's going to get some help covering his class this morning and we're going to go down to City Hall and I will literally beg them if I have to,' Tom chipped in.

When Tom wanted something he was a pretty formidable force to be reckoned with and Katy felt sorry for whoever happened to be working the front desk that morning.

'I guess I'll round up the rest of the club then.'

'I've been thinking about that, I can talk to Cerys and Rhodri if you like?' Tom offered. 'Sorry, I got a bit carried away last night and wasn't really thinking about it being –'

'Awkward?' Katy cut in. 'It's fine Tom, really. It'll be good to clear the air and probably if I didn't face them now I never would, and that would be a shame.'

'Okay, well I'll phone Sophia and Jenny before we go to City Hall.'

'Thanks,' Katy said.

'We're really going to do this?' Owen said with a deep intake of breath.

'Course we are,' Tom said and gave him a light kiss on the cheek.

'Right, then we better get scrubbed up,' Owen said authoritatively.

While the boys left to get showered and changed Katy opened up Tom's fridge to see what was available. It was immediately clear that Tom didn't spend a lot of time at his place anymore and that when him and Owen were there presumably they were living on takeaways. In the vegetable compartment Katy found the remains of a block of cheese that fortunately wasn't any mouldier than originally intended. In the cupboard over the sink she found three bread bags, each with only the ends of the loaves left. Katy had to be slightly creative in removing the furring greened edges on a couple of the slices, but all in all they were just about passable. She cut the cheese thickly and placed it in between each pair of slices and then lightly buttered the outsides. Katy then transferred the sandwiches to a frying pan and pressed down on each firmly so that the bread gently fried and the cheese melted and oozed over the crusts. It wasn't going to be the most gourmet breakfast ever, but after the night they had all had a grilled cheese sandwich would be most welcome.

When Owen and Tom finally emerged from the bathroom Katy couldn't help but audibly inhale in surprise. Owen was clean-shaven and his strong jawline was clearly visible for the first time since she had met him. He was wearing a dark tweed jacket and tie with formal trousers. But the bigger shock was Tom. His normally over-styled hair had been arranged in to a conservative side parting and instead of contacts he was wearing thick rimmed black spectacles and a light blue suit.

'Wow. Tom I didn't know you even owned a suit, you both look incredible!'

'What do you think – would you say no to these faces?' Tom asked through a wide mouthed-grin.

'Well let's just hope you need to speak to a woman or a gay man,' Katy said smiling as she admired the transformation.

'Here's hoping,' Owen replied a little more seriously.

The three of them ate their breakfast hungrily, with Tom interrupting every few moments with some new plan or idea to redo the stage. Though Katy admired his enthusiasm she was more worried about how they were going to get a basic frame together, let alone all the frills and trimmings that Tom seemed to be considering.

He finally came to a pause as he negotiated a particularly gooey strand of cheese that spilled out of the sandwich and clung to his lip. Katy took the opportunity to look at Owen and saw him smiling at Tom. It was a look of pure love flavoured with the smallest hint of awe and Katy recognised it instantly. Tom had finally found someone who saw him just the way she did and she couldn't have been happier for him. And in that moment she realised that whatever happened that day, or the next; whether they pulled off some kind of miracle with the stage, or whether they failed miserably, Tom would always have Owen to stand by him and love him as fiercely as she always had. So when they finished eating and were saying their goodbyes and wishing one another luck Katy gave Owen an enormous hug and silently thanked him for being the man her friend had waited so long to find and so richly deserved.

Chapter Thirty-Three

Once back at her flat Katy quickly showered and dressed, all the time avoiding sitting on the bed for fear that the moment her body touched the soft downy duvet she would be powerless to ward off her overwhelming desire to sleep. Putting on socks became an almost Herculean struggle but once she had conquered that task she felt a little more ready to tackle the rest of the day. She phoned a taxi and then tried to untangle her hair and make it look half reasonable. For a moment she toyed with the idea of using the blue eye shadow she had worn for the ball in an attempt to hide the small suitcases that had taken up residence beneath her eyes but she soon decided against it. For one she wasn't sure she had the energy or physical dexterity to draw on smooth lines, but there was another reason too – it was going to be a long, hard day and perhaps a little look of desperation might help the cause.

The taxi turned out to be a sensible decision as Katy quickly came to in front of Cerys' driveway with a sympathetic looking taxi driver gently nudging her awake. If she had taken the bus there was every chance she would have woken to find herself in some remote depot miles from where she needed to be. She thanked the driver and paid him his fare before turning her attention to the small whitewash cottage ahead of her.

The noisy crunch of gravel as Katy made her way towards the house was soon eclipsed by a chorus of barking from inside. There was no chance of ever making a discreet arrival at Cerys' and the front door was open before Katy had even had a chance to knock. The dogs greeted her enthusiastically and Katy only hoped that their owner would be as pleased to see her.

'Katy,' Cerys said with some surprise.

Katy smiled, unsure whether to extend a hug or a handshake. In the end she simply stood awkwardly rooted to the spot with her hands in her coat pockets until Cerys beckoned her inside.

'Sorry, I wasn't sure whether I should have called or…'

'Tea?' Cerys offered abruptly.

'Um, yes, thank you.'

Katy took a seat as Cerys filled a small pan with water and placed it on the stove top. She then fetched two mugs and warmed them under the hot tap before dropping a tea bag in each.

'Milk?'

'Please.'

Katy watched as Cerys awkwardly transferred the boiling liquid from the pan in to each mug, holding the saucepan handle with both hands. Katy wondered if she should offer to help but didn't want to appear rude.

'Thank you,' Katy said, as a steaming mug of tea was pushed towards her, leaving a small smear on the large wooden table.

'I wasn't sure I'd see you again, after your ran off at the winter festival. I'm glad you've come over,' Cerys said.

'I really am sorry for what happened with Rhodri, and for David showing up like that unexpectedly…and the fight and well all of it really. I never meant to hurt him. I never meant for anyone to get hurt. But it feels like all that I've done since coming home is to make things worse for everyone. To be honest I didn't know if you'd want to see me again.'

'Why ever not?' Cerys asked.

'Because of what happened to Rhodri – he's like a son to you.'

'Yes,' Cerys sighed sadly. 'But he's not my son. He's his own man and he…well I – I worry maybe I was a little overbearing. That maybe I got in the way of something between the two of you by keeping you apart and telling you about Claire.'

'No, not at all, I was trying just as hard to stay away, I just wasn't very good at it,' Katy said.

'Are you with the doctor now?'

Katy was caught off guard by the sudden change of tact and took a sip of her tea whilst she considered her response. It was a question she knew she needed to answer. Not just for Cerys but also for her, but there had been little time to think with the fire.

'No,' Katy said eventually. 'We're not together, but he's a good man. I know it might not seem like that to you or Rhodri, but he is. And it's been hard on him. We were together for four years. For him, it's like he's been in limbo this past year. Whereas for me, everything changed when I went away, and it's only since coming back that things have been so confusing.'

'Then there's still a chance for Rhodri? If you and David aren't together?'

The sudden U-turn shocked Katy. She had come to the cottage expecting at best an argument, and at worst to be thrown out without the chance to even explain herself.

'I was wrong,' Cerys admitted, 'I knew from the first time we met that he liked you. He may be thirty-five but he's just the same as when he was ten, moping around like a lovesick puppy. And after what happened with Claire I wanted to protect him from that, especially with you being...*conflicted*. But either way he's fallen for you and the fact that you're here means that your mind's not made up yet.'

'Well actually,' Katy said quickly, 'there was another reason for my visit. Not that I didn't want to come and see you both and say sorry.'

The disappointment in Cerys' face was obvious and Katy wasn't sure how much more of it all she could handle. As pleased as she was that Cerys was suddenly on her side she could no longer pretend that it was just David's happiness in her hands. Whatever happened at least one of them was going to be upset as a result.

'You'll still go and see him though won't you?' Cerys asked hopefully. 'I'm not sure he'd forgive me if he knew you were here and I didn't convince you to go next door.'

'Of course,' Katy promised.

'Excellent!'

Cerys' reply was much brighter and closer to her usual booming volume in tone. 'So why are you here then?'

'It's Tom, well Tom and Owen really.'

'Owen?' Cerys interjected. 'The big chap, looks like a rugby player?'

'Yes. Tom's boyfriend,' Katy said, hoping she wouldn't have to go over the whole explanation again. 'He's a teacher and Owen's class were planning a big nativity show this Wednesday. They built a big outdoor stage and Tom decorated it and everything looked perfect. But then last night it caught fire: drunks, or kids, or something. And it's all gone, and it's probably too late or just plain impossible, but we wondered if there was any way we could do something – the Christmas Club I mean, to make sure the show goes ahead.'

Cerys' face cracked in to such an enormous smile that Katy almost wondered if she had misheard. Between arson and devastated school children Katy couldn't see much cause for celebration. Cerys however had taken the news like a tonic and was on her feet and practically buzzing with energy.

'Of course we can do something, especially for Tom! Lovely boy. Of course Rhodri will help as well and I'm sure the girls will too and we'll have Owen's show back on in no time. So, what do you need me to do?'

Katy suddenly froze. She had been so focussed on the idea of trying to get Cerys and Rhodri on board that she hadn't given any thought to what she actually wanted them to do.

'Um, well we need a new stage I guess. Something big enough for the kids to stand on safely and it needs to be weatherproof and well I guess Tom can probably decorate it, but I can't think what it would be or what we could use. It took them weeks to build the first one out of wood and there's no time for that.'

Katy fell in to a despondent silence. It was like the first meeting of Christmas Club all over again – Cerys looking at her expectantly and Katy unable to come up with anything at all to say.

'Hay bales!' Cerys suddenly boomed, slamming the table with a closed fist and causing Katy to jump.

'I'm sorry?' Katy asked, wondering if it was a suggestion or simply a rural take on a Eureka moment.

'Hay bales,' Cerys said, as if it was perfectly obvious. 'We've used them for plenty of summer plays and concerts in the village. Good as a stage, good as a seat. You can arrange them anyway you like, and if you stack them right they're safe as houses.'

Katy gave the idea some thought. There was a chance it might just work.

'And you know who has plenty of hay bales?' Cerys asked coyly.

Katy smiled knowingly. 'Rhodri?'

'Exactly,' Cerys beamed, 'I guess you'll have to go over to the farm after all.'

'I was always going to go you know.'

'Well now you've got a good reason. Now run along and don't waste too much time on apologies. The boy'll just be glad to see you and he won't thank you for feeling sorry for yourself and raking over things that have been and gone. You'll find him in the top field, and by the time you're back I'll see what else I can pull together.'

Katy thanked Cerys profusely, even as she was being shooed impatiently out the door. Once again Cerys had come to the rescue and for the first time since Tom had woken Katy with the idea, she began to feel like they might actually have a chance.

Katy clambered over the wooden gate that joined the two properties, with Cerys watching on from the doorway. She hopped down on the other side in to a thick muddy puddle and turned to face the hill ahead of her. There was still a thin stubble of crop where the field had been harvested and Katy had to pick her way between the shorn off stalks with care. Although she didn't look back she could imagine Cerys still staring at her with impatient eyes, willing her to speed up.

As she moved from one rather muddy field in to another it suddenly occurred to Katy that she had no idea where the 'top' field was, or just how many fields there were to the farm. She hoped she wouldn't end up straying on to someone else's land and find herself staring down the barrel of some disgruntled farmer's gun, or having to flee from herds of cows or barking sheepdogs. After a good ten minutes of walking steadily uphill Katy turned puffing to admire the view. Cerys' cottage lay in the vale to her right and down to the left she could clearly see the outline of Rhodri's farmhouse; a sprawling rectangle of grey stone and slate in a garden of green. Beyond this was the village; a broad sweep of houses clustered like a scatter of ill-sewn seeds springing up from the landscape. And then there was nothing but rolling green hills and pockets of woodland until far away in the distance she could make out the town of Bridgend to the right and to the left the dense coil of Cardiff springing out in to the shimmering sea. It was beautiful and it was exactly the kind of view she had sought out when travelling, without realising that there were such wonders on her doorstep, a few miles from home.

Katy took out her phone to take a photo and casually glanced at the screen. There were no messages. She had hoped to have heard from Tom and was keen to tell him Cerys' idea, but it would have to wait. Beautiful views, crisp clean air and miles of countryside came at a price, and in this case that price was mobile phone reception.

After taking one last look across the valley Katy carried on up the hill. The slope was steep and seemed to go on forever. Just as she was beginning to think she had taken a wrong turn somewhere she saw a movement on the brow of the hill to her right. She changed her route and started to tack across the field diagonally, heading towards the figure on the horizon. As she got closer the features crystallised in to the familiar bulk of Rhodri, who – despite the cold, was wearing only a thin white t-shirt and muddied blue jeans.

In his left hand he held a long handled sledgehammer, which he held halfway up the shaft, swinging it periodically to drive a large wooden fence post in to the ground. In the cold air the sloping rises of his muscled arms glowed a healthy lobster-pink from exertion.

When she was close enough to be heard Katy called out to alert Rhodri to her presence. The last thing she wanted was to take him by surprise and for either of them to end up on the receiving end of the hammer by mistake. At the sound of her voice he stopped what he was doing and turned to face down the hill.

'Katy,' he said, sounding surprised.

'Cerys said I'd find you up here.'

'She said to come up?'

'Yes,' Katy said, hoping that she could help to close any distance that had opened between them.

'Well Winters, you're a sight for sore eyes,' he said, putting down the hammer and walking towards her.

'You must be freezing out here in only a t-shirt.'

'Only when you stop – it keeps me busy and outta mischief that way.'

He was standing only a few feet away from Katy; close enough for her to see the dark purple rim of a bruise under his eye and to see the warm fug of air from his breath.

'I'm sorry about what happened the other night,' she started, but before she could go on Rhodri had raised a hand in protest.

'You think I care about that? I'm just happy to see you, I wanted to call but I thought I should give you some space, Time to figure things out.'

Up close he was almost unbearably attractive, his dark eyes as richly textured as the soil he worked in. His face was lightly freckled from the sun and his skin gently furrowed, shallow enough that it didn't age him but enough to accentuate the strong features of his face.

'Cerys thought you might be able to help with something.'

'Of course,' Rhodri said quickly.

'You don't even know what it is yet.' Katy chided.

'I don't care, whatever it is I'll do it. Like I say – I'm just glad you're here and I'd do anything to help you, you know that.'

'Well it's more for Tom really...and Owen.'

'But it's not Tom here asking though is it? So I'm still chalking this one up as a favour for you Winters.'

Katy smiled, unwilling to argue the point. She was just happy to be in Rhodri's company once again and that the awfulness of the previous week had been forgotten.

As they walked down the hill in the direction of the farmhouse they chatted easily. There was a comforting tone to Rhodri's voice that warmed Katy through to her toes, despite the biting wind. And though he was sorry to hear what had happened to the stage and genuinely sympathetic to Owen and Tom's plight, Rhodri struggled to hide his pleasure at seeing her again.

When they reached the barn Rhodri opened the door with a flourish and Katy was greeted by the sight of countless hay bales, piled high in golden towers and bound with thick blue twine.

'How's that then?' he asked proudly.

'My God Rhodri. There's enough here to build ten stages. And you're sure we can borrow it?'

'Course you can. Cows aren't going to know.'

Katy felt a flicker of excitement. The chances of them actually pulling it off had just grown considerably.

'Don't suppose you fancy testing them out? See if they're up for the job?' Rhodri said, playfully jumping on the nearest bale and stretching himself out before gently patting the hay beside his hips.

Katy was suddenly grateful for the shadowed gloom cast by the enormous metal barn door and hoped it was enough to hide the flush of red heat to her cheeks.

Rhodri's t-shirt had ridden up to reveal a taut ripple of muscle and a wiry fuzz of dark hair that crept up from the low ridge of his jeans. Like the first time she had met him, she was aware how well clothes clung to him; the fabric of his jeans bulged and strained in all the right places and sent a flicker of excitement racing through her.

'I'm not much of an actress, even for a hay stage,' she said, deliberately leading them away from the real meaning behind his offer.

'Well, you can't blame a guy for trying.'

Katy heard Rhodri's mood dip in his voice. She stepped in to the barn and sat on the bale adjacent to the one on which Rhodri lay.

'You know things would have been different don't you? If I'd just come back and David wasn't around and everything was more straightforward, then-.'

'Yeh. But they're not straightforward are they?' Rhodri said, interrupting her.

'No, they're not.' Katie said sadly.

'Are you and him…?'

'No. No we're not, but I need to speak to him, there just hasn't been a good time with the fire and everything. I saw him at the weekend and things got, well, more complicated.'

'You've got a knack for that haven't you?' Rhodri said, not unkindly.

'It seems I do.'

'You know about my wife,' he said thoughtfully. 'The funny thing is, when she left me I couldn't understand how either of them could do it. And as angry as I was with her it's him that really got me. We were mates and he took everything from me and that's what I couldn't get my head round – how someone could do that to another bloke, much less a mate. But now I think I understand. David – I know he must be an all right guy. He has to be for you to like him this much, and I know he's a doctor an' all. He must be a good man is what I'm saying. And I know you were together long before I came around and that you've got unfinished business. But now I'm the other man in all this, and even after everything I went through I finally get it. And if it was only David I had to worry about I wouldn't give him a second thought. I want to be with you Katy and the fact that David's on the scene – it's not enough to keep me away: to make me not want to see you. The only reason I've kept my distance this past week is because of you, because you're not like Claire. And if you and I got together and you felt you hadn't been fair on David I know it would gnaw away at you. You're a good person Katy – too bloody good if you ask me. And I won't make you question that. But if you want to give this a go I'm here and I will do my best to make you happy. Because no one can make me smile like you, or make me excited about holly wreaths or driving to and from Cardiff just to spend time with you. And I don't doubt you're completely crazy at times, but I'm pretty crazy about you. And that's just how it is, and I'm not telling you to make you feel guilty, I'm telling you because you need to know how I feel.'

Suddenly Rhodri looked incredibly awkward and embarrassed. It was the most he had ever said in front of her and Katy knew how hard it would have been for him.

'I feel the same,' Katy said eventually, 'In all the time we've been together I've never felt like I had to be someone else, someone other than me. It's just so…'

'Easy? Yeh, it is. And it was never like this with Claire, in fact I don't think it's ever been so easy to spend time with anyone before.'

'I was going to say different.'

'Different in a good way?'

'Yes, a very good way.'

This time it was Katy's turn to be embarrassed. They sat in silence for a few minutes and she wished she could reach out to him in the way she wanted to. But in that moment it was enough just to be close to him, and to share in the open admission of feelings that they had both been harbouring for days.

Chapter Thirty-Four

Like all magic the spell of the barn was easily broken and the moment they stepped outside reality flooded back in. In the short walk back to Cerys' cottage Katy felt the closeness they had uncovered retreat back in to the shadows and take the form of unspoken desires once more.

The door to the cottage was open and Katy followed Rhodri through the doorway, unconsciously echoing his stoop as he ducked to avoid the low beam, even though she was nowhere near tall enough for it to be a problem. Cerys wasn't in the kitchen and so they passed through to the living room in pursuit of a sound that whilst Katy couldn't place, was definitely familiar. It was only when Katy saw the mounds of differently coloured material that she recognised the noise as the whirr of a sewing machine.

'What on earth is this Cerys?' Rhodri asked sounding bemused.

'Curtains. Every theatre stage has to have curtains. And then there's a canopy to go over the top to keep out the rain.'

Katy took a step forward to admire the work. It was incredible – Cerys had already sewn metres of old bed sheets, duvets and other scraps of material in to an enormous patchwork quilt.

'Sometimes being a hoarder pays off,' Cerys added a little guiltily.

'They're amazing!' Katy said and rushed over to give Cerys a hug as she thanked her.

'And how did you two get on?'

'Good,' said Rhodri sounding pleased.

'Yes there's plenty of hay. I just wonder how we're going to get it all there.'

'Tractor of course. I'll get the lads to give me a hand and we'll get it all on to the trailer in the morning.'

'But you can't just drive a tractor full of hay in to the middle of Cardiff!' Katy exclaimed, much to the amusement of Cerys and Rhodri.

'You bet I can and I'd like to see any of those city boys try and stop me. We've got a show to put on!'

It was impossible not to get caught up in Rhodri and Cerys' enthusiasm and Katy couldn't wait to tell Tom what they'd achieved. She only hoped that they wouldn't be causing Owen too much of a headache in getting permission to unload and set up their hay bale stage.

'Is there anywhere I can get a mobile signal?' Katy asked.

'There's a spot up the end of the lane, near the layby. There shouldn't be much traffic at this time of day. Or you could go back over the gate and you can usually pick it up all along the far side of the farm near the treeline.'

Katy opted for the lane, as she didn't fancy the idea of having to yomp across the muddy field for a second time in one morning. Rhodri offered to go with her but she left him preparing lunch for the three of them whilst she headed down the gravel path alone.

It was a beautiful crisp morning and the sky was a cloudless blue. Katy had almost forgotten her tiredness amidst the excitement and the beauty of the Welsh countryside. The hedgerows on either side of her were a tangle of thorny green bushes studded with bright red-berried jewels. Even the wildlife seemed to have been swept up in the excitement and the hedges bustled and squeaked with a throng of robins, crows and field mice. Katy walked along with her left side hugging the bushes, being careful not to scratch herself on the clawing briars, but also staying out of the middle of the road. As much as she believed Cerys that the road wouldn't be busy, she had also seen both Rhodri and Cerys drive and knew that quiet didn't necessarily mean slow.

Katy needn't have worried about finding the right spot, as soon as she stepped into the layby her phone leapt in to life in a chorus of bleeps and hums. First there was a wave of missed calls, swiftly followed by a series of texts announcing that she had new voicemail messages. She dialled the number on the screen and listened as an increasingly excited Tom provided updates from City Hall. Within the space of three messages Katy was taken on the full journey of Tom's morning. It began with Tom and Owen waiting to be seen, next came Tom reporting back on the first meeting, whilst Owen went in to a second on his own and it finished with the two of them practically yelling with excitement down the phone. Katy checked the time and decided to call Tom back immediately in case there was anything that needed to be sorted to get vehicular access to the site. Tom's phone went straight to voicemail – undoubtedly he was already recounting their victory to everyone in his phonebook. Katy left a short message letting Tom know that all had gone well at the farm and that the following morning a mountain of hay bales would be arriving, accompanied by curtains and a canopy to ward off any winter rain.

When she had finished her phone chirped again to announce a further voicemail. She redialled the number and listened as David's voice came breathily on to the line.

Katy, it's David. I've just had a patient in talking about a fire in the city centre last night at the stage. Please call me to let me know you're okay. I know yesterday morning was a bit of a mess, I know things keep getting messed up and maybe it's me, or maybe you're right, maybe we can't go back to how things were, as much as I want them to. But please call me as soon as you get this. I'm worried.'

Katy called David on his mobile, something she usually avoided doing during surgery hours. David picked up on the fourth ring.

'Katy, you're ok?'

'Yes, I –'

'Can I call you back in a bit; sorry I'm with a patient. I just had to know you're alright.'

'Of course.'

Katy rang off and settled herself in for a wait. She didn't want to call anyone else in case that stopped David getting through, so she decided to text her mum instead. If by any chance the fire happened to make it in to any of the papers then her mum would instantly fear the worse. She would have visions of Katy's body being dragged out in some horribly charred state, or imagine her engulfed in plumes of smoke. It had been the same ever since she had left home. Whenever there was any form of bad news from Cardiff, Katy's mum instantly assumed that she would be at the heart of it; lying under a crashed car or at the frontline of a protest march gone wrong.

When Katy had gone travelling it had opened up a whole new world of dangers for her mum to dwell on that Katy had never even considered. Suddenly she was at risk of obscure spider bites, tropical diseases and bizarre medical oddities, the like of which Katy had never heard of. But there was always some neighbour's son, or friend's cousin who had fallen ill abroad, and if they had then Katy was bound to as well. At first Katy had felt incredibly guilty about her mum's worrying, but as time went on she managed to become more stoic about it. She even started to suspect that being on the lookout for global danger was something of a fascination for her mum and one that allowed her to show off a near encyclopaedic knowledge of disasters. And whenever it was confirmed that Katy was alive and well and not the victim of an unexpected crocodile attack in the middle of Sydney's main shopping district, her mum displayed a near Blitz-like euphoria; that despite all the dangers the world could throw their way Katy was not only surviving but thriving in the face of near death.

Once she had pre-emptively allayed her mum's fears about being a victim of arson Katy started drafting another text. But before she could finish the phone started ringing in her hand.

'Hi, sorry about that.' David said. 'I was with a patient, but I had to know you were okay.'

'It's fine, and I'm fine too. Tom called me last night, but by the time any of us got there the police and fire services had already cordoned off the whole area.'

'You should have called me, I would have come down.'

'Sorry, it was all a bit sudden and unexpected. And I didn't know if you'd want to speak to me yet. I was going to call you today I promise.'

'Katy I'm always going to want to hear from you. Look about yesterday, I know I came on a little strong. Well a lot strong actually. It's just hard sometimes, I know what I want – what I've *always* wanted – a good job, a family…and you. But I know sometimes I can be a bit pushy. But I promise from now on – if there is a now on, I'll be more chilled about things. It's just I love you Katy, I always have and I want to be with you and I guess ever since you came back I've been hoping you felt the same. But I've had some time to think and hearing about the fire – I guess I just want you to know that I love you, but if you don't…you know, feel the same, then I don't want to lose you again. This last year, not being in each other's lives it just doesn't make sense. And whilst I'm not giving up on us, I guess what I'm saying is it's over to you now and you won't get any more pressure from me. Just promise me you'll think about it and if it's not going to happen then promise me you're not just going to jump on the next plane out of here again.'

Katy felt the icy cold air catch in her chest and a deep sigh raced up her throat. As a teenager; insecure and overly conscious of her slightly rounded tummy and awkward clumsy limbs, Katy could only have dreamed of two attractive men competing for her as an adult. And two declarations of love in one day would have been an unimaginable fantasy. But now it was happening, it wasn't at all how she imagined it. There was no thrill in the pursuit, or excitement at the idea. What she felt was sadness and a terrible overwhelming feeling of guilt. Because neither David nor Rhodri deserved what was happening. They weren't the two-dimensional imagined fantasy men constructed by her teenage self; with pop star bodies and film star faces. They were real people, with hopes and feelings and they could be hurt, just as easily as she could. And most of all they were both good men with big hearts, and the truth was that she would be lucky to be with either one of them. And the biggest tragedy of it all was that if she was faced with either one in isolation and at another time in her life there would be no dilemma and no decision to be made. But Rhodri had appeared just as David was coming back in to her life and both of them at a time when she was never less sure of herself and what she wanted. Travelling had opened up the world to her and she needed time to figure out what was right; where her career lay, what she should do with her life, and what relationships, if any, to pursue.

But none of that she could put in to words to David. She didn't know how to say that she loved him, but that at the same time she was also falling in love with Rhodri. And how could she tell either of them that it wasn't about them and which of them was 'better' as men always seemed to assume? It was about her and at the age of thirty-one she was finally beginning to figure out who she was and that was what mattered most right now. But instead she said; 'No planes, I promise.' Whatever happened there would be no more running away.

'Good,' David said, and she could tell he meant it. 'How are Tom, and Owen? They must be devastated.'

'Yes, well they were – but we're trying to get the show to go ahead.'

'How? I heard the stage was completely destroyed.'

'It was. We're building a new one'.

'I thought the play was Wednesday?'

'It is.'

'Bloody hell Katy, how are you going to build a stage in two days?'

'Well, um, Tom suggested we pulled all the Christmas Club back together to do it. I'm up at the farm now. Cerys is making curtains, Rhodri's going to make a stage out of hay bales and Tom's roping in Sophia and Jenny as we speak.'

'Wow, that's quite something Katy. What do you need?'

'Sorry?'

'What can I do to help?'

'Well I've no idea how we're going to bring it all together yet. Owen and Tom have spent all morning getting the okay for us to set up, but we still have to build the whole thing tomorrow.'

'I'll be there.'

'Are you sure? What about work?'

'I've not taken a day off since I started. I'll phone round and get someone in to cover the afternoon. I'll be there, tomorrow and Wednesday…and there'll be no fisticuffs, I promise.'

'Thank you David, thank you so much.'

'Anytime Katy. You know I'm always here for you, whenever it is, whatever you need, I'm there. Look I have to go now, I've got another patient, but I'll see you tomorrow. And if you need anything before then, you know where I am.'

'Okay, bye David, and thank you again.'

'See you tomorrow.'

When she had finished Katy took five minutes to compose herself. She rubbed her face, bringing warmth back to her cheeks and then blew gently on her hands. As she stood at the roadside she tried to keep the words her mum had spoken on the phone the previous week in mind – life would go on and the world would carry on turning, for David and for Rhodri, as well as for her. She was doing her best, she just hoped that was enough to minimise the fall out.

Chapter Thirty-Five

Back at the cottage there had clearly been no let up in activity. Cerys was surrounded by huge swathes of material and was feeding sheets through the sewing machine faster than seemed possible. Even Rhodri seemed to have been roped in and Katy laughed at the sight of the six-foot tall burly farmer swamped in floral duvet covers and holding up chintzy fabrics like sacrificial offerings at the altar of Cerys' sewing machine.

'Ah Katy,' Rhodri said, a small swatch of material sticking out of the corner of his mouth. 'We should get you back to Cardiff. You'll be alright here till I get back yeh Cer?'

Rhodri didn't really wait for an answer before shedding the layers of fabric from around his shoulders. Not that Katy could imagine Cerys was going to object to the two of them heading off in the car together alone. It was very clear that as firmly as she had tried to keep them apart Cerys was now very much in support of them.

'Brilliant,' he said, taking her silence as agreement and he hastily snatched two freshly made rolls from the work top before shooing Katy towards the front door.

'I'll see you tomorrow then Cerys?' Katy called over her shoulder as Rhodri nudged her from behind.

'Yes, I'll have all this done by then.'

'Thank you!' Katy shouted, just as Rhodri closed the door behind them.

'I hate sewing!'

'I'd never have guessed, you hid it so well.' Katy laughed.

They hopped back over the fence, Rhodri helping Katy down on the other side, and headed back across the field towards the farmhouse.

'I'm getting a little tired of walking across your fields today,' Katy puffed.

'I can carry you if you'd rather. I'm very good at fireman's lifts...and you look *much* lighter than a sack of grain,' he said smiling.

'You really know how to make a girl feel special don't you.'

'Hey, I said lighter.'

'I'll give the lift a pass thanks.'

'No moaning about the walk then.'

'Fine you win.'

'I can carry you then?'

'No I meant –.' But it was too late, Rhodri had picked her up and she was over his shoulder in an instant and her shrieked protests were soon rendered meaningless by a fit of giggles.

'And you said to hurry right?'

'No!' she cried, but again her plea was ignored.

Rhodri started to race across the field at an alarming pace, running with huge leaping strides that caused Katy to gently bump against his broad back.

'Stop it,' she squealed, but again her laughter gave away how much she was enjoying herself.

'Sorry, didn't catch that,' he replied, running even faster.

They tore across the field in minutes, but despite the speed and the muddy terrain Katy felt utterly safe in Rhodri's hands and right up until the moment he set her down by the 4x4 she never feared she would fall. Sickeningly he didn't even seem tired from the exertion and he casually got in to the vehicle beside her without so much as a drop of sweat on his forehead.

'So is that part of your usual workout routine then?'

'Yeh, but you're a much easier passenger than Cerys!'

Katy told him to stop teasing her and to start driving. He gave her a disappointed pouting look as he stoked up the engine and then passed her one of the rolls.

'What's in it?' she asked.

'Chicken, tomato, tuna and cucumber.'

'Which one is this?'

'What do you mean?' Rhodri asked.

'Well is it the chicken and tomato or the tuna and cucumber one.'

'Take a look.'

Katy carefully opened up the rather full roll trying not to spill any of the contents.

'Wait, this has all those things in it.'

'That's what I said – it's a chicken, tomato, cucumber and tuna roll.'

'That sounds disgusting.'

209

'That sounds fecking amazing and if you don't want it all the more for me.'

'So you have chicken *and* tuna in the same sandwich.'

'Yep, double the protein – it's hungry work being a farmer you know.'

Katy tentatively took a bite fully expecting to hate it.

'Well?'

'It shouldn't work.'

'But...?'

'It's so good.'

'Told you.'

Katy hungrily ate the roll, telling herself and Rhodri that it was purely exhaustion that allowed her to tolerate such a bizarre concoction. But deep down she knew it wouldn't be the last tuna-chicken sandwich she ate.

'So where to then?'

'I don't know. I've left Tom a message but he's not got back to me yet.'

'Well what are you going to do next?'

'I don't know really. You and Cerys seem to have the stage pretty much under control. I guess Tom will decorate it and Owen's sorted out all the permissions. I'm not really sure what I can usefully do.'

'Nonsense, I thought you wanted to be a writer.'

'How do you know that?'

'You told me at your flat when I came round to decorate the tree.'

'Did I?' Katy asked a little absentmindedly as she tried to recall the conversation.

'You did, and it strikes me this is exactly the kind of thing for a writer – getting the word out that the play's going ahead. And letting everyone know that the finest straw in south Wales will be on display...and the most handsome farmer providing it.'

'Is that right?' Katy laughed. 'But seriously, I don't know if I can do that. When I sell stuff in work it's just photocopier toner and crap like that – things people already need. I don't know if I can get people to come and see a play.'

'Sure you can.'

'Well it's nice that you think so, really nice actually. But I think I'd be more likely to believe you if you'd actually read my work.'

'Now hang on,' Rhodri said taking an enormous bite of his sandwich. 'I've seen an excellently crafted example of your work.

Which I know to have been written under the influence of *copious* amounts of alcohol and even then you were able to write something that touched the hearts of literally eight people.'

'Eight?'

'Yes, eight: Cerys, Sophia, Jenny, Chris, Tom, you and me.'

'Okay, well firstly that's seven…and you can't count me.'

'Ah but I missed out Owen – that's eight!'

'Nope doesn't count – he just came along to the after party, he's not an official member. And Chris doesn't count either – he's been a reluctant bystander at best. And Tom was only there for moral support. And I'm not counting you! You were just Cerys' driver for the night! So I make that three: Cerys, Sophia and Jenny.'

'I'm hurt Winters – just a driver. Is that how you see me?'

'Well you are driving me right now…but I'd say more driver slash caterer slash hay provider. A kind of all round country butler.'

'Cheek! Well I definitely count. Frankly I think I'm the ruggedly good-looking glue that holds the whole club together. So we'll settle at four. But either way you brought people together and look what you've achieved as a result.'

'What would I do though?'

'I don't bloody know; send emails, call up newspapers, go back on your favourite late night drinking forum – just have a go.'

'You genuinely think I can do it?'

'Absolutely!'

'Okay, then home it is Jeeves – but it's going to be a long night and that means coffee, and chocolate and quite possibly wine.'

'Supermarket it is m'lady.'

Rhodri took every shortcut known to man, and some that Katy suspected had never been tried before, to get her to the supermarket and home without getting caught in traffic. In the end she wasn't entirely convinced that it was any quicker than if they had gone the most direct route, but she appreciated his effort. When it came time to say goodbye they both lingered at Katy's front door seemingly unsure of what to say. Katy wanted to invite Rhodri in for a coffee, but she knew that she had a lot to get done and that it would be just as hard saying goodbye to him an hour later as it was then, even though they would see each other again the next day.

'I guess I should get to work.'

'Me too, those hay bales won't load themselves on to the trailer.'

'No. Thank you Rhodri – for everything. I don't know what we'd have done without you and Cerys.'

'Thank me tomorrow when they're all delivered and in place. I'll see you about 11? Once the traffic's died down.'

'That's great, thank you.'

'Well, goodbye then,' he said and leaned in to kiss her, his stubble gently tickling her face.

'Till tomorrow.'

Katy watched Rhodri turn and walk down the short path to the gate where his 4x4 waited just outside. She waved and then unconsciously brushed her cheek where he had kissed her. Her skin was still warm to the touch, still glowing from his kiss, even though the rest of her was freezing cold.

When he pulled out in to the street she finally opened the door and walked inside, silently missing him already.

Chapter Thirty-Six

Katy woke to find the winter sun streaking through the curtains, which she had hastily and unsuccessfully pulled shut around 2:00am. She was still fully dressed from the day before and her face was puffy and creased with pillow marks. But as bad as she looked she felt incredible.

First Katy had emailed or texted everyone she knew in the city; friends, former colleagues, even casual acquaintances. After that she had moved on to the newspapers and the magazines, firing off emails and extolling the virtues of the show and how it was rising phoenix-like from the ashes of the former stage. Finally she had scoured the internet for every local forum, social media channel and blogging site she could find and either posted directly on to the page or messaged the owner in the hope that they would share the news. By the end of the evening she felt confident that she had done everything she could to reach anyone who had been planning on coming to let them know it was still on. There would also be plenty more people who hadn't known about the play but now would as a result of her efforts.

As soon as she had woken the following morning she checked her phone and was delighted to see scores of replies where people had seen her message overnight and come back with a friendly hello or a query for more information. She quickly responded to all the messages that warranted an answer and forwarded some of the more interesting emails to Tom for Owen to see. Then she showered, trying to coax some life in to both her hair and her tired limbs and quickly threw on some clothes.

The clock on her phone showed 10:33am when she finally ran out the front door, a half eaten piece of toast clutched firmly in her left hand. She quickly wolfed it down and then proceeded to run, simultaneously ignoring almost every bit of advice her mum had ever given her about exercising after eating and the basic rules of road safety for pedestrians. At 10:59am Katy arrived panting at the site of the nativity, just in time to see a tractor and an enormous trailer part a crowd of confused bystanders as it made its entrance on to the street. Sat proudly in the cabin of the roaring, spluttering tractor was Rhodri, goading anyone to get in his way and loving every minute of it.

'He wasn't kidding then about the tractor.'

Katy looked around to see Tom standing beside her, transfixed by the progress of Rhodri through the narrow pedestrian lined street.

'No, I guess not. Where's Owen?'

'Right there.'

Katy looked in the direction Tom was pointing to see Owen running across the square urging people back and waving Rhodri through at the same time. Even Owen was dwarfed by the enormity of the tractor, which looked like a historical remnant from the early days of mechanised farming.

'Should we help?' Katy asked.

'Probably,' Tom replied. 'But I'm kind of interested to watch how this one plays out and besides I'm not sure I want to get any closer to Rhodri in that tractor than I already am.'

'No, he doesn't seem to have noticed how close he is to either side.'

'We've already asked the restaurants to take their chairs in and the shops to move any signs. Short of cutting the fronts off buildings we can't make any more room.'

'Don't give him any ideas! Oh come on, we can't just leave Owen to it.'

Katy and Tom joined Owen at the front of the crowd of people, guiding them back from the path of the tractor, even if it was a little hard to tell exactly what that path might be.

A loud honking sound from behind caught Katy's attention and she turned round to see Rhodri waving enthusiastically at her from the cabin of the tractor. She put on her most serious face and waved him forward, but as much as she tried to look stern she couldn't help but smile. Rhodri was never anything less than delighted to see her and he wasn't afraid to show it. His was the kind of honest affection that was never rationed or withheld, but given generously and freely.

Come on! Katy mouthed to him through the window. The tractor lurched forward in response and the trailer followed, narrowly missing a lamppost. Katy silently pleaded for him to be more careful but decided it was best she didn't engage Rhodri directly any more – the less distractions he had the better.

Eventually the tractor and trailer lurched to a stop and without any damage to property or human casualties as far as Katy could tell. Rhodri proudly jumped from the cabin and hugged Katy before moving on to greet Tom and Owen. There was a ghostly white hue to Owen's complexion and Katy was a little worried Rhodri's good humour and relaxed attitude to the task might not be the best thing for Owen's nerves.

'Perhaps we should get the bales unloaded, then you can take the tractor back to the farm,' Katy suggested.

'She's a hard taskmaster this one isn't she. Not even five minutes to catch your breath or stop for a coffee. You any idea how long it's taken me to get in. Queue a mile long behind me. She's a faithful workhorse this old thing but not built for speed.'

Katy had visions of an endless chain of disgruntled Christmas shoppers sat at the wheel of their cars cursing Rhodri from behind as they slowly meandered in to the biggest city in Wales behind a prehistoric tractor.

'I can imagine...best we get a move on then, so you're clear long before afternoon rush hour,' Katy pushed.

'OK, OK, blimey Katy – best be a coffee in this for me when we're done.'

'Of course,' Katy promised. 'I'll get you a takeaway one for the journey home.'

Owen gave her a look of pure gratitude and then steered Rhodri away.

The two men positioned themselves on the trailer, lifting the heavy bales and throwing them down to the ground. Rhodri and Owen threw the bales around effortlessly making it look easy. But for every bale they were able to move singlehandedly, it took both Katy and Tom to shift it away from the trailer and towards the stage area. Katy couldn't believe that a rectangular block of dried grass could be so heavy. She was painfully aware that more of the burden was falling on Tom, with the bale sloping down in his direction, but she couldn't lift it any higher at her end. What made it worse was that occasionally someone passing by would kindly offer to lend a hand and each time they would have to turn them down. Owen had been very specific that only people he had agreed on were allowed to move the bales and even then only under supervision. The terms set down both by the school and the authorities for their little venture had been very strict and Owen wasn't going to risk breaking them.

Every time Katy and Tom returned from carrying one of the bales there seemed to be at least three or four new ones waiting to be moved and it soon became clear that they wouldn't be able to clear the backlog. Owen threw down a final block and then followed it to the ground, casually leaping from the truck and landing squarely beside Tom.

'Need some help?'

'Yes please.'

With the three of them working on moving the hay bales they were able to keep up with Rhodri and clear the waiting bales that had built up whilst it had just been Tom and Katy. Owen carried the hay bales with ease, moving more quickly on his own than Katy and Tom could shuffling to and fro holding an end each.

In the end they moved all of the bales away from the trailer in less than an hour and Katy breathed a big sigh of relief. It wasn't just going to be Rhodri that needed a coffee; she was in desperate need of not only a drink, but also something sugary and stodgy to go with it.

'You move those things all by yourself at the farm?' Tom asked, sounding impressed.

'Sure, I have some help around harvest time but mostly it's just me.'

'Wow, clearly Katy and I aren't meant to be farmers. I swear it was like moving twenty sofas dealing with that lot.'

'I was moving them on my own too you know,' Owen chipped in sulkily.

Tom walked over to his boyfriend and gave him a kiss. 'I know, big strong boy,' he said teasingly, before adding more seriously, 'It was kind of hot though.'

'Yeh?'

'Yeh – definitely!'

Sensing a distinct possibility that the boys were losing all focus and that Rhodri would happily linger until he ended up causing a blockade that lasted the rest of the day, Katy decided to move things along; 'Right, coffee's all round, my shout.'

Rhodri eagerly volunteered to give a hand and the two of them walked to the nearest café leaving Owen and Tom to continue gushing over Owen's show of strength.

'They're not that heavy you know,' Rhodri said as they joined the queue.

'They bloody are!' Katy replied, still exhausted.

Katy returned with a latte for Tom, a strong black coffee for Owen and an enormous tray of sugar glazed doughnuts. Rhodri followed closely behind with his and Katy's drinks. Katy allowed Rhodri five minutes of peace as the four of them sat on the hay bales strategizing exactly where and how they would build the stage. The fire service had done such an excellent job at removing all traces of the fire that it was impossible to tell where exactly the first stage had been. There was no debris left behind and the rain overnight had washed away any soot or ash that might have given them a clue.

'I think we'll just have to make a start and do the best we can,' Owen said eventually.

'I could stay and help you know, you'll get it all in place much quicker with me about,' Rhodri offered.

It was true that having Rhodri about would definitely make lighter work of the task, but Katy could see Owen's anxiety about the tractor obstructing the city centre for any longer than necessary.

'We would, but there's some stuff I really wanted to go through with Cerys, and we can't fully finish the stage until we know the size of the curtains and the canopy she's made. We can make a start but if you could fetch Cerys that'd be a massive help and then you can help us finish the stage.'

Katy's words seemed to do the trick and Rhodri appeared happy with his new task. It was after all Katy reasoned, something that only Rhodri could do, whereas the rest of them could at least make some progress on the stage in his absence. Rhodri returned to the tractor without a fuss and Katy and Owen followed so that they could help direct him back out of the narrow street. Katy wasn't convinced that Rhodri took any notice of their gesturing and shouting, but it felt like they were trying to help at least.

After a slightly terrifying ten minutes where Katy feared for the life of at least six different pedestrians, herself included, Rhodri was back on to the main road and facing in the right direction. He gave her a last enthusiastic wave and then disappeared round the corner.

'That was possibly the most stressful experience of my life. Give me a room full of screaming ten-year-olds over your fella in a tractor any day,' Owen said.

Katy laughed and put her arm round Owen as they walked back to Tom who was busy explaining what they were doing to a group of enquiring shoppers for what felt like the fiftieth time that morning.

'If everyone that's shown an interest in what we're doing turns up tomorrow then it's going to be one very packed show,' Tom said.

'Yeh, I just hope everything's going to be ready in time,' Owen said.

'It will be,' Katy said confidently.

They arranged the hay bales in a single layer to form a large rectangular base around the size of a small city bus. Over short distances and with no need to lift them Katy and Tom were able to push and drag the bales in to place on their own and the three of them made quick work of it. It was only when they attempted to add height with a second row of hay bales that Katy and Tom started to struggle again and the pace of construction slowed. For a while Owen took on all the lifting so that Tom and Katy would bring the bales over to the stage and then Owen would lift them in to place. But even this soon became too much for all of them and they had to take more and more breaks.

'I hate to admit it but I think we may have to wait for Rhodri to come back,' Owen said.

Tom and Katy readily agreed and the three of them slumped on to the bales and passed round a bottle of water, which they all drank from thirstily.

'I need to pick up some timber for the frame. Any chance you could stay here with the stuff Katy? I could do with Tom's help lifting at the other end.'

'Sure, is there anything I can do here?'

'Take a break, you both look knackered. Don't lift anything on your own okay. We shouldn't be long.'

'Do I get a break too?' Tom asked hopefully.

'Yep, about ten minutes – just about as long as it takes to drive to the DIY store.'

Tom fixed Katy with a melodramatic pout and rolled his eyes, clearly envying her the rest. He took a last swig from the water bottle and then trailed off in pursuit of Owen, who was already well on his way to the car park. Katy watched him disappear in to the steady drift of people milling around the city, hopping between shops and offices, largely oblivious to the Herculean task that Katy and her friends were undertaking.

Feeling unable to slack off whilst everyone else was hard at work, Katy got out her phone and checked her messages for the first time since she had left the apartment. She had eleven new emails and three missed calls. She returned the phone calls first; one was from a community newsletter wanting to write a piece on the nativity and asking for more details, the second was a similar enquiry from an online listings page and the third turned out to be a wrong number. Once she had dealt with these Katy moved on to the emails. She became so engrossed that it wasn't until someone cleared their throat directly in front of her that Katy broke her stare from the phone and looked up to see Rhodri standing over her.

'Hey, you're back! And Cerys, it's so good to see you!'

Both Rhodri and Cerys were laden with huge piles of fabric material and apparently that was just the first load. Katy quickly put her phone away and started to carefully take folds of the fabric from them and stack them on to the hay bales. What Katy had initially thought to be multiple curtains turned out just to be one enormous sweep of material that criss-crossed between Cerys' and Rhodri's arms in overlapping folds. The two of them must have walked from the car side by side with Rhodri stooping the whole way to stay at Cerys' level.

'I don't know Winters, I leave you and the others for an hour or so and I find they've buggered off leaving a job half finished and you're sat on your phone making friends.'

'Tom and Owen have gone to fetch wood and we've made a good start on the stage. Anyway what do you mean making friends? I'm publicising the play, just like *you* suggested.'

'Who are this lot then?'

Katy turned round to follow the direction of Rhodri's gaze and was horrified to see that on the loose bales that they hadn't yet moved and even on the far side of the stage from where she had been sitting, people were sat down on their phones, eating sandwiches or just taking a rest from shopping.

'It's not a bench!' Katy cried.

One teenager looked up at her with fleeting interest and then returned to his phone and no one else even acknowledged that she had said anything. Just as Katy was about to try again she was eclipsed by a booming yell from Cerys.

'Everyone off the hay! You can help or you can clear off and sit somewhere else!'

Katy winced a little in embarrassment having never been one for public confrontation, but she had to admit it worked. A few grumbles and dirty looks were thrown in Cerys' direction but she gamely stared each of them out and in less than a minute the hay bales were clear.

'Thank you.'

'Not a problem. Just need to show them who's boss.'

Katy suspected that whenever Cerys was around people always had a pretty clear idea of that and so when the last of the material was taken from their hands Katy asked Cerys if she minded staying with the stage whilst she went back to the car with Rhodri. Cerys happily agreed and Rhodri also seemed excessively keen about the idea. Katy only hoped that the two of them weren't getting carried away.

'I hope it wasn't too much work for Cerys, all this sewing,' Katy said when they were out of earshot.

'No, truth is I think she loved having something to do. She was glad you asked, and I think she was flattered you went to see her. She's very fond of you. Since Claire left, well she doesn't have a lot to do. Helping is in her blood, and farming, and she'd gladly muck out the animals and yomp around the fields all day if I let her. But farming's a young man's game. You know yourself from lifting those bales earlier – they're heavy; see I admit it. She likes having stuff to do, but it's the company also. She can't be happy just having me for conversation.'

'She loves you, and you're very good to her. I'm not sure everyone would look after their mother-in-law after what happened.'

'Not Cerys' fault what Claire did though is it?'

'No, but all the same, I'm sure she wouldn't have expected it and I'm sure she appreciates it.'

For the first time since Katy had known Rhodri he seemed to stiffen up and become tight-lipped. He clearly didn't want to talk about the matter any more – Cerys was family and that was all that mattered to him.

'I hope it's not a problem but David's coming this afternoon. In fact he's due anytime now. He's promised there won't be any trouble – he wanted to help.'

Katy knew the topic of David wasn't likely to put Rhodri at ease but she had to tell him and it seemed as good a time as any to say something.

'Course, though I'm not sure what help a doctor's going to be.'

Katy let the remark go unchallenged. Considering that the last time they had met David had punched Rhodri, a little jibe didn't seem like too much to worry about. Even so when they got back to the stage with the rest of the material Katy was relieved that it was still just the three of them and Cerys and David hadn't been left making awkward conversation.

Cerys had carefully separated the material in to three piles; the two curtains and the cover that would form a roof. Between them they unravelled one of the enormous curtains. It was made of countless pieces of material all carefully stitched together. Katy recognised some of the patches as duvet covers and bed sheets, but there were other things in there too; a picnic blanket, an old tablecloth and even a slightly tired looking woollen jumper. It was an eclectic and slightly chaotic mix of fabrics and colours, but somehow it worked. Cerys had managed to combine the rustic charm of a homemade quilt and the vibrancy of a harlequin's outfit in to one epic project.

'It's fantastic Cerys, it really is. I can't believe you did it so quickly. You must have been up all night.'

'It was a late finish but nothing too bad, they do look rather good don't they?'

'Perfect,' Rhodri concluded.

As Tom and Owen still hadn't returned with the wood to make the curtain frames, Katy suggested they carry on with the stage. Rhodri established Cerys as supervisor and positioned her in the centre of the bales so that she could direct them quickly in to place. Between them Katy and Rhodri then lifted each block and placed it on to the existing base layer. Katy was well aware that Rhodri didn't need her to help share the burden and that in reality she probably made the task more cumbersome than if she had just stepped back and watched him tackle it. But he never made her feel that way and he even threw in a few grumbles and neck rubs that Katy suspected were entirely for her benefit.

At 2pm David arrived. He looked a little unsettled and Katy suspected that he, like her, wished that Tom and Owen were around to help diffuse any potential tension.

'Hey, sorry I'm late. Surgery went on longer than planned – you know how it is.'

Katy was unsure how to greet David, normally she would have given him a kiss but she was aware of the watching eyes of Cerys and Rhodri and she didn't want to stoke the embers of any resentment by appearing too affectionate. In the end she settled on a hug and awkwardly introduced David to Cerys and then Rhodri. To her relief David was uncompromisingly gracious and after he had shaken hands with Cerys he offered Rhodri the same courtesy.

'What needs doing then?'

Katy hesitated to answer. Until Tom and Owen were back there really was very little to do but work on the stage and she wasn't sure how best to keep the two men apart.

To her surprise it was Rhodri that came to the rescue; 'I think Katy could probably do with a hand if you don't mind. The bales are pretty heavy.'

Katy mouthed a *thank you* to him and then quickly brought David up to speed on what they were doing. Katy wasn't convinced that she was any more use to David than she had been to Rhodri, but she was just happy that they were all able to be in the same place without punches being thrown. The two men were never going to be friends, but after the last time Katy was more than happy to settle for civility.

By the time Tom and Owen finally returned they had pretty much finished the stage, with only a couple of bales missing from around the edge. It was two bales high and fairly evenly constructed. Rhodri had even made a step on each side of the stage using an extra bale, to save the kids having to clamber or jump too high.

'Wow, it looks great guys – it's huge isn't it? Sorry we were so long, traffic's really bad and it took ages to get all the right wood.'

After admiring the stage Cerys showed the boys what she had been working on and Katy watched happily as Cerys practically basked in the glow of compliments dished out by Tom and Owen. All in all the day was going better than Katy had hoped and only the failing light threatened to thwart their strong progress.

'What next?' Katy asked Owen – keen to keep up their positive momentum.

'I could do with a hand rigging up the frame for the material. Sophia said she's sorted us out some lights and that they'll be on standalone frames, so we only need to worry about supporting the weight of the curtains and the roof.'

'I can help with that,' Rhodri replied and David swiftly followed suit.

'Then I can start work on the backdrops with the girls,' Tom added, patting the huge white dustsheets that were rolled up under his arm.

If Cerys had looked happy earlier she practically exploded with joy at being referred to as a girl. In the short time since she had known her, Katy had seen Cerys flourish in the warmth of new friendships. It was fantastic to see sparks of her personality resurface that had perhaps been hidden for too long. And as much as Katy hoped that the play was a success, if nothing else came of Christmas Club but bringing some happiness and company back in to Cerys' life then the whole thing had been well worth it.

Katy linked arms with Cerys and stood primly in front of Tom. 'The *girls* reporting for duty. What do you need?'

'Well if you can each take a sheet and just paint whatever comes to mind. You know the nativity; stables, starry skies, camels in the desert, sheep in fields; that kind of thing.'

Katy gave Tom a worried look. 'You want us to actually paint? I thought we'd just be laying down some base colours for you to work on.'

'There's no time for that; I could never paint them all by tomorrow. Just do your best – keep it bold and fun and you won't go far wrong.'

'But Tom, what you did – the first stage it was so wonderful, there's no way I could do anything like that.'

'Me neither,' Cerys added sounding worried, 'I'm no artist.'

Tom smiled at them both and unrolled one of the dustsheets on to the pavement. 'Here, how about I do you some outlines to give you something to work with?'

He dabbed a brush in to a small pot of paint and made broad black brushstrokes across the white sheet. The outline of a stable quickly appeared, with two windows and a large wooden door in the centre. In the foreground he roughly outlined some hay bales and then textured the floor with a firm stamp of a thick bristled brush running the width of the sheet. He passed the sheet to Cerys and then proceeded to unravel another one which was quickly transformed in to the outline of a long winding road passing between steeply rising hills dotted with small towns.

'I don't know how you can do it so quickly,' Katy said admiringly. 'Are you sure you wouldn't rather have a go at doing them yourself, I'm worried I'll ruin it.'

'Not at all. I can't pretend I wasn't gutted when the stage went up in flames. But it's gone now and this new stage is a joint effort and that goes for the painting too.'

Katy took the sheet from Tom and picked up a brush with trepidation. For a few moments she just stared at it wondering where to start, until she decided there was nothing for it but to go for it. Soon the large blocks of white started to be replaced by the green of hills and the greys and browns of rooftops and buildings. To Katy's left Cerys was tackling the barn with similar bravery and to her right Tom was working on a beautiful desert scene complete with palm trees and spitting camels.

As the light started to fade they increasingly had to rely on streetlights and the warm glow of restaurants opening up for the evening trade to see by. Katy had already moved on to her second scene; a starry sky with the star of Bethlehem glowing white in the centre when she was nudged gently by Tom. Katy looked up, instantly seeing what had caught Tom's eye. David, Rhodri and Owen were all ten feet off the ground perched amongst the rafters of the wooden frame they had constructed. Rhodri and Owen had both stripped to their t-shirts, leaving a pile of discarded jumpers and coats between them. David was still wearing a thin sweater but had rolled the sleeves up to reveal two toned arms, one clutching a hammer and the other a fistful of nails.

Rhodri – who was nearest to the streetlight – had a thin glisten of sweat just visible on his forehead, which he wiped clean with the palm of his left hand. Balanced under his other arm was a full-length piece of timber, which he held in place using only his triceps and the cleft of his upper torso. To Rhodri's left was Owen – who was leaning far in to the centre, pushing his chest forward so that the material of his jeans tightly hugged the firmly rounded buns of his bum.

'Oi, you two, back to work,' Cerys said sternly, 'I know what you're doing.'

Katy and Tom gave an embarrassed laugh and quickly returned to their painting before the men spotted that anything was up. Even then Katy noticed that both her own and Tom's progress on their second canvas slowed as they both stopped to steal regular glances at the boys – purely to check on their safety of course.

It was 7:30pm by the time they finally decided to call it a night. The pubs were already starting to get busy and none of them fancied having to try and explain their exploits to drunk people. Besides they were all shattered and it was too dark to see anything clearly. The timber frame was up, as was the canopy and the curtains would be hung first thing in the morning. Under Tom's direction Katy and Cerys had nearly finished two scenes apiece and Tom was putting the finishing touches to his third.

'So that's it then? Rhodri asked.

'Yep, it's all we can do for tonight,' Owen said tiredly. 'Thank you so much everyone. Providing Sophia comes through with the lights and Jenny has made good on her promise to sort the props and costumes we lost in the fire we should be fine. Really, I can't thank you guys enough. Let me buy you all a drink.'

Katy felt her heart sink. She could tell Owen was genuinely touched by the effort everyone had made and it was lovely that he wanted to repay that – but she was exhausted. All she wanted to do was sink in to a hot bath, eat her body weight in pizza and collapse in front of the television with a glass of wine.

'Cerys and I should be getting back if that's okay?' Rhodri said.

'And I've got surgery first thing tomorrow, but I'll be here from one o'clock tomorrow for any last minute things.'

'Okay, well thanks guys – if you're sure. But I definitely owe you one tomorrow in that case,' Owen said.

'If you boys don't mind I think I'd rather wait till tomorrow to celebrate too. I don't think I shall be long before bed,' Katy added, grateful that the others had paved the way with their excuses.

'Do you need a lift home?' Tom said.

As soon as he had asked the question Katy witnessed a flicker of disappointment cross David and Rhodri's faces as they realised they had missed an opportunity. But Katy was glad it had been Tom to ask, she knew she could say no to him and he wouldn't take it personally. As tired as she was she was looking forward to the walk home alone and a chance to reflect on the day without having to make idle conversation or have any more emotional farewells on her doorstep.

'Oh, but we can't just leave things can we? What if someone decides to take another match to everything.' Katy suddenly said, fearing her quiet night in was about to disappear.

'Don't worry, that was one of the conditions for allowing us to rebuild. I've got security for the night and they should be arriving anytime now actually.'

On cue a van pulled up, coming to a stop in exactly the same spot as Rhodri's tractor had been parked earlier. It was a dark black van with thick silver writing on the side, which read *Three Bears Security*.

'Well that doesn't make sense,' David said, sounding confused. 'The three bears were rubbish at security.'

As Tom and Owen descended in to fits of laughter, a sliding door on the van opened and three men stepped out, each with a dense beard, thick muscular arms and firm barrelled tummies tucked behind smart black coats.

'Friends of yours?' Katy asked playfully.

'You could say that,' Owen laughed.

'I still don't get it,' David said. 'I mean Goldilocks walked right in to their house and stole from them. How does that make them a good choice?'

Katy laughed and said her goodbyes to Cerys and Rhodri before turning to David. 'I think I'm going to leave Tom and Owen to explain this one. I'll see you tomorrow.'

Chapter Thirty-Seven

Katy woke to find the world covered in a thick layer of frost. Through the misty white of her windowpanes she could see the ground far below sparkling like diamonds in the lamplight. Even the enormous clunky radiator in her bedroom wasn't enough to keep the wintry air at bay and so she quickly hopped in to the shower. The water took an age to heat up and she spent the first 30 seconds squeezed in to the corner of the cubicle to avoid the icy spray.

When she was finally warm Katy reluctantly prised herself from the shower and quickly towelled and dressed herself before the chill air could work its ill upon her body. The kettle went on straight away and soon she was sat in an armchair, fingers warming against the steaming mug. It was 6:30am; long before they were due to meet and though exhaustion had ensured she slept, once she had woken there was no chance of dozing off again. Of course she was nervous – and excited – about the nativity, but there was more to it than that. Katy had decided that she couldn't leave things the way they were any longer. She was going to talk to David and Rhodri after the nativity. It was a relief to finally be getting things out in the open, but having decided upon her course of action she was keen for the day to begin. She felt the same nervous anxiety that had churned her stomach before a school exam, the type that only resurfaced in adulthood at job interviews and blind dates.

A little before 7:00am she decided to phone Tom. As expected he was already awake and so Katy decided to go round to his flat so that they could await the coming storm together. By the time she arrived at the apartment Owen had already left for work and Tom was dressed and ready for the day. Katy could see the nerves etched in to his brow and his anxiety manifested itself in a chaotic chorus of toe-tapping and fidgeting. With Owen in school the responsibility for the final set-up had been left to Tom, and Katy could see that the burden weighed heavy on him.

'It'll be okay,' she said.

'I know, it's just this means so much to Owen, and the kids, and I want it to be perfect.'

'Well perfect might be pushing it. But given that three days ago we didn't have anything I think we're doing pretty well.'

'God that sounded terrible, I'm not being ungrateful, I mean what everyone's done – you, Rhodri, Cerys and David, it's been fantastic. I just really want this to work out.'

Katy steadied her friend's tapping knee and put an arm around his shoulder. She understood exactly how he felt, as the same anxiety was racing through her at the thought of speaking to Rhodri and David later. She knew what it was like to want something with all your heart, hoping things would work out when all the odds seemed set against you and worrying about how it would effect the ones you loved. But all either of them could do was wait now.

Katy tried to distract Tom from fretting by offering to cook him breakfast, but neither of them felt up to eating. In the end they decided to head over to the site earlier than planned. It was the right decision, like most things the waiting was the hardest part and Katy felt better once they were doing something. Two of the men from the security team were standing in front of their van when Katy and Tom arrived. Their faces were barely visible between their thick woollen hats and high collared winter coats.

'Oh, you look freezing. Are you alright?'

'Ah, we've had worse jobs. Owen booked us a room in the hotel across the street so we've all had a chance to get some kip and the van's pretty well set-up.'

Katy eyed the meagre pile of blankets on the back seat and the single electric fan heater and decided that the men were made of far sterner stuff than she was. Whatever career doubts she was having, clearly night security wasn't going to be a viable alternative. At the offer of a coffee both men perked up considerably and one of them even removed his hat, revealing a finely cropped head of hair in the process. Katy returned not only with hot drinks, but also with two enormous bacon baps and the news that they could clock off sooner than planned. The men reacted as if Christmas had arrived a week early. After a brief round of enthusiastic goodbyes and a quick stop at the hotel to leave a message for their slumbering colleague the van pulled away and Katy and Tom were left to inspect the hard work of the previous day.

The stage was finished and the hay bales had been covered in thin sheets of wood to avoid small feet getting trapped in any of the cracks. The wooden frames were still standing firm and only one of the curtains was left to hang. The biggest area of risk was the lighting and Katy hoped that before long Sophia would be making an appearance. In the meantime they returned their attention to the painted backdrops, which still needed a few finishing touches.

At 10:00am they were joined by Jenny; who was followed by a huge pile of cardboard boxes on legs, which turned out to be a slightly disgruntled Chris. If it hadn't been quite so early Katy would have offered to get him a pint to try and sweeten him up, but she decided she would leave it to Jenny to pacify her husband. The boxes were set down on the stage with a heavy thud and Chris gave a huge sigh as he pointedly stretched his arms and back. The gesture seemed to go unnoticed by Jenny, who was keen to show off her handiwork. From the first box she pulled a handful of angel costumes. Each outfit was brilliantly white and finished off with a pair of lace wings edged in gold ribbon. In the next box were some simple cloth outfits in browns and greys for the shepherds and vibrant purple and silver robes for the wise men. The last two boxes contained props and were bursting with gold coloured gifts and wooden swords, leather style money pouches and small toy animals.

'Jenny this is amazing. Thank you so much,' said Tom.

'It was kind of fun actually and Chris did a lot of the work – making swords and trawling the charity shops for bits and pieces.'

'Well thank you *both*,' Tom corrected.

Chris seemed to perk up at the recognition of his efforts and even volunteered to give Tom a hand hanging the last curtain. Katy and Jenny arranged some of the props around the stage and put up the backdrop of Mary and Joseph's house ready for the opening scene. The four of them then tackled the remaining pile of hay bales, positioning them in to rows in front of the stage for people to sit on. They ended up with six rows of bales and enough space for at least 40 people, if any more than that turned up then they would have to stand.

Just as Katy and Tom stepped back to admire their efforts Katy felt a tap on her shoulder. She turned round to see Sophia standing behind her empty-handed.

'Sophia, hey. I thought you were hoping to get some lights?'

Katy could hear the strain in Tom's voice as he fought to keep his emotions in check.

'Oh, I did. The university has a pretty good theatre club and I managed to borrow their sound system. I just needed some help bringing them along.'

Katy looked up to see a procession of muscular young men in incredibly short shorts and tight polo shirts carrying metal gantries and ten or more sets of lights, each around the size of a large holdall.

'Wow,' said Tom. 'That's…a lot of stuff!'

'Sophia,' Katy said, 'they don't look much like drama club students.'

'Oh, they're not,' Sophia said casually. 'This is the university rugby team. I thought they'd come in handy.'

Katy laughed as the men trotted by. Without fail each of them gave Sophia an appreciative look as they passed and the braver amongst them jostled to be noticed with a smart remark or an exaggerated show of strength. Katy and Tom may as well have been invisible for all the attention that the boys gave them. One of them asked where they should set up and Tom didn't even attempt to hold their attention, he simply relayed the information to Sophia and watched as the boys hung on her every word.

'You've been busy since the winter carnival,' Katy said with a wink.

'Yeh, James, the one at the back with ginger hair, he lives on my corridor. I ended up going out with him and a few of his teammates for a drink at the weekend. It was fun and then when I got Tom's call they just kind of volunteered to help.'

'God I feel old,' Tom moaned.

'C'mon Grandpa,' Katy smiled. 'Let's make sure they can keep their eyes off Sophia long enough to get these lights up.'

The arrival of Sophia and her small army of rugby players triggered a huge change in pace. Suddenly there were a lot more people on hand and the lighting went up more quickly than any of them could have imagined. The boys raced through tasks with the eagerness of excited puppies and Katy and Tom found they were struggling to keep up with their demand for new jobs.

By the time Owen arrived with thirty children and a gaggle of parents in tow the stage was up and the lights were all in place and switched on. Tom quickly brought Owen and the headmistress up to speed before the site was given the final safety check. To everyone's relief they were good to go and Owen instantly ushered the excited children up on to the stage and pulled the curtains across so they could finish rehearsing and change in to costumes.

As the activity on the site snowballed so too did the interest of the people passing by, fuelled in no small part Katy thought by the presence of eight strapping twenty-somethings in shorts. Seeing an opportunity Katy ran in to the nearest shop and emerged a minute later with a few sheets of A4 paper and a black marker pen. She scribbled the rough street address of the stage on the bottom and the time of the nativity and then handed the sheet over to Tom.

'What's this?'

'Our flyer, you've got two minutes to draw something Christmassy at the top of the page.'

'Two minutes?'

'About one minute fifty seconds now.'

Realising that arguing wasn't going to make any difference Tom swiftly got to work. Taking a second piece of paper Katy then wrote the word *reserved* in large capital letters. She then gave Tom a little longer to finish before hovering over his shoulder to tell him that his time was up. He handed her the piece of paper, which had been completely transformed with a drawing of a donkey carrying Mary along a wide road under a starry sky.

'Not bad, you know you should think about taking up art professionally,'

'Thanks Miss,' Tom said. 'Now care to tell me what this is all about?'

'You'll see, just get everyone together and I'll be back in a sec.'

Five minutes later Katy returned from the same shop staggering under the weight of an enormous pile of papers stacked in to two piles; one about five times thicker than the other.

'Right everyone,' Katy said, trying to sound louder and more authoritative than she felt. 'Boys: take a handful of posters each and work your way out from here. We want as many people to come to this play as possible and I don't care what you have to do to make that happen. Pose for selfies, take your tops off...carry the women of Cardiff here over your shoulders if that's what it takes. Just be charming and get as many people as you can. Sophia you take a bundle too, we do want some men to come after all! Holly, Chris: put *reserved* signs on the hay bales – I think this place is about to get pretty busy and I want all the parents to be at the front. As soon as you're done with that you're on the streets handing out flyers too. Everyone clear?'

There was an enthusiastic chorus of *yes's*, particularly from the rugby playing contingent of Katy's impromptu taskforce. She quickly handed out the flyers and then turned her attention to Tom.

'Ready for this?'

"That depends what you have in mind.'

'I'm pretty sure it's about to get very crowded, and someone's going to have to keep everyone in order.'

Tom didn't look too convinced, but as people started showing up it soon became clear that neither of them had any choice in the matter. Both Tom and Katy found themselves running from side to side and backwards and forwards answering questions, reassuring people that things were starting shortly and keeping the hay bale seats clear. When Cerys and Rhodri showed up they were swiftly roped in to the task as well, freeing Katy up long enough to talk to some of the local media outlets that had started to arrive in chaotic flurries of tripods and cameras.

At some point Katy was vaguely aware of David out of the corner of her eye, but there was no chance of stopping to talk to him. The next time she looked she saw that he was helping parents to seats and flagging down passers-by with a wave and a well-patterned spiel. Katy felt her heart grow with love for him that little bit more – knowing that even after everything that had happened, all the hurt and uncertainties, he was still there for her.

She allowed herself a brief moment to scan the crowd and picked out the familiar faces of Anne, Simon and Adam all huddled together near the front of what was becoming a sizeable host of people. And then the chaos really began. A whoop from across the street drew Katy's attention and she looked up to see Sophia, Jenny and Chris flanked by the rugby boys leading a group of at least sixty or seventy people towards them.

'My God,' she whispered under her breath. The woman who had been interviewing her suddenly swivelled round to capture the advancing mass on camera. The rugby boys were loving every minute of it, cheering and whipping up the crowd behind them and drawing the attention of those already waiting.

Katy checked her watch; it was 1:50pm. She made her excuses and then looked around to see if she could see Tom. The hay bales were completely full and there were people standing on either side of them. Eventually she spotted him near the front and quickly made her way over.

'There must be two hundred people here!'

'I know, it's crazy. Are they nearly ready? I'm worried we'll have a riot on our hands if we don't start soon.'

'Five minutes. One of the parents is just fetching the collection buckets and then it's curtains up.'

Gradually Tom and Katy were joined by the rest of the members of Christmas Club as first Cerys and Rhodri and then Sophia, Jenny and Chris appeared at their side. Finally David joined them at the front, a little tentatively at first but Tom soon stepped aside to allow him in to the circle.

'Well we did it guys,' Tom said as he handed out the buckets that had just been passed to him.

A muted cheer rippled round the group. They had achieved everything they set out to do and far more besides. Katy could see that Tom's eyes were welling up and as he spoke his voice wobbled with emotion'

'Thank you everyone, you don't know how much this means to Owen, and to me. I won't ever forget this day and whatever any of you need, whenever it is, I'll be there.'

Katy felt her own eyes start to prick with tears. Suddenly she wanted nothing more than to get away from the rest of the group before she lost control and surrendered to the tide of emotion that had been building all day.

'We should spread out for the collection,' she managed, although the crack in her voice was clear to hear.

She walked away, ignoring the concerned looks on her friends faces, but she should have known that wouldn't be enough to deter Tom.

'What's wrong?' he asked as he caught her up.

'Nothing, just the same as you – a little emotional that's all.'

'It's more than that Katy. What's wrong?'

'Nothing Tom really, it's yours and Owen's big moment, I want you to enjoy it.'

'How can I when I know you're upset. You heard what I just said to those guys – whatever, whenever I'll be there and that goes for you more than anyone.'

'I'm going to speak to them after the play – David and Rhodri. And I know I have to. It's just that when we were all standing there a moment ago, it suddenly occurred to me that maybe that was the last moment we'd all be together like that. In a few hours everything will change and I just wish there was another way.'

'You've been keeping this to yourself all day? Why didn't you tell me? We could have talked about it, I could have helped.'

'Because this is what matters today,' Katy said indicating the stage and the assembled crowd. 'I'll be okay, honestly Tom, please just enjoy the play.'

Katy kissed Tom on the cheek just as the curtains were pulled back to a loud applause. When Owen appeared on the stage she took the chance to slink away and positioned herself near the back of the audience on the left side. She saw Tom look round in concern but she gestured for him to watch the stage, hating that he might miss Owen's big moment because of her. Thankfully Tom stayed in place and Katy tried to focus her attention on Owen as well and ignore the clamouring fears in her head.

Owen did himself proud and even managed to squeeze in a few jokes to warm up the crowd before handing over to the headmistress to make the final introductions. She was a kindly looking woman in her early fifties and she spoke with a soft Welsh lilt that Katie found soothing.

When she finished speaking, the headmistress' spot on the stage was taken by a small child of no more than nine or ten who was wearing a blue headdress and cream robe. The crowd instantly fell in to a hushed silence to allow the child to be heard and from that moment on they were rapt. The children were wonderful and there were very few missed entrances and forgotten lines. Even the backdrops Katy had helped to paint didn't look too out of place and everyone seemed to be enjoying themselves. Katy only wished that she could watch with the same carefree contentment, but her mind kept rehearsing the conversations she was about to have. And it was clear that she wasn't the only one whose mind was on other matters. Tom kept looking back throughout the performance, but so too did Rhodri and David, and all of them looked concerned.

Before Katy knew it the play had finished and the audience was cheering and clapping as the children took a final bow. In a haze of applause Katy heard her name and the names of her fellow Christmas clubbers as Owen thanked them for stepping in and saving the day. But rather than taking the moment to celebrate what they had achieved Katy used the attention to kick off the collection, launching her way in to the audience with her bucket in hand.

Coins were thrown in with a satisfying thud and there was even the occasional note in amongst them. Soon Katy's bucket was filled with a metallic splash of silver, bronze and gold and getting heavier with every moment. For five blissful minutes she watched pound after pound roll in, knowing that all of it would help Owen's school. But then people started to drift away, returning to their shopping or heading for coffee and cake.

Katy's section cleared first and she was left holding her bucket with no one to collect from. Rhodri was still mopping up the last of the contributions on his side but edging swiftly towards her. To her right David was closing in on her as well. She started to panic; unsure if she was ready to face them and who she should speak to first. Suddenly Tom was by her side. He took the bucket from her hand and ran it over to Sophia, before heading back in Katy's direction. He took Katy's hand and swiftly led her away from the stage and the watching eyes of David and Rhodri.

'We can't leave; I don't want you to miss out. You should be with Owen.'

'Owen has thirty hyped up children to worry about. He's not going to have time for anything else right now.'

They walked quickly away from the stage area, blending in with the departing spectators until they came to a side street. There was a long granite bench and Tom and Katy sat down hand-in-hand. To all the world they probably looked like a couple resolving some tiff, and in many ways they were. Katy and Tom had been near constant companions for over a decade. Far longer than any other relationship either of them had had. Since the early days of adulthood it had always been the two of them.

'You okay?'

'I know I have to talk to them. And the longer I leave it the worse it gets. But maybe today isn't the right time; I don't want to ruin anyone's day. I never expected any of this to happen. None of this was ever supposed to be about finding a boyfriend; it was about doing something different, something for me. I wanted to settle back in and figure out my career and just be me for a bit. The last thing I wanted was to hurt people's feelings.'

Tom put his arm round Katy and gently kissed the crown of her head. He had always been able to calm her down, always known what to say and that a hug could heal as well as words ever could.

'Katy you can't plan these things. You can't help when you fall in love, or who with. Look at everything you've achieved since you've been back. Look at Cerys; she's a different woman than when we first met her. And look at today; none of this would have happened without you, so stop being so hard on yourself. Do you remember what you said to me, all that time ago, when we were in university and I was trying so hard to be someone else; when I was angry at the whole world because I didn't know how to be me?'

'Yes,' Katy said quietly.

'I didn't choose to be gay Katy, just as you didn't choose for any of this to happen. But things are happening and whatever you feel for David and Rhodri it's real, anyone can see that. You can hide away from it and miss out because you don't think you deserve it, or you can embrace it and accept whatever comes, casualties and all. You taught me to be brave, you helped me accept who I am and you never made me feel like there was anything wrong with that and I love you for it. But you need to take your own advice now Katy. You can't shy away from it any longer. You have to choose and it will be hard I know. But I'll be here for you, every step of the way, just as you were for me once.'

'God, it's really happening isn't it?'

'Yes.'

Tom squeezed her hand and then asked quietly; 'You won't tell me who it is will you?'

'No, not until I've spoken to them. But haven't you guessed?'

'I think so; I think I've always known which way you'd go deep down.'

'And?'

'I think it's the right decision.'

'So do I,' Katy said quietly. And with that she stood up, pulling her coat tight against the wind. She embraced Tom and the warmth from his body gently spread to hers and she closed her eyes, savouring the last moment before things changed. The two friends had finally grown up and whatever happened Katy had the feeling that things would never be quite the same again.

She saw David and Rhodri standing near the stage, a little apart from one another, each with their own friends. They looked up almost as one, both anxious, both clearly wanting to speak to her and to check she was okay. Her eyes moved between the two of them and she felt her heart race at the enormity of the moment. But finally her eyes settled on him and he returned her gaze and in that moment she knew it was the right decision, she knew there was no turning back.

Christmas Eve

One year later…

Chapter Thirty-Eight

Katy sat on the train station platform watching the arrivals sign ticking over. Nearly every train was delayed. There had been a heavy snowfall overnight and much of the country had been blanketed with a thick carpet of white. Cardiff had been no exception; every rooftop of the city was covered and heavy flakes continued to fall.

She checked her phone for what seemed like the hundredth time but there were no new messages and the minutes weren't passing any quicker. The train had originally been due in at 15:35pm and it was already 16:20pm. Luckily Katy had been having regular progress updates and had stayed in the warm as long as possible, only venturing out a few minutes before. She contemplated getting a coffee, but if by some miracle the train did suddenly arrive she would hate to miss that moment when he stepped out on to the platform. There was a small butterfly of nerves in her stomach; there was bound to be, but it was far outweighed by the buzz of excitement.

Katy looked around at the other people waiting. Some had bundles of presents and bags, presumably waiting to catch the train onwards to Bridgend, Neath or Swansea. But there were plenty like her too, with no luggage and only the expectation of loved ones' arrival causing them to venture out in the bitter cold.

At 16:30pm the arrival of the train from London Paddington was announced. Katy stepped forward, reminding herself not to be too excited and that he had had a long trip. Twelve hours on a plane followed by three on a train would have taken its toll. But as the train drew in to the platform she knew it was hopeless to pretend she could be anything but delighted to see him.

Katy scanned the coaches as the train rolled by and when she saw the letter 'C' she started walking up the platform, keeping pace with the door. An elderly woman exited first and a young man – possibly a grandchild – rushed forward to help her with her bags. Next was a young couple and then finally she saw him – she knew it was him even before he had fully stepped in to view. He was a healthy bronzed tan colour, completely out of odds with a cold December in Wales and his clothes were equally unseasonal. He was dressed in a light waterproof with tailored hiking shorts and walking boots.

'David!' Katy squealed and ran towards him practically jumping in to his arms.

He picked her up and effortlessly swung her round. 'Good to see you too Winters! It's been a while.'

'A while? It's been nine months!'

'Hey, nine months is nothing – some people bugger off for a whole year when they go travelling you know. Anyway there's someone I want you to meet.'

David stepped aside to reveal a similarly dressed woman with long blonde hair. She had brilliant blue eyes and a warm smile. On her back she carried an enormous rucksack, which she put down on the ground before stepping forward.

'Claudia. It's so great to finally meet you,' Katy said.

'And you, I've heard a lot about you!'

'Come on girls, I'm freezing here. Where's Rhodri?' David asked.

'Parked out the back, come on then, give me something to carry. I'm guessing snow's a bit of a shock to the system,' Katy said as they stepped out in to the open.

'Just a bit, it was 29 degrees this time yesterday.' David said shivering.

'And that was Bangkok?'

'Yep, last stop Thailand.'

'I can't wait to hear all about it.'

They put the bags in the back of the 4x4 and Claudia and David climbed in with them.

Rhodri leaned through from the front cabin to shake both their hands and then gave Katy an enormous kiss before starting up the engine. 'Sorry it's a bit of a squash back there,'

Katy laughed; 'They'll have been travelling in much worse than this lately.'

'Yes this is luxury.' Claudia added.

'What is it you do by the way Claudia?' Rhodri asked.

'I'm a doctor – that's how David and I met, volunteering in Malaysia.'

Rhodri smiled and then gave Katy a nudge. 'A doctor eh, they really are well suited.'

Katy heard a giggle from the back of the vehicle and the soft press of lips touching before David spoke; 'Yes, we are.'

Katy thought of the last time they had all been together. David hadn't understood when she had said they weren't right for each other. She remembered the tremble in his voice as he had asked her why, over and over again. For a moment she had feared he would push his way through the hay bales and direct his anger at Rhodri, a fight between them ruining another festive occasion.

But instead David had turned and walked away, merging with the departing stragglers from the nativity crowd. She had followed him, begging him to stop and talk. It was only once he reached the frosted bank of the River Taff that he had calmed down enough to speak to her.

'Did I ever stand a chance?' he asked bitterly.

'What do you mean?'

'When you came back – did you even want us to get back together? Because most of the time you were away it was all I thought about. And you…I think you just wanted to get away from me, from us.'

She couldn't look at him; instead she focused on the tensed white knuckles of his hands as they gripped the railings of the bridge.

'I'm sorry David. Please can't we go somewhere and talk about this properly.'

'Will it change anything?'

'What do you mean?' Katy asked.

'Will talking about it make it any different? Or will you still go running back to *him* as soon as you're done letting me down gently?'

His normally blue eyes had taken on a steely hue. Tears scratched at his cheeks. She couldn't answer him. Instead she watched him walk away, worrying she would never see him again.

She didn't speak to Rhodri that day, or the next. Despite the mounting missed calls and worried texts that filled her phone. When she did finally walk up the muddy path leading to Windmill Farm two days later, she promised herself she'd try and explain everything to him. She'd tell him how she'd wanted to kiss him that first day holly wreathing, and every time since. That she wanted to be with him, and that she was sorry for not telling him sooner. But she couldn't just abandon David; she couldn't lose his friendship again.

But none of that happened. The moment Rhodri opened the door she wrapped her arms around him and melted in his arms and she only withdrew when her lips finally and urgently found his.

For weeks Katy's mood had alternated between elation at her growing relationship with Rhodri and the guilt that dug away at her whenever she saw David. Then sometime after New Year's something changed within her. It was too difficult to feel bad about David anymore. Rhodri made her too happy for that. And when she stopped punishing herself and trying to hide her happiness from David, the frostiness that had settled between them slowly started to thaw.

For the first time in weeks they were talking again; really talking. And Katy's travels filled the void left by the end of their relationship. With each conversation David grew more and more interested – asking about hostels and volunteering and her favourite countries. But most of all he focussed on what it had done for her: her newfound confidence, her happiness, and the sense of freedom.

At the start of February Rhodri and Katy had gone round to David's for dinner and she'd spotted a travel brochure on the table. A month later he was gone.

Chapter Thirty-Nine

The roads were quiet and so despite the snowy conditions they made it back to the farm in a little under half an hour. Whilst Katy showed David and Claudia the guest room, Rhodri went next door. He reappeared five minutes later with Cerys in tow. They were both laden down with all manner of pies, pastries and cakes.

'Wow, what's all this?' Katy asked.

'Well I know you wanted to cook Christmas dinner yourselves, but I thought it couldn't hurt if I made some extra for Christmas Eve.'

Katy smiled and led Cerys and Rhodri in to the kitchen where there was already a mountain of food.

'It's a good job we've got a full house.'

With Cerys' attention on David and Claudia, Rhodri mischievously held some mistletoe above Katy's head and leaned forward expectantly.

'You know it's been a year now, you don't have to trick me in to kissing you with mistletoe anymore,' Katy laughed.

'It's fun though.'

'It is,' Katy agreed, and to prove the point she wrapped her arms round Rhodri and kissed him gently on the lips.

'You sure you don't mind not being at home with your family for Christmas?'

'Of course not,' Katy replied. 'I wouldn't miss this for anything – our first Christmas together since I moved in. And anyway it is a family Christmas; you and me, Cerys, Tom and Owen and David and Claudia all together. It sounds perfect.'

'It sounds very you,' Rhodri laughed.

'What do you mean?'

'Chaotic, a little crazy, but pretty perfect too.'

'Crazy?'

'Oh come on, your ex-boyfriend and his new girlfriend, my ex-wife's mum and your gay best friend.'

'You're right. That does sound perfect. Everyone we love under one roof for Christmas.'

At that moment David, Claudia and Cerys joined them in the kitchen. Rhodri handed out tall fluted glasses and Katy liberally filled each one with sparkling champagne.

'To David and Claudia, welcome home! And to everyone *Happy Christmas*!'

Katy's toast was met with a chorus of cheers and clinking glasses. She took a large sip of her drink and then giggled as the fizzy liquid bubbled in her mouth and tickled her nose. She had meant what she had said to Rhodri – it really was the perfect Christmas. A year ago she had worried she had broken David's heart and seeing him happier than ever was the best Christmas present she could hope for.

'How's your writing going Katy?' David asked, interrupting her thoughts.

'Slowly. Between college and this one keeping me busy working on the farm there's not always much time. But I write articles for magazines when I can and a few of them have been picked up.'

'That's great. Proper farmer's wife now aren't you? I couldn't believe those pictures you sent of you holding that newborn lamb.'

'Farmer's girlfriend,' Katy corrected.

'For now,' Rhodri said smiling. 'But she's not a bad worker, I think she's worth keeping around.'

Katy was just about to make a smart comment back at Rhodri when there was a knock at the front door. 'Saved by the bell,' she said playfully. 'Right everyone, top up your glasses and put on your coats, we're going outside.'

Rhodri groaned melodramatically and rolled his eyes at David, but they knew better than anyone not to argue with one of Katy's ideas. Tom and Owen didn't even have time to take their coats and gloves off before Katy was ushering them back through the door and towards an outbuilding adjacent to the farmhouse. On the side of the old stone and slate building was a modern metal staircase. Katy led the way, calling behind her for everyone to hold the handrail on their way up.

'Um, have you noticed its snowing Katy?' Owen shouted.

'Yeh, it's bloody freezing,' Tom added.

'Not really dressed for this,' David chipped in.

'No point arguing lads, just grin and bear it and let her have her way – it's normally easiest,' Rhodri said.

Katy flashed Rhodri a smile and then stepped up on to the roof of the building. It was covered in a coarse black surfacing that had been recently cleared of snow and then gritted. Katy shook a fine dusting of snow from some terracotta pots and then produced a lighter from her pocket and proceeded to light potted candles across the roof. There were seven chairs up there too and a large hamper from which Rhodri pulled blankets.

'Wow, look at the view,' Claudia exclaimed as she crested the rooftop.

Although it was night time the snow covered landscape shone silvery-purple in the light of the moon. Spidery tree branches dipped under the weight of fallen snow and against every hedgerow pillow-like drifts were forming. The nearby village was illuminated with firefly-sized lights as the glow of open fires and fairy lights escaped from houses where families had gathered to celebrate Christmas. And all around the sky was filled with tumbling, dancing snowflakes.

'I'd like to propose a toast,' Rhodri suddenly announced. 'To Katy, who I love dearly. For bringing us all together and for coming up with ridiculous ideas like this – that never fail to delight.'

Katy smiled with embarrassment as her assembled friends raised their glasses in her honour. As they did so Katy couldn't help but allow her gaze to flicker across to David. They had had many conversations by phone and email since he had left to go travelling and no matter how many times he had told her he was happy it was another thing to be able to see it. And Katy couldn't have been happier with David's response to the toast, he wasn't even looking at Katy as he raised his glass, but gazing lovingly in to the eyes of Claudia who was sat on his lap nestled against his chest and sheltering from the cold.

There was a brief silence as everyone paused to drink in the view – and the champagne. Finally David spoke, a little hazily as if waking from a dream and picking up from Rhodri's toast as if there had been no break in conversation.

'Talking of bringing us all together I wondered if Sophia and Holly might have been here. Do you still see them much?'

'We all got together to work on the holly wreaths again, but to be honest everyone's so busy. Sophia has a boyfriend now – do you remember the rugby player from her halls? James - well it's him. And Jenny and Chris are busy doing up the house they just bought.

I'd love to see them more, but Rhodri and I are flat out with the farm. Without something to bring us all together I guess it's just difficult to get people to make the time.'

'Well if you'd actually given us a minute before dragging us up on to the roof we might have been able to help you out with that,' Tom said smiling.

'What do you mean?' Katy asked.

'On three?' Owen said to Tom.

Tom nodded and then counted them in. Simultaneously they pulled off their gloves to reveal a pair of rings on the fourth finger of each of their left hands. They were matching silver bands with complementary strips of dark and light metal.

'We were thinking a summer wedding. There's going to be a lot to do in six or seven months. We'd need a lot of help – know anyone that might be up for it?' Tom asked.

'I have just the team for the job.' Katy said, struggling to fight back tears.

There was so much Katy wanted to ask. She wanted to know every detail of the proposal, to look at the rings and to hear every one of the thoughts she knew Tom would have already had about the wedding. But there would be time for all of that. It was Christmas Eve and they had two days of good food, good wine and excellent company ahead of them. She looked around her friends surrounded by the people they loved and all of them happy. And then her eyes rested on Rhodri and she found he was already staring at her, watching her sharing in her friends' happiness. She smiled back at him, and mouthed the words 'I love you' to him, and in that moment she knew that that Christmas and every one after would be magical, because she had found the man she loved for always.

-THE END-

About the Author

Nick Frampton lives near Exeter in Devon, England. His debut novel The River was published in 2017 and is the first title in an epic new fantasy series.

The Cardiff Christmas Club is his first romance novel.

As well as writing, Nick loves getting out and about on the beaches and moors of Devon, attending food festivals with his baker-husband and is overly fond of watching 90s/00s verbose American high school dramas.

Nick travels whenever he can and he's the co-author of Your Big Adventure: a guide for anyone planning a gap year.

Web: www.framptonbooks.com
Twitter: @framptonbooks
Facebook: www.facebook.com/framptonbooks/
Goodreads: Nick Frampton

Printed in Great Britain
by Amazon